The Tales of Six Tigers

The Tales of Six Tigers

A WINDOW ON THE COVERT AMERICAN
WAR IN SOUTHEAST ASIA 1971-1975

• • •

C. R. McDaniel

ISBN: 1519614292
ISBN 13: 9781519614292

Dedication

To all the Tigers that ever were, living and dead.
To the many people who provided me assistance,
especially my friends Dale Jamison, Tim Harvey, Eric Davidson,
Keith Fulgium, and Kurt Ginsel,
without whose encouragement I could not have written this novel.
And to Rebecca Harvey, without whose help the task of writing this
book would never have been completed.
And lastly, to the occasional dram of inspirational Jack Daniels.

Prologue

• • •

I TAKE A SIP OF Jack Daniels, a toast to the old team. The smoky taste of the whisky takes me back to Southeast Asia and the time I spent there. For a moment, I am back in that time, young, strong, and fearless, surrounded by my brothers in arms. They are all gone now, done with this life and on to the next. I am the last of the Six Tigers.

The memories come back, crystalline and sharp as knives. They flow through my mind, reflections of a reality I once knew. My time to join them will come soon, but today, I choose not to allow our story to go to dust with me. I finish my drink and begin writing *The Tales of the Six Tigers,* a window on a covert war in Southeast Asia.

C. R. McDaniel

AKA Snake, AKA Red Dog

CHAPTER 1

Welcome to Fucking Thailand!

• • •

There are no facts, only interpretations.

— FRIEDRICH NIETZSCHE

THE FLIGHT TO THAILAND WAS a bitch. I took a 727 from Dallas to San Francisco, a 707 from San Francisco to Guam, Guam to Manila, Manila to Tan Son Nhut in Vietnam, and finally an old DC-3 from Tan Son Nhut to Udorn Royal Thai Air Force Base (RTAFB) in Thailand by way of U-Tapao and Korat. If there was runway between the US and Udorn, Thailand, I think we landed on it.

As the plane touched down, the copilot looked back through the cockpit door, pointed to a hangar, and told me I should meet my party at the Air America Hangar. I walked down the stairs, stood on the runway, and looked around. I was feeling really covert and had the theme music from television series *Mission Impossible* running through my head. I stretched, hoisted my duffel onto my shoulder, and started walking toward the hangar.

Two airmen were walking toward me from the back. They yelled, "You McDaniel coming in from Tan Son Nhut?"

"Yes, that's me."

"Good! Because we are going to kick your ass, so get ready. Welcome to fucking Thailand!"

The covert feeling evaporated, and the theme music in my head stopped. The larger guy was probably a little over six foot and maybe 220 pounds. The smaller guy was maybe five-foot-ten at best and pretty skinny. I was not about to run from anything on day one. I put my duffel down and walked toward them.

I moved in to get to Big Boy first. I was pretty sure he was a boxer by the way he moved and held his fists, and when I saw his cauliflower ear, I was certain. I had to set him up and take the first strike. I stopped about eight feet from him and settled into a "come on, let's box" fighting stance, waiting until he got one or two steps closer.

Just as he came within striking distance, I slipped my right foot out and pivoted into my real fighting stance, called *back cat*. Suddenly, I wasn't a boxer anymore, and he was in my striking range. I took a quick hop, left foot replacing right, closing the distance between us. I raked toward his face with my hands, giving him a reason to keep his guard up. While I made the feint to the head, I launched a rising back kick. It came up under his guard, catching him in the solar plexus. He doubled over. I held his head down, slid my left leg under him and heel-kicked him in the nuts. He collapsed. Then I grabbed his hand, reversed the finger joints, and applied pressure, twisting the arm to lock the wrist and elbow. He howled in pain as I used the joint locks to keep his attention. His skinny friend retreated; deciding he did not want to play. Welcome to fucking Thailand indeed!

I was debating whether I should dislocate Big's arm and give chase to his buddy or just interrogate him a little when the door to the small office along the edge of the hangar opened and Mr. Nash appeared. I had seen him once before, at the very start of training. He was official and imposing in his starched white shirt and grey slacks, a man to be reckoned with. He walked over to us and said, "Welcome to Thailand, Mr. McDaniel. Just call me Nash. Can I call you Mac? Looks like you passed this little test with flying colors. You can let him up, it's okay." As he spoke, Nash leaned over and gave me two pats on my shoulder, the Hapkido signal to release a hold, which I did instantly. I was surprised by the taps but even more so when Nash pulled out some folded bills and gave them to Big Boy, who beat a hasty exit.

"Come on, Mac, you're in the guest house. You need to get cleaned up before we go eat. I want you to meet some friends of mine, John and Bruce."

"You guys certainly have a strange way of greeting new people. What would have happened if I had really hurt him?"

"I never thought about it till now," said Nash. "This was just a gentlemen's wager to prove your training. I was sure you would win; at least, that was the report I got back from all of your instructors. And I was right; you just kicked his ass in about ten seconds without taking a single punch, and he doesn't seem too damaged either, except maybe his pride."

I couldn't argue with the logic, I had won, but maybe I was good or maybe I was just lucky, and fucking lucky seemed like a real possibility. I always had that worm of self-doubt deep in my belly, eating my guts, spoiling the perfect moment. It certainly was a hell of a welcome to Thailand. I had expected some hazing would come from the team before my first mission, but I wasn't expecting it to start so soon. These guys didn't play nice.

Nash and I entered the AA guest quarters; it was like a nice motel. I took a hot shower—my first hot shower in almost nine months—and it felt great. Even though I had been traveling for a week and would have preferred to linger, I hurried. I couldn't keep Nash waiting. I put on my Class "A" uniform with the SAT logo on the shirt, the only clothes I had, except for the jeans and shirt I had flown in and jungle fatigues. I decided to wear my grey beret with the silver Southern Air Commando (SAC) badge. I was still really proud to have won it. In the training program, it meant I was certified. Here, it was just another shiny piece of metal.

I must have looked completely stupid to Nash—bright-eyed and bushy-tailed with ignorance, arrogance, and innocence mixed in equal measure. We made small talk about the trip as I dressed, and then we walked over to the restaurant, Club Rendezvous, to get something to eat and a beer. I had expected primitive accommodations, but this place had a pool and nice restaurant separated from a "high class" bar by a wrought iron partition. This place was not only American, it was upscale, and everyone there was American.

"Watch the language here," Nash said as we walked in. "It's a family place. And no swimming without a swimsuit either. We've had problems in the past with some of our more exuberant employees. We have to keep the Air America boys here happy." I got a hint of some intercompany rivalry. I had been warned to keep a low profile, stay out of trouble, and not socialize too much with spooks from other organizations. Having different chains of command did not make the current spooks happy, and the military were never happy about civilian "augmentation" groups anyway.

Nash directed me to a corner table where two men my dad's age sat drinking beer. They stood as we approached. Nash introduced them as John and Bruce, and we shook hands. More beers came, and I drank one quickly.

"Well, Mac, you certainly passed the entrance exam with flying colors," Bruce said. "Cost me a pretty penny too, betting against Nash. Nash only bets on sure things; I should have known better. That guy was a golden gloves boxer, and you kicked his ass in less than a minute."

"Just a lucky kick," I said.

Boxer yes, fighter no, I thought. *You do what you are trained to do. Boxers train to box. They play by a set of rules. I didn't have any rules to play by, and I knew his, so it wasn't really a fair fight. Just like us fighting the Communists who have no "rules of engagement." You can't win fighting that way. This is getting too close to politics. I have a job, and it isn't making policy or even thinking about policy. I'm a fighter, not a thinker, and I'm here to do what I'm ordered to do.*

I assumed these guys were really high up in the organization, probably some of the OSS boys' club. I suddenly realized so was Nash. This was an elite group for a new guy to be eating with. I figured I'd better watch my manners and my mouth. I remembered my father's advice: "Don't lead with your tongue." I knew that my fight had just been old-fashioned entertainment for these guys, and I really did not care.

"We will provide everything you need before you leave, except the kit, which you will pick up at the base," Bruce said nodding. "This is all important company business, and we will pay you and the team a big bonus if you can get the lost device back. It was a one-of-a-kind prototype and almost priceless to us."

"I will do my best, sir; I am sure the entire team will." I started to feel a little drunk as the beer hit my empty stomach.

"Yes, I'm sure of it too, and I am sure you will do well with this team. They are aggressive but also very professional. You will fit right in," said John.

That told me something. I was about to meet a bunch of aggressive motherfuckers. That little worm of self-doubt started eating my guts again. *How did I get myself into this? Was I just completely stupid?*

"Let's eat something; Mac here must be starving," said Nash. We all ordered steaks and baked potatoes, and I drank another beer while we waited for the food. When it came, I consumed my steak and baked potato in record time, followed by a large piece of pie.

"Did they train you to eat, or does it come natural?" Bruce asked.

"Training, sir," I replied. This got a good laugh.

After dinner, Jack Daniels was substituted for the beer, and I had several. While we made small talk, the white shirts quizzed me about my training. It was difficult to explain the training, so I just said we did a lot of PT, running, and combatives as well as a couple of months in the jungle. Bruce noticed the scar on my right arm; it was a thin, angry red line, curling from the middle of my forearm around to my elbow.

"Where did you get the scar?" he asked.

"I brought my arm to a knife fight, sir," I replied. (It was really just a minor knife training accident.) Everyone laughed. Soon, I would have a lot more scars to talk about, and not all of them on the outside.

"So how did you get the name Red Dog?" Bruce asked.

"Must have something to do with my hair, sir," I answered, removing my beret. I had hoped that that moniker might not follow me, but it seemed that it had, arriving even before I did.

The talk turned to the war and how we were going to lose it. "The politicians and diplomats are killing us by holding the military back." Then, with the alcohol kicking in for everyone, I sat and listened as they told old stories about the OSS in Europe during World War II. I loved hearing these tales; these guys were the real deal. I wondered if I would be on the other side of the table in thirty years telling war stories with my friends. Actually, I was surprised I had made it this far. I had no idea where I was going or how I would get there. I had come close to dropping out of training on several occasions, but had managed to hang on until I got stronger and began to do well.

After everyone had finished eating, Nash said, "Mac, why don't you go on back to the guest house? You've had a long day, and we have some company business to discuss that would only bore you. And I am sure you need to catch up on your sleep after the trip."

"Yes, sir, you're right. I am really tired."

"OK, then let's meet for breakfast at 09:00; that will give us time to talk some before you leave."

I was beat and a bit drunk, but I made it back to the room without having to ask directions. I stripped off my clothes, and as I lay on the bed, I thought about how I got into this crazy, fucked-up situation.

CHAPTER 2

How Did I Get Here?

• • •

The mark of the immature man is that he wants to die nobly for a cause,
while the mark of the mature man is that he wants to live humbly for one.

— J. D. SALINGER, *THE CATCHER IN THE RYE*

I WAS A SMALL-TOWN BOY with small-town values. My dad fought in World War II, and my grandfather was in World War I, so it was just a natural progression for me to end up in Vietnam I guess. I graduated from a small, north Texas high school; my class was just ninety-six students.

I devoured books, especially science books. My first real break in life was winning second place in the state interscholastic league science contest. It wasn't first, I missed that by two points, but it still won me a four-year Welch Foundation scholarship in chemistry.

I went to North Texas State University, which was my nerd heaven. Master's Hall, the chemistry building, became my new home, and I managed to be one of only two freshmen to get a job working in a research group. I soaked it all up like a sponge. I had a bright future opening in front of me—first graduate school, then a postdoc, then a university teaching job. I thought I was primed for big things.

But then it was 1969, and the Vietnam War was raging in Asia. On December 1, they held the first draft lottery, pulling days of the year out of a hat and assigning each day of the year a number. We watched the numbers being pulled in a packed TV room in the dorm. Afterward, everyone got drunk: the people with high numbers celebrated, the people with low numbers just needed a drink. I "won" the lottery with a forty-nine, which made it a certainty that I would be drafted and sent to Vietnam.

While I had resigned myself to fate, I was really worried about going into the army; I even considered ROTC. But it was too late for that. None of my friends were selected—just me— so I didn't have much of a support group; we really didn't talk about it. My girlfriend, Karen, had been the youngest delegate to the 1968 Democratic Convention in Chicago. She had been gassed by Mayor Daley's storm troopers, and the word *antiwar* did not come close to describing her or her family. I really liked them, and they liked me, but their answer to my situation was "Go to Canada." I felt that I had to do my duty to my country. Going to Canada was not an option for me. With my future going off to war I just could not get closer to Karen and we drifted apart and split up in the middle of training. It was the first collateral damage of my decision not to run away but to work for Southern Air. .

I started trying to get myself ready by running, exercising, and trying to gain some weight. I was really skinny and couldn't put on weight easily (those were the days). I drank a lot of milkshakes, ran long distance several times a week, and took Tang Soo Do karate classes to try to get some sparring skills. I didn't tell anyone about the martial arts classes; I was afraid they would laugh at me. Then I got a break: one of the young professors I had met playing handball invited me to train in Shotokan karate. I didn't have much money, so I jumped at the chance of free training.

We met in an empty dance studio with a bar and mirrors. We practiced several times a week, mostly at night. At first, the instructor probably just wanted a target, but I was more than happy to be one. Since I had been taking Tang Soo Do, I picked up the Shotokan quickly. At least I wouldn't be a complete nerd when I had to go. Now I knew how to fight.

I graduated at the top of my class and was done with school except for a clerical error that kept me from actually receiving my degree until the next graduation. I didn't care; I was too worried about the next step in my life and how I would survive Vietnam. I was getting ready to tell my dad and sister that I was about to be drafted, but I had one last academic job to complete: I had to present a paper at the American Chemical Society in Austin, Texas. It was a last hurrah for my academic life. I drove to Austin and found my hotel, a big drum-like building on the river. I was heading for my room when a tall man in a swimsuit carrying a towel over his shoulder called to me.

"JR? JR! It's me, Tom from Southern Airways." I looked at him closely, and then I remembered. Tom was one of the guys I had known from working at Southern Airways (SAT) in Mineral Wells during the summers as a high school student. He was a young helicopter instructor pilot who had been friendly with the summer kids.

"I didn't recognize you with all the hair," I said.

"Well, it's me for sure. I'd like to catch up on what you have been doing if you have time. Hey, let's meet for a drink after my swim; you can drink, right?"

"Sure, I'm twenty-one now."

"Great, meet you at the bar downstairs at about eight?" How he recognized me with my long hair I will never know.

• • •

When I got to the bar, Tom was already there, and I took the barstool next to him. We shook hands and he said, "What would you like to drink? This night is on me. I ran into a lot of money recently, and I think I still may owe you for that favor you did me at Southern."

"What favor was that?" I asked.

"Putting me in your car that night when I was drunk and base security guys were looking for me."

"That was nothing."

"Well it saved my ass. I would have been kicked out of the program if they'd found me drunk again."

"OK, great. Give me a gin and tonic," I said to the bartender.

When it arrived, Tom said, "Let's move to a booth where we can talk." Once we settled in, he started with: "So, how is your dad?"

"Same old routine, not much of a change there. Still working for SAT. I just finished my degree, so I guess I am a chemist in need of a job. But it looks like I am about to get one. I'm headed for Vietnam, my draft number was forty-nine, my deferment is over, and I just did my physical. I'm just waiting on the letter from the army."

"Well, that is pretty bad news. But hey, there may be another possibility. I might be able to get you a deferment of sorts. Well, at least a better job than the army, if you're interested."

"Hell yes, I am very interested in not having to slog through rice paddies and get shot at for three hundred dollars a month. But I am pretty sure I'm already drafted."

"Don't worry about that, this will get you deferred. And I can't guarantee you won't get shot at, at but the pay is a lot better—about fifteen hundred a month."

"Fifteen hundred dollars a month? Jesus! Who do I have to kill for that kind of pay?" I asked.

"Maybe the same guys you would be killing in Vietnam, just at a better rate of pay."

"Tell me more." I was ready to say yes.

"Well, it is working for Southern again, but in a different department."

"You mean for 'the company'?" I had heard that Southern did a lot of government contract work. That must be what this was, I guessed.

"If you can pass the physical," he laughed. "The training is worse than army boot camp and you still look pretty skinny. Can you still run?"

"For fifteen hundred dollars a month I can fly and I could put on a lot of weight," I said. To tell the truth, I had put on ten pounds in the last nine months. In high school, I had been emaciated; thanks to eating like a fiend more recently, I was now just skinny.

OK, let's go get something to eat and talk a little more. This may happen pretty fast," he said. "When are you available?"

"I am available right now. Today."

"You have to promise me one thing: you cannot tell your father or any of the guys that I helped you with this. And you should not tell him what you are doing."

"He may find out anyway and kill us both; he still knows a lot of people at Southern."

"We will have to move quickly, but we still have a day before you get your draft notice if I know the army, and I know the HR department very well," he said with a wolfish smile.

"So you mean you are sleeping with the HR department?"

"Sure. You can meet her tomorrow; her name is Cathy, and she is a real fox."

● ● ●

The next day, I drove to Dallas and met Tom and Cathy at Bobbie McGee's Conglomeration on Mockingbird Lane. It was a crazy restaurant. The waiters and waitresses were all in costume—our hostess was Tinkerbelle in an almost-see-through, fluffy dress. She took me to the table where Cathy and Tom were sitting, and Tom introduced us. Cathy was really built, as they say, and knew how to show it off in a low-cut mini-dress. The waiter arrived, dressed in purple tights and a vest with no shirt. Tinkerbelle reappeared, and they started goofing around while we ordered. Tom ordered steak and crab legs for everyone at $8.95 each, which was pretty pricey considering a McDonald's Quarter Pounder was fifty cents at the time. This was an exotic place for someone who had spent the last four years either in class, at work, or in the library. Eating out had meant the local burger place and heavy drinking was fruit juice and 190-proof alcohol stolen from the lab.

Cathy said my signing up was great since it completed her recruitment quota; she had been one man short, and now she would get her bonus. I thought it was great too; from having no job prospects and my ticket to Vietnam punched to making $1500 a month was unbelievable. She took all my information—full name, draft number, address, social security number—and said she would get the letters out first thing.

"Go on to your physical with us before the official letter comes, and if you get any communications from the army let me know immediately and don't report anywhere or reply unless I tell you to." When we left the restaurant, Cathy gave me a large packet of papers from the trunk of her car. It was all pre-employment and physical exam stuff, complete with detailed instructions which I followed on where to go and what to do. I completed everything and I was on my way.

CHAPTER 3

Training: The Beginning of Hell on Earth

• • •

The purpose of training is to tighten up the slack,
toughen the body, and polish the spirit.

— Morihei Ueshiba, founder of the
Japanese martial art of Aikido

There were about thirty of us, all about the same age—early to middle twenties. We appeared to be from everywhere: some had army haircuts, others looked like hippies. I was close to the middle, longish hair but not down to my shoulders. However, it was a true flaming red, which marked me out from the start. I was pretty apprehensive, but I tried to make conversation with some of the other members of the group. Two guys in white shirts and dark blue ties arrived, and everyone got seated and quiet.

"You gentlemen are here for training prior to assignment to overseas operations in Asia. The training here will be difficult, more difficult than the basic training many of you have had in the military. It is possible that some of you will choose to drop out, and for those who do, that may mean loss of deferment and a trip into the regular army. For those who remain, you will be paid your full salary during the training period, and it will be deposited in bank accounts for you every two weeks. You will not require any money during the first ninety days of training and will have limited contact with anyone outside the compound.

"The first three months you will be ours for twenty-four hours a day, seven days a week. You will be expected to comply with all orders; failure to comply will certainly get you dropped from the program. This is not the army. It is worse than the army, but it pays better...much better. Before we go any further, would anyone care to leave now?"

No one moved a muscle. Fifteen hundred dollars a month was an enormous amount of money.

"If you want out at any time, just let one of your instructors know, but please remember that everything you do here or see here is covered by the agreements you signed; we expect you all to maintain secrecy about everything you see or participate in, including training. You work for the government now. If you have a car here, follow the bus to the training facility and please park in the designated parking area. You will not need or have access to your vehicle until training is complete or you wash out.

"Be aware, no contraband substances are allowed. These substances include food, drink of any sort, alcohol, tobacco, and drugs. If you have any of these in your possession, please get rid of them in the trash cans provided here. You were instructed to have only the clothes you are wearing, and no luggage is allowed, so please dispose of anything of that nature, even if it is in your car. You have fifteen minutes before we depart. Training has officially started."

The training facility was off Ed Bluestein Boulevard, close to Bergstrom Air Force Base; it looked like an old part of the base. The buildings were wooden affairs, with peeling white paint. I wondered if they had been relocated from an old base. There was a twelve-foot chain-link fence with black aluminum strips like venetian blind slats running through it and razor wire around the top and in coils circling the base. I parked in the designated area, got out, and walked to where everyone was assembled. You could tell the military types; they seemed to understand what was about to happen and were cool, calm, and collected; or at least I thought so. I was nervous; the butterflies in my stomach were flying high.

Two men in green fatigues walked out of one of the buildings and over to the assembly area. "My name is Mr. Russell, and this is Mr. Sykes. We will be your instructors. Be aware, we expect you to comply with any orders we give without delay and to the best of your abilities. If you cannot meet our requirements here, you will be removed from the program immediately. Now, please form up into groups of six!"

We looked at each other, and I stepped into a group of five to make up the required six. We were the first six to form, and

Mr. Russell yelled at us get into the barracks in Bay One. We ran into the old building, which was filled with steel lockers and bunk beds arranged to form a *U*. Footlockers occupied both ends of the beds. The floor was gray painted wood, with two six-inch-wide white stripes marking the aisle. Two rooms with large windows into the bay occupied the back, and the stripes passed into a large tiled area, presumably a bathroom, at the back of the building. Which was Bay One? We had no clue, so we stood at the first bay close to the door on the right side. Group 2 arrived and took the second bay near the door. The rest of the groups tumbled into the building, followed by Russell and Sykes. Sykes looked at our group and asked, "What's your number?"

"One, sir!"

"Then why are you not in *Bay One*?"

One of the shaved head guys answered: "Sir! This recruit did not know where Bay One was. Sir!"

"Wrong answer, Jarhead." He looked at me. "So what is your answer, Red?"

"Sir. We are in Bay One. Sir."

"Well, it looks like Jarhead here is uninformed and maybe a bit dim, and Red here is definitely a smart mouth. Now listen up: Bay One is where I say it is, and it is at the back on the right. Bay Two, where are you? Get to Bay Two, back on the left. Bay Three, you are by sheer dumb luck in the right place." And so it went until we were all where we needed to be. "OK, no talking; find your racks NOW!" We all grabbed a bed, now called a rack.

"Gentlemen. Please strip completely and put all your clothes in the paper bag on your rack." Everyone rushed to comply.

"Now, gentlemen, please step outside with me." Thirty-six naked men surged for the door. I do not remember ever being naked outside before, certainly not with thirty-five other men. This was definitely not like gym class. "Now, form up!" We tried to form lines, but we were not fast enough, or where we needed to be, or in the right size lines. I tried to remember Dad's advice—stay in the middle of the formation. Well, the men of Bay One were the first rank of the formation. Not only were we naked, but we were Front Rank Naked, and I was in the pole position—the left end, the absolutely worst possible place to be.

"Are all of you idiots? I want a formation six abreast starting here. Is Bay One the only group that can hear?" The other groups jumped to get arranged, and thirty-six naked men stood in ranks.

"I am going to give you all your numbers. Please remember this number. To assist with this, Mr. Russell will write your number on your left arm. We will start here with Red. You are BAV-1. Jarhead, you are BAV-2..." and so it went until we were numbered and named from BAV-1 to BAV-36. "Now, we will try to march to the training hall. Most of you have been in the military, so this should be easy. Everyone else, just follow the guys next to you. First, put your right foot out and now your left. Now repeat right, left, right, left, right, left. Where are you going, boys?"

"Training hall, sir!"

"I can't hear you, and you have stopped. Did I tell you stop? No I did not! Everyone drop and give me fifty push-ups." Down into the dirt we went, thirty-six naked men lying in the dirt doing push-ups. This was not good. As a first rank, we had no issues, we dropped and went forward a bit, but the ranks behind us had no place to go but down and literally had to put their faces in other people's butts. Everyone was calling off push-ups; we were nowhere close to being in unison.

Sykes became completely unglued and launched into a stream of well-practiced profanity. *All together now, up on the one count, down on the two count.* The entire formation now began to move as one, up-hold-down, as Sykes counted off push-ups. "Anyone need to quit yet?" Sykes asked. Just for additional enjoyment, Russell began to spray the formation with a large water hose. "How about now? Face it, some of you will not make it. Some of you cannot take it—you might as well quit now." Well, fifteen hundred a month was a princely sum, and no one quit, even if it required a naked mud wallow. For me, quitting would be a sentence to the army anyway.

Having covered our bellies with mud, we proceeded to the adjacent building. It was a large Quonset hut affair with a concrete floor that had been waxed and polished until it shone. Two barbers appeared with two folding chairs, which they placed on the concrete slab in front of the training hall. They plugged their clippers into extension cords and proceeded to shave our heads two at a time. Even the people with shaved heads got shaved again. When finished, we stood waiting for the entire formation to complete their haircuts. It did not take long, about fifteen minutes, but the mud was drying in the hot sun. The wet hair made the clippers pull and bog down, but the barbers just continued. I was lucky I was number one. The hair was now gone, and if you had a beard or mustache it was now just stubble. The hair collected around the chairs and mixed with the mud. Six more men appeared in green fatigues, carrying several large boxes.

"Gentlemen, please meet Mr. James, Mr. Jones, Mr. Roberts, Mr. Campbell, Mr. Brown, and Mr. Harris. These men are my training assistants. Please respect them as you would me. They will directly supervise you in many aspects of the training. You may not enter my Training Hall as filthy as you are. Bay One step up"

We stood on the concrete slab in front of the building while they used water hoses in a less than kind method to wash us off. I now understood we were truly in the process of being reborn. We had left the old world behind with our clothes and were being baptized into training. We took towels from the boxes to dry off with and were told to drop them in the empty box and reform in the hall, which we did. In the hall, there were folding tables with stacks of clothes and boots. Sykes appeared at the door and walked to the front of the formation.

"I will call your name and you will find your equipment behind your name on these tables. Stand in front of your equipment." He began calling out last names and people began to break formation and stand in front of the tables.

"Now, you will find you have seven pairs of white socks. Put one pair of these on. You have seven pairs of OD (olive drab) boxer shorts. Please put one pair of these on. You will find seven white tee shirts; put one of these on. You will find three sets of OD fatigues, trousers, and blouses. Put a blouse on; button it up. Take two blousing bands," he held up two green string-looking things. They were elastic bands. "Put one on each leg under each knee and pull on your trousers. You have a garrison belt. Put it on, but do not buckle it." There were two belts; I had no idea what a garrison belt was, so I watched Jarhead select his and followed him.

"Next, put on your jungle boots. Stuff the pants into your boot tops. Drop your trousers, blouse the trouser legs over the outside of your boots, and secure them with the blousing bands you have cleverly put around your legs. Pull up your trousers and button them. Adjust the waist with the pull-tabs on the sides and buckle the belt. Now you know how to get dressed. You will dress exactly in this manner when dressed in fatigues. Every day, the same procedure will be followed: socks first, underwear, blouse, and then your trousers. You will not deviate from this procedure. For mornings, when we run in shorts, the procedure is socks, jock, shorts, and shirt. The uninitiated among you may ask why you always start dressing with your socks. There is, it turns out, actually a reason. Feet tend to get fungal infections in the tropics. Athlete's foot, especially in tropical areas, can be serious and especially when wearing boots, even jungle boots. If you put on your socks first, this infection will not be transferred from your feet, by way of your trousers or underwear, to your crotch, causing a second fungal infection. Jock rot and especially Jungle Jock Rot, gentlemen, can be more than just a bit of an itch."

It was now 6:00. "Pack up your equipment in the duffel bag," said Sykes. I watched some of the other guys carefully roll up the fatigues and tee shirts, and I followed their example. We finished as quickly as possible. "Now, one more thing: you will find a pair of dark grey wool trousers, a light grey shirt, a gray Eisenhower jacket, and a dark gray beret. You may not wear these until told, and you will be punished if you so much as put the beret on your currently worthless heads."

"We will now attempt to march you, carrying your duffels on your left shoulder, to the dining hall. Today is Sunday; you will have thirty minutes to eat your meal. Normally only fifteen minutes will be allotted for eating. Eating is to be done in silence. If you do not know how to eat properly, the training assistants will teach you."

We formed up and marched to the dining hall, stacked our duffels, and entered. There were six tables of six, and at one end two tables with three chairs each flanked a single table with two chairs. These were for the instructors and assistants. "Every Bay has a numbered table; stand behind your chairs please. You will find we will feed you very well here, and you will eat what is presented. Now be seated." I had expected some nasty cafeteria or reheated frozen food, like the dorm food at school, but it looked like they were really going to feed us like kings; well, at least until we started eating C rations, that is.

"Some of you are fat. I will work the fat off your lazy asses. Your training assistant has a list of who you are. Starting Monday, you will eat less and work more until your fat asses are history. Some of you are skinny; you will eat more and work harder until you have some muscle and you toughen up." He rang a bell, and the kitchen doors opened. Dishes on large trays carried by several waiters appeared. Plates were set in front of us: a large, charcoal-grilled steak, mashed potatoes, green beans, and plates of bread and dishes of butter. The smell was almost overpowering. But no one started to eat. Every table was served, and pitchers of ice water and glasses appeared.

"Well, it looks like you know how not to eat until instructed. This is good. When I ring the bell, begin." He rang the bell, and we all inhaled the food. It took less than thirty minutes to consume the entire meal. When we were done, the plates were cleared and a dessert course consisting of large slices of chocolate cake and black coffee was served and consumed just as quickly.

"Tomorrow, training will start. You will now return to the barracks, stow your clothing, and have the remainder of your equipment issued. Each training assistant will now take his Bay and depart from the dining hall." The training assistants appeared, and we drew Mr. Harris, a tall, rather thin guy, definitely a runner, who looked to be about twenty-five years old.

"Follow me, gentlemen." We walked back to the barracks. I had thought we would be marching around everywhere, but that did not seem to be the case. When we got back to the barracks, Harris asked which of us had been in the military. I was the only one in the group who had not been through basic training. "OK, so, Red, you are my problem child. I hope you are quick on the uptake. The good news is we don't give a shit about most of what you learned in basic like marching and saluting everything you see. Since you have not had any bad training to get over, you may be the best student, but you have to be physically up to speed and smart. You are marked to add pounds, and add pounds you will until you are at least up to one seventy-five when we are finished. Your body fat percentage is less than ten percent, so you just need to add bulk. Protein powder is available to all, but you, Red, are required to drink at least two quarts per day. Miller, I mean Jarhead, you are marked as fat and you need to lose ten to twenty pounds of fat and replace it with meat. According to the doctor's report, your body fat percentage is close to thirty percent. This is unacceptable; you need to get to twenty percent or less. You will eat less than the rest of the team and run more until you are cleared as the right weight. If I catch you cheating, I will run you to death or out—is that clear? Some of you other guys are close to being outside the correct weight and you probably know who you are, so we will watch it and train hard.

"The rest of your gear is on your racks. You have the large paper bag with your clothes. If you have a car, please give me the keys; you will not be able to use your car for at least three months. We will see that the batteries are removed and the charge maintained. You have razors, toothbrush, soap, and powder. You have a pair of track shoes, shorts, jocks, hats, and everything else you need. So tomorrow, before breakfast, which is at five thirty, we will have a little run. Figure on at least five miles to start with, so control the pace. If you go too fast at first you may be walking at the end. From this point on, you are not individuals; you are a team. No one finishes until the last man finishes. Except for Mr. Sykes's little test run tomorrow, that is. You will be in an individual race on the leg back to the base. That run will separate the men from the boys.

"There is a rhythm to the training. Monday mornings are always endurance exercise. Monday afternoons will be stations in the training hall. You will learn about that soon enough.

"Lights out is at eight p.m., so get ready. If you need to go to the head, go now before the rush." We sauntered down the long center "hall" to check out the bathroom facilities. These consisted of a WWII-vintage urinal trough along one wall, with six vintage WWII toilets standing opposite along a seven-foot half wall. Six sinks and mirrors occupied the back wall, and there was a shower with two rows of six showers, each dropped down from the ceiling. We headed back to our racks.

We had a minute to talk to each other before lights out, and I was eager to meet some of the team members. We hadn't been allowed much time for conversation. "What are stations in the training hall?"

"I'm sure we will find out soon enough."

• • •

At 4:30 a.m., a very loud whistle blew and the six assistants appeared, yelling at us to get up and get ready to run. I rolled out of my rack and opened my footlocker to remove my running shorts, jock, shoes, and socks. I knew I could do ten miles at a seven-minute pace without any problem at all. Hell, I might be able to do it at a six-minute pace if I got my adrenaline up enough. I did not think many could keep that pace.

Mr. Harris said, "No shirts is OK. Wear the black TRAX track shoes with the three white stripes, and don't try to go too fast at the start. You can always speed up. Someone will stop, and it had better not be you. Sykes is a real runner, including marathons. That is twenty-six point two miles gentlemen. He is fast, and he will cut some of the herd out for sure."

We formed up outside in a six-by-six square. The six assistants formed up on our left. Mr. Sykes arrived, and he looked like a runner, lean and in shape, but with large arms. He was wearing black shorts, no shirt and the same black track shoes we were.

"Now we have a little run gentlemen," he said. We jogged down the road toward the gate. There was barely enough light to see the road, just the occasional light from the very occasional pole. Running in formation was not natural to me. It was like running in a pack, and keeping together was not easy. With effort, I managed to stay exactly at Harris's shoulder. Being on the front row did have one benefit: there was no one in front of me to run over. The pace was slow to moderate. We ran through the gate and turned onto a blacktop road next to what looked like an old runway. We were following Sykes, and he began to pick up the pace. We kept up, and in a few minutes I fell into running mode, becoming detached and just hitting the rhythm of the pace. We continued to run in formation for at least forty-five minutes. This was not an easy trick, as I had never run in formation before and the pace was not my natural pace. Then Sykes stopped. I judged it to be almost five miles from the base. He turned to face us and said, "Now it will be every man for himself on the way back home. Run back as fast as you can; first team member back gets his team something special, but if you don't beat me back I will give you all something special. Go!"

Almost everyone took off at a really quick pace. Steve, who was also from Bay One, and I ran alongside each other and talked a bit. I said, "They are running too hard. They will never make it back at that pace." We kept up a steady run at about a six and a half to seven minute pace. Mr. Sykes was behind us. "Probably biding his time for a kick at the end," I said. Fifteen minutes, Steve and I started to pass a lot of people. Five more minutes and we passed the mass of runners in the middle of the pack. Slowly, we continued to move up. Sykes was moving up too. He was only a quarter of a mile behind us, and we were pushing to keep ahead of him. There were only three guys left ahead of us, and we were pushing the pace a bit. About half a mile from the gate, the road turned uphill, and Sykes was quickly closing the distance to us. I told Steve, "We need to kick now or he will take us on the uphill." We picked up the pace as much as we could, catching and passing the other three. One of them picked up his pace and closed with us. Sykes was about ten yards behind us, but he was not closing the gap much now. I could see the gate. Steve and I turned it on with all we had left, and so did Sykes. We were sprinting now. I was way past my normal endurance and in the runner's high state of feeling no pain. We crossed into the camp just a step or two ahead of Sykes. He kept running, so we kept going until we got to the barracks, where we collapsed. Sykes was about thirty-five, and he'd just kicked the asses of thirty-four guys ten years younger than him.

"Good run, Red, and you too," he said, looking at Steve. Some of the others were coming in now. Finally, Harris arrived in a pickup truck with six guys in the back. Woe unto them as they walked past Sykes. "Your performance is unacceptable in the run. You have six weeks to bring it up to standard or you can quit now. Some of you can't take it, and some of you won't make it." Three of them chose to quit right then; they each rang the bell in front of the barracks. Three chose to stay and would be given special attention. I realized that this was a ten-mile test and that we would have more of these to weed people out before training really got serious.

• • •

We filed into the dining hall and found our table. All six of my group was still there. Plates of eggs, bacon, and toast began to arrive, along with cups of black coffee and large glasses of water. I was 100 percent spent. I had no appetite at all; I just wanted water and lots of it. We were waiting for the service to complete when Harris walked up with a large plastic jar of strawberry-flavored protein powder, which he opened and stirred into my water. It looked nasty. He then took all of Jarhead's bacon and put it on my plate. It looked greasy. Orange juice arrived, and Harris stirred protein powder into my OJ as well. The bell rang, and we started to eat. Harris looked at me and said, "Eat first; drink as little as possible until the very end." I followed his advice and ate all the bacon. Then I ate the sausage and started on the eggs. I was shoveling it in, but we were at the ten-minute mark. I ate the bread and drank the OJ. I was right, it was nasty with synthetic strawberry. I managed to finish the OJ, but the water was still there. I only had two minutes and was worried about throwing up, but I continued to drink and barely finished as the bell rang.

We formed up outside. What I needed was some time to digest the meal, but it quickly became clear that that wasn't going to happen. I started to wonder what Harris would do if I were to vomit it all up as soon as I really started to exert myself again. I had never had problems with eating or drinking before a run, but I had never eaten this much before one either. We were marched to the other end of the camp where, in a lawn area, we found seven twelve-foot-long wooden logs which had had the bark removed.

The trainers told us to stand by the logs. Some teams had only five men due to the dropouts. A pickup arrived and new guys arrived to take the place of the dropouts.

"Now we will begin. Lift the log to your left shoulders." It was damn heavy, but we managed to lift it. The taller guys were bearing most of the weight. The trainers noted this and said, "Shuffle your team to put the tallest guy at the back down to shortest guy at the front." Somehow, we managed to do this without dropping the log. This put the weight on everyone more equally.

"Now let's have some fun," Mr. Roberts said. He seemed to be enjoying this. "Follow along with us." The trainers pushed the log up over their heads, and we followed their lead with ours. They went down to the right shoulder, we followed, and then back up above the head. Next, we moved the pole completely down to the left, passing the shoulder, and down to the knee, and then up again above the head. My arms were burning. I could feel saliva dumping into my mouth, and I swallowed. I refused to spit. Next we bent down and back up, and then we started to walk while pressing the pole up and down. I began to think I was going to vomit, and I contained the urge, but at least three people did not. The exercises continued with squats, sit-ups, and holding the damn thing over our heads for long periods. Finally, after an hour that felt like an eternity, we put them down. I really hated the pole exercises, well until met the canvas sack of sand.

After a bathroom break, we formed up and marched back to the training hall. Coolers of Gatorade sat outside the hall. We broke ranks and drank. I thought to myself, *At least Harris didn't stir protein powder into this.* It was 8:45, and the day had just begun. My stomach had calmed down, but I really needed to go to the bathroom; breakfast seemed to have made it through my system in record time. I asked Harris if I could make a trip to the toilet. "OK, but you have about five minutes, so hurry." When I got back, we marched off to a set of bleachers where we all sat down.

"Now, to exercise your minds a bit, we have Morse code practice. Anyone here know Morse code?" Hands went up. I knew dot was *E* and dash was *T* and dot-dot-dot was *S* and dash-dash-dash was *O,* but that was about all I remembered. Suddenly, however, dot became *dit* and dash became *da.* We began our first lesson on da dit da communication with a paper handout of the code for the letters and the numbers.

A PRC-25 radio arrived. "Anyone use the old prick 25 or PRC-77?" Hands went up. I felt stupid and untrained yet again. I got my first lesson in proper radio communications and radio etiquette.

At 11:45, we broke for lunch: fried chicken, French fries, and green beans. Harris came over and dropped an additional chicken breast on my plate and added the strawberry-flavored protein powder into my water. I managed to eat everything except a few French fries, but the taste of the fake strawberry lingered in my mouth.

After lunch was Stations in the training hall. Around the perimeter of the hall, various apparatuses were built into the walls, each designed to handle six participants. A pegboard with holes and one-and-a-half-inch pegs to fit into the holes, a dowel board with the last dowel offset an additional six inches from the others, thick ropes hanging from the ceiling, and pull-up bars. Each trainer stood at a station. Sykes stood in the middle of the floor with his whistle. Bay One stood with Harris at an open location on the floor. "This station is push-ups. When Sykes signals, drop down and start. I will call the cadence." Sykes blew the whistle and we dropped down and started: *up–hold–down–one, up–hold–down–two*. In five minutes, we had cranked out about forty push-ups with good form, and the whistle blew, on to the next station. We moved to the pegboard. You took a wooden peg in each hand and put them into holes in the board to pull yourself up the wall, pulling the pegs out and putting them in higher holes as you moved. Keeping your arms bent at no more than ninety degrees was crucial. If you let yourself hang from a peg, you would never be able to reach up to the next one. On to the dowel board, where we hung from the top dowel and did leg raises to ninety degrees on a slow count: *up on 1 hold, down on 2*. Whistle! We moved to an open spot on the floor where we did burpees, which I knew from high school PE as a squat-thrust. I felt saliva pouring into my mouth, the prelude to a good exertion-induced barf; eating in fifteen minutes and then immediately going to 100 percent exertion was designed to make us barf. Not throwing up was going to be a constant challenge.

The whistle blew and we went on to the rope. We lay on the floor and grabbed the rope, moving it back and forth to create waves. At the top of the rope was a bell that you had to ring constantly. Whistle! Sit-ups. Whistle! Leg raises. Whistle! Dip-push-ups, where you spread your arms and legs and rolled forward to put your chest on the floor. I was so tired that I was barely able to do these, and I had done them all day long in Karate class for years. Whistle! Sign language. Harris did the signs for A, B, C, and shit and we parroted them back *A, B, C, SHIT; A, B, C, SHIT.*

The whistle blew and we were at the pull-up bars. I was able to do five, which was not sufficient; ten was the minimum. By this time, everyone in the hall was sweating even while sitting. After about forty-five minutes, Sykes called a water break, at which I rediscovered how wonderful water tastes with no protein powder in it. My arms hurt, my legs hurt, my back muscles hurt, and my shoulders were killing me. Outside, it had started to rain and we could hear the drops amplified by the tin roof. Mercifully, the temperature was dropping.

Sykes yelled at us to form up outside, and we moved out into the rain. "We are going to go for a little buddy run," he informed us. "Bay One, Red, put Jarhead on your shoulders." I squatted down and Jarhead loaded up on my shoulders. Then I got up, just barely able to stand. He was damn heavy. Fucking lose some weight, you fat ass. "Now BAV3 get BAV4," Sykes said, and so on until there were eighteen pairs. Sykes pointed to the dirt path circling the camp. We headed off at as fast a pace as I could muster; people were passing us. *Damn, Jarhead, you are really heavy, as is the rain that is still pouring down.* The runners were churning the trail around the camp into a deep, heavy clay mud. The water collected in places and the footing was really bad. Jarhead and I were about in the middle of the pack when the guys in front of me slipped and went down. I tried to avoid it, but I slipped and joined the pile up. Jarhead and I disconnected and he landed a perfect belly flop in the mud. We sorted it out and continued around.

Then it was my turn to get carried. Around we went, churning up the dirt track thoroughly. Now down, and it was time for the wheelbarrow. I picked up Jarhead's legs and he walked on his hands while I followed. This was really slow. He fell twice, getting a face full of mud each time. On my turn, I went too fast and planted my face in a puddle of muddy water. At the bottom of the small hill, my right hand slipped, and I was completely flat in the mud. Finally, we finished.

Third time round was "carry on your back." I wrapped my legs around Jarhead's waist and my arms around his chest and off we went. Then I carried him around the track. When we made it back, we were exhausted in every way you can be. We stood in the rain, letting it cool us off and wash some of the mud off of our faces. I didn't know if I could take much more. We returned to the barracks, and there were the three trainers with hoses on either side of the concrete slab going into the barracks. By now, we knew the drill. We stripped and got hosed down before entering the barracks. The towel boxes were back and we dried and dropped off the wet shirts in an empty box, shorts in a third, jocks in fourth, socks in the last one. I sat naked on my rack; we were too exhausted to talk. I felt myself tightening up, and I stood up to stretch. Steve followed suit and soon Bay One was all in. We knew tomorrow would come soon, and we couldn't be still.

Three more men rang the bell and left the program. The culling of the herd was in full swing. We'd lost a quarter of our number, and it was only day one.

Harris came in and told us to dress for dinner. We begged Tylenol from Harris, and he passed out two to each of us. I took them without waiting for water. "You guys did OK today. Tomorrow is Combatives after the run. If you enjoyed today, you will love tomorrow." At least we all had something to look forward to.

The rain had stopped; we hurried to the dining hall, avoiding most of the deep mud, and took our seats. We started to discuss day one. The consensus was that this process was designed to get rid of a lot of people and cut down the class. We all committed to sticking with it for at least a month. I was not looking forward to Combatives, if Sykes was involved, I figured it could be mud wrestling. I had done fine on the run, but I had started to believe Sykes was out to get me, since I was one of the few men without a couple of years in the service. It was a long time until I realized Sykes was out to get everyone, not just me.

The food was amazing, or maybe the exercise drove my appetite—stuffed pork chops with corn and green beans and plates of stuffing. I got two large stuffed chops and a heap of stuffing. Jarhead got one chop and no stuffing. This time I did not get water and protein powder. I got milk with three packages of instant breakfast and several spoons of protein powder. It was like a milkshake. I cleaned the plate in fifteen minutes and sucked down the milkshake and a glass of protein powder–free water. We were stuffed and beat to death physically.

We formed up again and marched back toward the barracks, but we did not stop. Instead, we went back to where the logs were. *Oh, shit,* I thought, *I will throw up for sure if we start this again.* The front that had brought the rain had also brought cool, dry weather. There was a large amount of wood piled in a fire pit, and it had just been lit. *Are we going to walk through hot coals? Jump over flames?*

Sykes and Russell appeared along with the trainers. "Break ranks and listen up!" Sykes barked. "Red, Steve, and Roy, front and center! I told you all that anyone who beats me in the run will get something special. Here it is." He opened the coolers; they were full of beer. "Three of you beat me, and here are three beers for every man. Time to enjoy a little camaraderie. Now everyone get one, and let's drink a toast to day one being over."

Then the six trainers got together and started to sing. They sang a song called "The Corps," which I had never heard before:

THE CORPS! THE CORPS! THE CORPS!

The Corps, bareheaded, salute it, with eyes up, thanking our God.
That we of the Corps are treading, where they of the Corps have trod.
They are here in ghostly assemblage. The men of the Corps long dead.
And our hearts are standing attention, while we wait for their passing tread.
We sons of today, we salute you. You sons of an earlier day;
We follow, close order, behind you, where you have pointed the way;
The long gray line of us stretches, thro' the years of a century told.
And the last man feels to his marrow, the grip of your far off hold.
Grip hands with us now though we see not, grip hands with us strengthen our hearts.
As the long line stiffens and straightens, with the thrill that your presence imparts.
Grip hands tho' it be from the shadows. While we swear, as you did of yore.
Or living, or dying, to honor, the Corps, and the Corps, and the Corps.

They sang it a second time with the rest of us joining in as well as we could without knowing the words.

From time to time as training went on, we had fire pit meetings where we drank beer and sang songs together. Singing together was a bonding experience, and we developed quite a repertoire by the time training was over.

• • •

Four thirty in the morning came quickly on day two. We rolled out of bed. I was in a great deal of pain. I hurt everywhere—legs, arms, back, and chest. I put on my shorts and the track shoes. Sykes was not there, but we went running again anyway: out at a moderate nine-minute pace, and this time back at the same moderate pace, probably no more than five miles. I felt much better after the run; everything seemed to have loosened up.

Breakfast was just like the day before. I was beginning to be able to consume lots of food quickly. I craved bread and ate several slices. My appetite seemed to have increased along with my exercise level. Then we returned to the training hall for Combatives, which turned out to be a nice term for getting beaten up by several people in a row.

I had thought the training in Moo Duk Kwan Tang Soo Do was pretty hard. This was a Northern Korean style with heavy Chinese influence. I was proficient but not a real expert. I had a blue belt, which was the equivalent of first-degree black, since no students were allowed black; that was reserved for the Master. I had worked out with others, like my college roommate, a Judo black belt, who taught me the basics of throwing. I had learned the basics of Shotokan, especially "entering skills," which were about getting in close…I had also learned how much a cracked rib hurts.

I thought I had a lot of experience in both kata and free sparring (fighting) and had big calluses on both my knuckles and feet as well as several damaged bones to show for it, but I did not know what to expect here. We had trained with low or no contact except for bags and makiwara boards, which were lightly padded two-by-six-inch posts you struck to develop focus and body tolerance. When struck, they would move back, but just a little bit. I had spent a lot of time striking a makiwara and developing power, focus, and big knuckles. I had been hit before, but mostly when things got a little out of control. I expected things here would start at out of control and then get worse. I was right.

Sykes joined us after the run. We formed a circle around him, and he began explaining what Combatives are. "We will have some free sparring to start with. Anyone who has prior boxing or martial arts experience, hands up." I raised my hand, as did most of the rest of the group. I knew Sykes had all our papers and knew who had what experience.

"Red, where did you get those big knuckles from?" He was really observant.

"Moo Duk Kwan Tang Soo Do and a little Shotokan sir", I said.

"Have you ever fought in a tournament?"

"Yes, sir, I have."

"So what did you score?"

I felt myself turning bright red and said, "Sir, I was ejected from the tournament for illegal tactics to the face."

"Well, there might be hope for you after all!" Everyone laughed. "Well, Red, you are up first. Anyone else?" Several volunteers appeared, but it looked like everyone raised their hands.

"Okay, Bear, come on over here." A hairy behemoth came to the center. He was a monster, definitely Neanderthal genes in this guy—a knuckle-dragging boxer and a bar fight machine.

Sykes said, "Listen up. Here are the rules: *there are no rules.* Try not to strike the head, neck, or nuts; we are here to spar, not to kill. The referee whistle will start and stop the sparring when it is determined there is a loser." We did not have cups or mouth guards; I began to think this could get really nasty. "Anytime you decide you have had enough and want out of the program, just go outside the door and ring the bell a few times. Someone will help you ring the bell if needed."

Four large mats were pulled together to create a fighting square. I was really nervous and had full butterflies in my stomach. I entered the square and began breathing deeply and trying to calm down. So there I was with the Bear, who I recognized as the very large and very hairy guy who had barely completed the run. He was probably motivated to kick my ass to make up for that. I was motivated to keep Sykes from kicking me out, as it seemed like he was pretty much out to get me and I figured he'd chosen Bear as his tool to throw me out. We shook hands and squared off at each other. God! His hands were enormous, and they would soon be pummeling the crap out of me. He had huge feet as well. Well, you know what they say about people with big feet…they have big socks, and he was wearing his socks. And wearing socks on this mat was like being on a wet floor.

Bear reminded me of my first Tang Soo Do instructor, a big bull of a man. Bear outweighed me by at least fifty, maybe a hundred pounds. It was a funny-looking match-up to be sure: the 170-pound skinny kid versus Godzilla. I hoped he was slow. He took a boxer's stance. I settled into "back cat," my fighting stance, which I had adopted at the insistence of one of my sparring partners. This was a normal cat stance, except you rotated the front foot to "point" the heel at the opponent and looked over your shoulder with one arm and elbow protecting your back and one in a high guard. "Never trade punches with a boxer; you will lose," echoed in my head. *Especially one who is a monster, and this guy certainly rates as monster. Okay, got to kick him fast before he hurts me. Always get the first strike; it might be your last. Aggression pays!*

Sykes whistled to start the match. Bear, the big boxer, came forward. I used a quick skip forward, left foot replacing the right with a little twist, and a rising back kick coming in from the floor and going up...almost what the Chinese would call a Tiger Tail kick. The kick was really good; it slid under his guard and connected perfectly with his solar plexus. He crumpled forward, and I did a 180 with a hammer fist to the back of the neck. I pulled the punch and just touched him on the back of the neck at cervical vertebra number three, just like I had been trained to do.

I looked at Sykes, but he didn't whistle; he just looked back at me with a grin and shook his head. *The son of a bitch is really out to get me, I knew it! Shit!* Bear was up again. I stepped away; he followed, looking pretty damn unhappy and damn enormous and damn pissed. He punched and missed; I scored a back fist to his shoulder. It made a nice pop, but it didn't slow him down at all. I stepped inside; we were very close. I was throwing elbows, punches, and hammer fists, but Bear was faster than he looked and simply closed his arms around me in a bear hug like a wrestler. I couldn't win in this kind of grappling; it really was like fighting a bear. He was so strong; he picked me up without any effort at all and began to walk toward the edge of the mat. Maybe he was planning to take me outside and just ring the bell with my head. I struck at him with my hands and tried to choke him, but he had no neck so that didn't work. I grabbed his face with my fingers and put the thumbs under his jawline, going after those wonderful little pressure points, the pain surged through him and he dropped me like a hot potato, but on the way down he managed to hold onto my wrist.

I needed to get away from him. I broke the grab, working against the thumb with a circle, and came back inside with a spear hand to the diaphragm. He was stunned for a second and I took his hand, grabbed his pinkie finger, and reversed it. He howled with pain and struck at me with his free hand. He contacted the side of my head with a glancing strike. I figured now I was good to go at him—after all, he hit me in the head. I turned him using the finger pain, staying on his side as he continued to flail at me across his chest. I released my right hand, which I was using to control the arm, and with my now free hand I gave him a palm heel upward to the chin. *Chin is not head, right? Chin is not off the list, right?* He struck my head after all and looked a bit woozy after the strike; I released his hand and started punching his chest and solar plexus. Punch, reverse punch, punch, reverse punch; I struck as fast and as hard as I could. He was so solid that he absorbed the strikes without even attempting to block. I disengaged, this was just not working; he slumped forward just a bit. I stepped back and hit him with a full-force spinning foot sweep. His sock-covered feet slipped on the mat and he went down on his ass. Finally, Sykes blew the whistle and announced "Bear, you are out!"

Shit, I just beat the bear—well, me and his socks. That means I get to stay another day. I am elated by my victory. I am sure this is part of "culling the herd." I still think Sykes has it in for me, but I will not give the motherfucker the satisfaction; they will have to carry me out dead.

I was winded but full of adrenaline. I needed to sit down. I stood with my hands on my knees, trying to breathe. "The next fighter is you," Sykes said, pointing at a medium-height dark-haired guy. Sykes motioned me back to the center of the square. *Shit, I have to go again with no rest: this is fight till you can't.* We shook hands. This guy was not a boxer. He settled into a typical fighting stance. I settled into my back cat. He opened with a roundhouse kick. I blocked it. He spun and threw a back kick, I stepped back and blocked it, and then he threw a spinning back fist and another roundhouse. I blocked and retreated. He kept throwing one technique after another, all connected, spinning right and left and coming forward. They were all good techniques. I kept blocking and stepping back. I had seen this shit before—this guy fought like Paul, my old sparring partner, a barrage of techniques all choreographed to fit together. I had just the right medicine for this shit. He was in the middle of a set of techniques, and I was approaching the edge of the mat. As side kick came in, instead of backing, I stepped in close during the moment of the spin when he's blind. Then I put my back against the outside of his thigh and slid into horse stance as the kick came in and struck him in the kidney with a strong elbow. That stopped the action. I spun 180 degrees to take his back, and he spun around to face me, still close. That was a mistake. I stepped into him, my left foot behind his right and struck him below both shoulders with palm heels at the heart and lung acupressure points. I pushed hard, and he fell back over my heel. Sykes blew the whistle. "Okay, two for two." Maybe Sykes would eject me for not doing enough pull-ups, but he would not, by God, be able to eject me for not running or fighting.

Now I was really hurting; the adrenaline was wearing off. Sykes picked a short, burly guy and motioned me back to the middle of the mat. If this was fight till you lose, it would probably be now, as I was approaching exhaustion. This guy didn't look like a boxer and I had reach on him, but I was really tired and he was fresh. We shook hands. I settled into a short forward stance. I wanted to kick and retreat and avoid contact. He settled into his fighting position. *Oh shit, he's a Judoka.* My roommate had been a second-degree black belt in Judo. He had taught me how to throw, but I could never throw him unless he allowed me to. He was built like a fireplug, short and stout; shorter and stouter than this guy. This guy wanted to grapple and throw me around or off the mat. He came forward and I crescent-kicked to clear the attack, followed by a back kick. I made contact, but he partially blocked it. He stepped in and under and grappled with me. He tried to hip throw me, but I rolled off and didn't go down. He raised his arms and grabbed at me, and I stepped in. I caught his wrist with my left hand and punched him in the armpit with my right. It must have hurt; he released me and stepped back. He stepped in again, and we traded punches and blocks. My ribs hurt. He kicked, and I jammed it on my leg by stepping up and in with a crane stance. I came down and struck back with my fist, but he blocked it easily. We clashed now, throwing fists and elbows from in close, and then we grappled again. My adrenaline was flowing; I felt no pain. He tried to twist and throw me again, but I resisted by sliding down inside onto one knee. I pushed up and we both fell to the mat side by side. Sykes whistled. "You are both out." There was a small round of applause as we left the mat. *Merciful heaven, we punched the shit out of each other.* I began to feel pain from virtually everywhere.

Sykes picked two more fighters from the group. I was standing with Bay One watching the action. I was completely spent, bruised, and bashed, watching the fighters wail away at each other. They circled each other slowly and then got into it again, pounding each other. It was brutal. I needed water. I needed my shoes and socks. They were grappling now, and both fell to the mat. One of them landed on top by sheer luck. Sykes whistled. "You're out."

Sykes pointed at me and asked, "Want to go again, Red?"

I heard myself saying, "Yes, sir." I heard my ribs say, "You are fucking crazy!" But I didn't think you could say no to Sykes. The fifteen hundred dollars a month passed through my mind; this guy was really getting his money's worth. We shook hands. It was another fucking boxer, but he looked winded. I settled into back cat again. He came on with his shoulder toward me. I couldn't hit him with the back kick, and I didn't have a powerful roundhouse. I was slow to strike, but he was not; he turned and kicked at me with a front kick, but it was a tired boxer's front kick and a bad kick as well——slow coming in and slower getting out. I caught it. *Yes!* I pulled it up toward the ceiling and pushed as hard as I could. He went down, but so did I when his other foot slipped and hit mine. Sykes whistled and yelled, "Up!" We struggled to disengage and got up. I was on all fours when he blew the whistle and threw us both out, calling two more guys.

I had my hands on my knees and was trying to breathe. I saw Harris, "Water?" I asked.

"Not yet," he said. "Hey! You are really doing great, you aggressive little shit. You must really have berserker blood in you!"

"Thanks, Harris. What I really have is dry mouth." The adrenaline rush was over...for now.

The fighting was moving along quickly; matches rarely took more than five minutes. The last pair finished after a long boxing and wrestling match. "Form up!" Sykes yelled. I limped to my spot in the formation. Catching the kick with crane stance on my leg had not been such a good move.

Harris looked at me and said, "You okay?"

I said, "No, sir, I am not okay; I am great!" Who was I kidding? I'd had the shit kicked out of me by a large number of highly motivated individuals. Another win like this and I'd be dead.

"Now that we've had our fun, we are going to begin training," said Sykes.

Great.

"Space out the ranks, front rank five paces forward, second rank four paces forward, third rank three paces forward, fourth rank two paces forward, fifth rank one pace forward. Those who have fought more than one match already, form up out here."

We all broke out of the ranks.

"Okay, now you all get to watch and have some water if you want." I really wanted water.

Six matches started at six mats, each refereed by a trainer. Everyone was going to get a little and give a little, with the same rules: you win, you stay. The Bear sat next to me and introduced himself as Larry. He said, "You really kicked my ass, but I don't know how! I guess you really are a tough little shit."

"Well thanks, Bear—I mean, Larry; you are certainly a tough big shit." We laughed and watched the brutality on the mats. Lots of punching and pushing, a little blood, and lots of wrestling—everyone was beaten and several were bloody. The bell rang and six people quit, but no one from Bay One. Just to help us keep count, their boots were lined up on a shelf high up across the back of the barracks wall. That was a third of the class gone on day two. No replacements showed up, so we only had five bays now. Well, that was until six men who had to drop out of the previous class from injuries showed up a while later.

"We will have Combatives every day for a while," said Sykes. "Just after the run." Now, the question was, could I do this again? I was not at all sure; I figured tomorrow I might not even be able to walk.

Sykes called formation, and we moved out for lunch. Today it was large plates of something called Pad Thai, made up of noodles with fried egg and bits of meat and other stuff, including some spicy peppers. I loved it—and I still do. I also got another milk with protein powder. Then we headed back to the barracks. We were given two hours to shower and rest.

Everyone looked like shit. I had bruises everywhere. When I went into the showers, Bear was standing under the water and said, "Hey! You really bruised my ass where I landed and my chin, look!" It was true. Where he hit the mat was pretty badly blackened. There were also a number of bruises on Bear's chest, which I assumed I had contributed to.

"Look what you did to my hand," I replied showing my blackened hand. We both laughed about it. My face and my hands were black and bruised. I had several loose teeth, and when I washed out my mouth I spit out blood. I really wasn't sure I could do this again. At least not right away.

Harris, seeing me spitting blood, brought me a glass of saltwater and aspirin to rinse out my mouth. I thanked him, and he said no problem and gave me two Tylenol, a gift from heaven.

● ● ●

The next morning, I barely made it out of my rack. I was scraped and bruised everywhere. I was a Technicolor portrait of abuse: red, blood-crusted scrapes; black, blue, and green bruises; still spitting a little blood from a loose tooth. We formed up outside, and Harris led the group at a nice slow pace, out and back for just about three miles. It hurt a lot, and I mean a lot, but I made it out and back again okay. We ate another huge breakfast and went to the training hall for Combatives. This time, Mr. Russell led the exercises. Mercifully, we stretched for thirty minutes, did breathing exercises, and then did stretching again. Then Russell announced, "You will learn the proper way to punch and the proper way to move." In five lines of six spaced on the floor, we moved from forward stance to forward stance, punching and reverse punching; back and forth the entire length of the hall for forty-five minutes. This form of training would continue for weeks.

"Now is the time for sparring," Russell said. "We will have six rings, gentlemen." The training assistants helped us arrange the mats. "Bay One, in first." We dispersed into the rings. Now six opponents would be selected. I was in the first ring, and Russell called, "Bear, get over here." *Motherfucker!* He was giving me Bear again. I figured they really wanted to get rid of me. Into the square came Larry the Bear. We shook hands. Somehow he looked bigger than before. *What to do now?* Without time to think, I slid into back cat. My legs were stiff; I couldn't fight at 100 percent, and I knew it. So did Russell. The whistle sounded, and Larry the Bear attacked. I cleared with a crescent kick and then a back kick. Bear blocked the back kick with both forearms, pushing me to the side. I continued the spin and hit him with a really strong spinning back fist; it made a very audible pop and sounded like a solid strike. Then suddenly, just like in the cartoons, I saw stars and heard bells and the world started spinning; I knew I was headed for the mat. I didn't know where it had come from. That was a problem with spinning techniques: there's an instant where you are blind, and Larry the Bear just stepped in and punched my lights out.

I was only out for a few seconds. When I came around, Harris was standing over me holding up three fingers. "How many fingers do you see?" I showed him the bird. He laughed and said, "You're out, Red!"

Bear proceeded to beat the shit out of a number of other people while I watched. Finally, he got down to Jarhead. They were both big boys, but Jarhead looked small beside the Bear. This was the last match, and Larry the Bear was tired while Jarhead was fresh. They pummeled one another for a long time, and then Jarhead snuck a punch in and Bear finally hit the mat. We were done and ready for lunch.

Large chicken-fried steaks with mashed potatoes and beans were served. I was starving and ate everything on my plate. Jarhead looked beat to shit. He looked at me and said, "Man that Bear is a monster!"

"Uh-huh. And he is going to kick our collective asses again tomorrow and the day after that for a long time, and I don't really know how to avoid it."

Jarhead gave me a look full of pain. "I got him when he was completely tired and beat up today. Tomorrow could be really bad. He punched your lights out."

"I guess so; I really don't remember much except the bells ringing and lightning flashing. I guess we have something to look forward to that makes the morning run look like fun."

After lunch, we headed to the rifle range. The instructors were ready with M-16 rifles. We were told to stand on the firing line while the instructors provided safety instructions:

- This is a deadly weapon; *never* point it at anything you do not want to shoot.
- Never have it off safe except when you are at the range and in firing position.

- Never have a round in the chamber except when you are ready to fire.
- Never aim past the two large posts to the left and the right. I will use a whistle to provide the signals.

I had read the manual, but I'd never fired an M-16 before. The rest of the guys seemed to be familiar with the weapon though.

"Now, we will determine your skill level" said Mr. Russell.

I already knew my skill level was very low.

"Bay One, up first." Harris handed each of us a weapon; I held mine the same way Jarhead held his...or at least as good an imitation of him as I can manage. Harris passed out empty twenty-round magazines to us.

"First, clear the weapon. Before you handle a weapon, the first action is always to clear the weapon," said Harris. I followed Jarhead's lead.

"The range is hot! On the line, load one round into the magazine. Lock and load." I shoved the round into the magazine and rammed the magazine home, locking it into the weapon. I watched Jarhead make the weapon safe by moving the selector to safe. Then I figured out how to pull the charging lever, since an M-16 does not have a bolt handle on the side like a hunting rifle, and let it chamber the round. I had seen this done before when I was a kid growing up in the country, where firearms were common. I felt Harris watching me closely and got really nervous.

"From a standing position, prepare to engage the target on my signal." I turned, following Jarhead's lead again. Single shot only. I turned the selector from safe position to fire. I put the rifle against my shoulder and my cheek against the stock. I looked through the sights, aligning the post with the target centered in the ring of the back sight. I expected a big kick and tensed up. I knew this was bad, though, and tried to relax.

"Ready on the right! Ready on the left! Ready on the firing line! At the command of fire, fire a single round at your target center of mass. Fire!" I thought I had the right sight picture; I had the post on the target and had it centered in the ring. I pulled the trigger. The rifle discharged, and I felt no significant recoil. The first target was only fifty yards away. I scored a bull's-eye, center of mass. *Well, it can only be downhill from here,* I thought, and it was.

"Now," Harris says, "when I give the command to fire, you will have thirty seconds to fire nine single shots at the target. Remove your magazines and load nine." He handed us each nine rounds. I pushed nine rounds into the magazine.

"Engage the magazine!" I shoved the magazine home. "Lock and load." I checked the selector, pulled the charging lever back, and released it.

"Prepare to fire a single shot only." I moved the lever to the fire position.

"Fire on my command." He blew the whistle. I got the sight picture I wanted and squeezed off another round. It hit the target on the paper, but not in the silhouette. The next eight shots formed a loose group—sort of center of mass, but really all over the target.

Harris then said, "Cease fire, cease fire. Make all weapons safe, clear the chamber, lock the charging handle, and ground the weapon." We followed the instructions and placed the rifle on wooden boxes at each station. Isn't it amazing how a single little *click* makes a killing machine safe?

This process was repeated with the rest of the bays. Standing next to me Jarhead said, "Where are they getting these range commands? They are not like the ones in the Marines." Shit. It was the blind leading the visually impaired.

"Gentlemen, we are done for today. Tomorrow, I will instruct you on how to zero and to properly sight in the M-16, how to fire the M-16, and how to clean the M-16. I will teach you how to aim and make long shots before you get the Sykes method of close quarters combat with a rifle. And over the next several months, he did and we did. I was never great with the rifle—acceptable, middle of the pack, but never great.

We made it back to the bunkhouse, which smelled like a Ben-Gay factory. I headed for the showers. I took a quick look and became convinced that I was the most battered and bruised person there. I was also starving. It was time for supper and bed.

The next morning, before the run, we had a quick checkup by a doctor. We all stood naked on the line in the barracks while this grizzled old flight surgeon took a look at us. Harris must have told him I had some bleeding in the mouth, because he checked mine carefully and gave me a shot of lincocin hydrochloride, a strong antibiotic. Harris repeaed this everyday for a week.

"Today, we will run in boots and fatigues" announced Harris.

I was sore everywhere; my legs, my shoulders, and my arms were all killing me. I loved my black track shoes; they weighed almost nothing, and I felt fast in them. This race would be an endurance test. Running in track shoes was to kill the big guys, running in boots and packs was to kill the rest of us. We ran out about two miles in formation—fast, but not a dead run; pretty good for wearing boots, I thought. Later on, I found out just how much I didn't know. The way home was another race. I finished in the top ten, not the top three, and my feet and legs really hurt. I had a hot spot on my heel. Getting back took some time, since there were a few slow boys in the group, including the Bear. Running was not the Bear's cup of tea. I encouraged him at the finish; he took two steps after the line and puked.

"At least I finished," he moaned, "and I'm not last."

Harris came over and said, "Tomorrow we do this with packs and sandbags."

Back at the barracks, Harris held foot inspection. A couple of us had developed blisters. He called over the medic, who had two syringes and a bottle of mercurochrome. First, he inserted a syringe and pulled the liquid out of the blister. Then he injected a small amount of mercurochrome and forced it out through the first hole. We were told to leave the blister alone—don't peel it off—and he gave out moleskin patches as well.

The packs (rucks) were issued and were always on your back and dragging you down. As the training continued, we added weight every week until we were running with a forty-pound pack and routinely humping an eighty-pound pack for miles. We learned how to properly adjust and pack a ruck with ammo and water so it didn't make noise as you moved through the bush. Sand was more comfortable to carry than ammo. The

instructors knew this, of course, so as soon as we showed proficiency with sand they switched us to water and ammunition.

Bear seemed to be impervious to the added weight; he
didn't get much faster, but he didn't slow down, which moved
him up in the rankings.

When you need help getting up, then you know the pack is
heavy enough. Eventually, we would do a fifteen-kilometer (9.3
miles) cross-country hike with a sixty-five-pound pack in under
four hours. This was not a promenade. I had run ten miles in
about an hour, but the loaded hike was many times more difficult.
It was not on a road, and while sixty-five pounds may not sound
like much, moving at speed with that much weight is really tough.

• • •

On day four, we went to the training hall for Stations and started with pull-ups...with Harris counting, "One, two, three, three
again, three again, three again." I could manage only three of six
tries. I was tied for last place with three other guys from Bay One.
Half of us sucked. Harris said, "Totally unacceptable." We rested
for five minutes while Harris reamed us. Then we were back on the
bar, and I did four! Amazing what a little motivation can do for you.
My lack of upper body strength showed, and what chest muscles I
did have were screaming at me. We continued the circuit: push-
ups, sit-ups, Burpees, sign language, and so on around the hall. We
added exercises with ten-pound dumbbells into the mix. Finally,
we were finished; my upper body muscles were still screaming.

"Okay," Sykes said, "form up and back to barracks—shower, shave, and shit, and get dressed for lunch." I could hardly wait to put hot water on my chest, arms, and back, even if it was only for five minutes. I was hoping maybe we could beg some more Tylenol from Harris. I figured on being beaten up by Bear that afternoon, so at least I had something to look forward to. On the plus side, I felt like I had gained some weight, even if most of it was just fluid from swelling sprains and bruises. There was no hot water in the showers though. It wasn't used up—it was just turned off. *Fuck it,* I thought. Even cold water felt good.

We ate lunch and then we formed up and moved to the training hall. Training was about to enter a new stage. Sykes had us sit in a semicircle around him and said, "So far, you have really not performed anything we would really call Combatives. We simply had everyone show us how they fight and got rid of your weak sisters. Some of you fight surprisingly well; some with training, like Judo, Karate, or boxing, are pretty good, and some of you may just be lucky. Red," he said, looking directly at me, "I admit I was surprised to see you beat the Bear. I also admit, sorry Bear that it was a thing of beauty, a sheer joy to watch, and it proves my point that training can make all the difference in the world. When he is fighting, Red here almost never takes his eyes off his opponent's *hara*—a point about three inches below the navel. The Chinese call it *tan t'ien*, the Koreans call it *dan jun,* and our Indian friends call it the *swadhisthana chakra*. It is the balance point of your body, and where it goes, you go. No head fakes can happen if you take your cue from the *hara*. Red had some good instructors, and that is why he was able to get the better of Bear here; well, at least once so far. You all still have a lot to learn, and I mean all of you."

Sykes then began the first of many lessons on what we called Combative Arts. This was a blend of various combat styles, including Karate, Judo, Akido, and dirty street fighting. Sparring changed and became a controlled activity designed to practice specific techniques, to harden the body to being hit, and to develop the strength needed for grappling. We ran lots of two-man sets, repeating specific techniques over and over. Over a period of about ninety days we became hardened and sharp.

Speaking of sharp, we were also taught knife fighting and use of a combat blade. The standard issue blade was the British Commando blade, a Sykes-Fairbairn double-edged stiletto knife; it was a beautifully designed knife. I do not know and never asked if Sykes himself was any relation, but I wouldn't have been surprised.

Sykes-Fairbairn double-edged stiletto knife

A few of us, including me, chose the Japanese chisel point Tanto as a primary blade for training and the Sykes knife as a secondary weapon. Some chose the Marine Corps Fighting Knife as the primary weapon. The Tanto was good choice, because it turned out Sykes was a master instructor of Tanto Jitsu, the art of the Japanese knife fighting. *"In the hands of a master, the blade, though seldom seen, is always present"* was the credo of Tanto Jitsu. We learned blade handling, hiding, and the seven classic strikes with the knife. I never attained even close to the proficiency of a master, but I was not bad either. Tanto Jitsu was also an exercise in concentration and breathing.

Tanto Knives

We fought with the actual blades most of the time. Initially, the blades were kept in their sheaths, but as we progressed, the edges of the blades were encased in a thin rubber tube with a long slit down its length. This was held in place with black cloth tape. Even with this thin layer of protection, I received a long cut on my right arm when just a tiny bit of the point of my opponent's blade made it through. It was a clean cut, about four inches long and not deep. It cut me like a razor, and it healed with just a small scar that I still have today. Fear of the knife in a fight abated as we became very used to the blade being present in two-man sets and the parry and thrust drills. Using the blade as an extension of the body and integrating it with strikes and locks took the most time. We also learned *kata,* or forms. These helped solidify our techniques onto the same movements, correct in the details of the parries and strikes.

Both the Sykes knife and the Tanto were weapons to cut the opponent, but the fighting styles were different. The Sykes knife was all about the point, you stuck it in and cut by ripping it out. It was held tightly with the thumb and first two fingers and less tightly with the last two fingers. Targets were major blood vessels like the carotid or femoral arteries or heart. I always thought the Sykes knife was more of an assassin's tool, a covert weapon, the "sneak up behind someone and kill him or her" knife. The Tanto, on the other hand, was a more overt weapon and was all about the blade and the cut. The knife was held tightly with the pinky finger and the finger next to the pinky, and the thumb and first two fingers had a grip but not the death grip.

in addition to the mechanics of the martial arts, the instructors, especially Mr. Sykes, also taught a sort of code of action—a Bushido or code of the organization as they saw it. "We have a debt and duty to our society. We are required to defend our beliefs, sometimes with blood," Sykes told us. I believed that we all saw that what we were doing was in line with these ideals and that we were defending our nation.

We trained hard in the martial arts. The core was Korean kicking with Japanese hand techniques. The style used dynamic tension, which we trained in using to resist punches and kicks.

One exercise exemplified the training: six men would lie on deck next to each other, about a foot apart, with their heels lifted and heads and shoulders curled up, while six other men ran across their stomachs, making the circuit several times. The key was to exhale, focus your *chi,* and tense just as each foot hit your belly. Then the roles were reversed, and the runners became the "floor mats."

Ultimately, I overcame both my pull-up deficiency (if fresh, I could do more than twenty pull-ups at the end of the ninety days), and I quickly gained more than fifteen pounds, all of it muscle. If I had had any fat, it was all gone, even though I was eating like a fiend and consuming massive amounts of calories.

Once we were physically ready, our training shifted to how to exit a helicopter, including the ability to free rappel. In small landing zones set up in the woods and in some farmer's fields east of Austin, we learned how to tie a Swiss seat harness, how to rappel from a helicopter into a landing zone, and how to exit a Pickup Zone (PZ) attached to a rope.

We were instructed in the art of stealth. We Americans had learned from the Aussies that in stealth mode you did not just hack your way through the jungle with a machete like Bogart in the African Queen, but instead you silently snipped your way through with secateurs (known to the country boys in the group as garden shears). The point man (lead person) did the cutting and the drag (last man) covered the trail. I was acceptable (maybe even good) at this, but the main benefit was that now I could really understand and appreciate the masters of stealth.

We went on a large number of field exercises. These generally involved packing an eighty-pound ruck, running an insertion drill from a helicopter, cruising around some farmer's woods for a few days, and then heading home. We got to test all the available C Rations and LRRP Rations and civilian food as well. Living on this shit without a fire or heat for a couple of weeks was more than a test. I knew that our deployed military in 'Nam did this for months, the poor bastards. We also had dried beef, beef jerky, sardines, tuna, and that marvel of science, the ziplock bag. These were new and very sturdy compared to the ones we get today. Supply used them to contain small parts, but they also worked great for keeping things in that you did not want to clank together and things you did not want to get wet, like jerky.

It was hard to keep or add weight when eating out of a can. I actually missed my constant doses of protein powder. My appetizer standby became tuna in olive oil, sometimes substituting sardines in olive oil and canned scrambled eggs with chopped ham for breakfast. The bottom line was that grease, protein and sugar were three of the important four food groups. Tropical chocolate was the fourth if you could get it. I liked M&Ms better, but they could be noisy unless they were stowed right.

My least favorite field exercise began with a hike down to the river in a light rain (I guess it was the Colorado, but I really cannot recall). We used our ponchos to make rafts for all of our gear and clothing and then floated them across the river with our rifles on top. I am, at best, a poor swimmer, but of course that was not something I was about to share. So this exercise was really scary for me. Fortunately, I made the crossing without help, since my pack floated well, but the water was cold, and I turned noticeably blue and shivering, with chattering teeth, just like in the cartoons. When I finally got out, I was greeted by, "Hey! Look at this! Red just turned blue on us!" followed by lots of laughter at my expense. A lack of body fat meant that cold and water together, for me, really, really, sucked.

Every time it rained, we were out in it. I later understood that during the rainy season dealing with rain was essential and getting used to it was important, but at the time I was sure it was just the result of a sadistic bastard running the show. A pine forest in Texas may not be exactly equivalent to an Asian monsoon, but the rain got damn wet during Texas tropical downpours, and it was definitely colder. In the winter, it was just miserable, and we were often not allowed to have coats or ponchos, so we got wet and cold. Wet at ninety degrees isn't pleasant, but wet at forty degrees is torture.

After months of physical harassment, the day finally arrived for the next step. We knew something was about to happen, but we didn't know what. We loaded up in a Southern Air Transport C-130 with all of our equipment and left our little base for parts unknown.

CHAPTER 4

The Jungle

• • •

On a hard jungle journey nothing is so important
as having a team you can trust.

— TAHIR SHAH

PARTS UNKNOWN TURNED OUT TO be parts very well known—a
small country known as British Honduras, which had two important assets: exceptional jungle and a British military camp in
the middle of it. The US Jungle Training Base in Panama was
booked up solid, and British Honduras was better. Both have
triple canopy jungle, but Honduras had dark Travellers rum as
well. Since I had recently received a Dear John letter from my
girlfriend, who was not happy with my extended absence, I welcomed a road trip. I thought it was a good way to get my mind
off my problems. And I was not the only one with girl issues, so
I did not feel alone.

A little explanation for those who do not already know:
when people talk about triple canopy jungle, they are talking

about the thickest jungle around. It consists of (at least) three layers: the forest floor, often covered with rotting leaves, the shrub layer, which is from the ground to about 50 feet, a second layer of trees and plants from 50 to 150 feet tall, and a final layer of the massive monster trees that penetrate the second canopy and reach heights of 200 feet or more. There is so much foliage above that very little light makes it through to the ground, often as little as 2 to 5 percent. In the darkest parts, the lack of light reduces the thickness of the understory, but at the edge of a river or a large stream where no large trees exist, the shrub layer becomes amazingly thick. The thickest understory plants are always found at the margins of rivers or streams or clearings.

Mangrove trees, a common water's edge or swamp plant, can even be found in salt or brackish water. These trees have a mass of multiple roots and grow into a virtual wall that is almost impenetrable. They support their own ecosystem of birds, snakes, lizards, and fish. Even bamboo can be thick and difficult to move through. Ironically, the smaller, thinner stuff (about the diameter of a finger) is the hardest to get through. The canes get so windblown and tangled that they become a huge knot. It is an obstacle to simply go around if at all possible, so bad that it is actually marked on some maps.

The rule of thumb in the jungle is that everything will bite, sting, stick, or otherwise hurt you. Every bug, fly, or snake seems to have a nasty attitude, as do some of the plants with thorns and razor sharp leaves...and did I mention the leeches? They climb up on the plants to hitch a ride on you if the plants are at all wet, as they are every morning. A wound from a leech can leak blood for a long time, as they have an anticoagulant in their bite to keep the blood flowing. That makes leech bits particularly prone to infection. And what about the mosquitoes? They are hellish in some places. They can get you through your fatigues without any difficulty. You can actually pull the fabric a bit and trap the little buggers in the act. Insect repellant works to remove an attached leech, but mosquitoes just lap it up and keep going.

You might say I was not fond of jungle insects.

We landed on a little strip where two trucks (Lorries) waited for us. We loaded up in the trucks and were off down a short track to the Airport Camp now known as the Price Barracks, a British post in Ladyville, British Honduras, bordering the beautiful blue Caribbean Sea. The post was made up of a series of sheet metal buildings with the distinctively British touch of a classic red British telephone box sitting just outside the barracks. Part of working with the Brits meant learning a new vocabulary. We dumped our gear (kit) in the barracks and discovered we were just in time for the afternoon *stand easy*, or brew. This was tea, brewed in an enormous metal kettle and served in mugs. We all stood around TUBBIN (thumbs up bum, brain in neutral) and met the trainers. Mr. Russell had accompanied us, as he was an expert in jungle warfare, but we would have some British instructors as well.

The first exercise was an evasion and escape that very afternoon. Everyone got a compass, a liter of water, and whatever we wanted from our packs that would fit in our trouser pockets. We were taken in the lorry down a dirt track to where a second dirt road intersected it. Here we formed up and were given instructions. Rule one was stay away from all the snakes as they are all "nasty buggers," especially the coral snakes and the infamously nasty fer-de-lance. The team of twelve instructors and Mr. Russell would give us a ten-minute head start. The objective was to make it five miles through the jungle to another road, which paralleled the one we were on, before the instructors caught up to us. The jungle was pretty thick in spots, but there was a long patch of almost open territory and a trail that made a sharp turn about one hundred meters ahead. We lined up, the whistle blew, and we ran.

While I ran, I took a camo stick out of my pocket and applied the green paint to my face and neck—no pattern, just green. I decided to take the high ground. Just as the open area necked down and the trail turned there was a large old downed tree with a few scraggly limbs remaining. It was covered with moss, which was growing where leaves and bark had mounded up against one side—a perfect hiding place. With my knife, I cut the moss just against the underside of the log. Next, I carefully pulled the moss-covered detritus up and inspected it for vermin. It came up like a blanket because the layers of large leaves had not decomposed but just sort of stuck together. I was able to remove some of the decomposing leaves on the bottom and push them under the detritus toward the end of my little ranger grave. Then I squeezed down into the area between the log and the ground, pushing my boots under some of the moss at the bottom and then pulling the "blanket" back into place over my body and higher up against the log rather than down under it. This took a few minutes, but I was pretty sure I was invisible.

The trainers came walking slowly up the trail, and I became completely still. They stood right on the top of the big log, and one of them even took a piss. Fortunately, my "roof" of leaves and moss was pretty watertight. I listened to them talking about how easy it was going to be to root us out and how this was not even a proper jungle...just a bit of thicket. Then one of them bet Russell a fifth of Scotch whisky if anyone one made it to the road undetected, and he accepted. "Johnnie Walker Black good enough?" said Russell.

"Yes, an excellent choice," said the voice. Had I been discovered? Did the guy who pissed on me know I was there? I didn't move. Ten minutes passed, and they all moved off down the path, tracking the rest of the team. I waited another ten minutes, just listening, and then I gently opened a small opening to peer out. I saw no one. I listened another few minutes and then slowly crawled out of the hide.

I moved to the edge of the jungle and worked my way back to where the lorry had been parked. I heard it start and drive off. I followed just at the edge of the bush. It turned and headed down the road toward the road we were to reach. I took my camo paint sticks out of my pocket and completed the application of the paint. On the edge of the dirt track, I made my way down the road as quickly as I could. I wasn't going to set any world speed records running in combat boots, but as long as I wasn't seen, I would beat everyone but the truck to the other road. I ran for about fifty minutes or so and then saw the crossroad ahead. I drank all the water in my canteen, as I had been sweating in hot humid air. Even with the wind coming down the road, it was steaming hot and you lost water to sweat like crazy.

From the dense jungle understory, I could see the lorry and two soldiers lighting a primus stove and putting water on to boil. They had built a small cleared area for the stove at the side of the track. They had their backs to me, facing out toward the lorry, and I moved as silently as possible to the edge of the bush, just a few meters from them. The wind moving the leaves helped to camouflage any sounds. The foliage at the edge of the road was very thick, with many big-leaved understory plants. I was well camouflaged with my Tiger-stripe pattern jungle fatigue and face paint, and I knew I was damn close to invisible in the thick plants.

Tiger-Stripe Camoflage Trousers and a Marine Fighting Knife

They had brought folding chairs, and they sat down and proceeded to brew up a large pot of tea. I waited and watched. When the tea was done and they both had a mug, they sat down and decided to have a smoke break as well.

Moving like a snake, I slowly exited the cover of the bush through an area of less growth. I made a few judicious cuts and then crossed the two meters just behind them undetected. I quietly put a hand on each guy's shoulder.

"Holy mother of God!" They bolted upright and the tea mugs went flying. Other interesting British curses poured forth; after all, the tea was hot. "You scared the shit out of me!"

"I am sorry to have scared you, but I assumed this was the rally point. I was watching while you made tea and thought I might get a mug if it's not too much trouble. I suppose someone also owes Mr. Russell a fifth of Johnnie Walker Black as well, but that would not be any of our business, I guess."

They were completely taken aback. "How the bloody hell (bloody this and bloody that was apparently some British curse similar to our fucking this and fucking that) did you get here so fast?"

"These boots did slow me down a bit, but I have been observing you all for a few minutes. I didn't want to just pop out of the bush and get shot, you know." I was given a mug of tea, and some cookies (biscuits).

"Okay, Yank, so honestly, how did you get here so quickly?"

"Well, I'm not a Yank. I am from Texas, and I will admit I did run part of the way; is that cheating?" I asked.

"No, no that is allowed, but they would catch you for sure. They have an Indian tracker or two with the group. There's no getting away from those boys."

"Well, I am part Choctaw and Cherokee; maybe it was professional courtesy."

"It will be another hour or two before the trackers are expected in," they said.

"That's fine," I said. "I brought my hammock." I pulled a balled up string hammock out of my pants. "Perhaps I can take a quick nap while we wait for the rest of the guys?" Of course I hadn't brought the hammock because I planned on taking a nap, but because it could be used as the base of a Ghillie suit by hanging leaves and such from the mesh. But I didn't have to tell them that. I strung the hammock between a tree and the lorry, sprayed some bug juice on the ropes connected to the tree to discourage the insects, and pretended to go to sleep just for effect.

The radio crackled, and one of the Brits picked it up and explained the "current situation" to Colonel Sir Richard, who was apparently somewhat unhappy with my presence. The rest of the team had been rounded up as quickly as expected. A couple of raindrops had come down on me, so I decided to get up and stow my hammock.

"Are we going to have a brew in the truck before the rain starts?" I asked. My new British buddies looked at me strangely, and just then the heavens opened up with a downpour. We sat in the back of the truck on folding chairs under the canvas top, sipping tea and discussing the football league and how Manchester City, my team, though not in the top ten, was at least better than better than Manchester United. Still, the winner had been bloody Liverpool, a team none of us liked. Then Russell and Colonel Sir Richard arrived with the remainder of the team.

"Well, lad, I must say, job well done!" said Sir Richard. "Job well done indeed, and you cost me a bottle of Scotch as well."

"Johnnie Walker Black as I recall, sir," I said. "Sorry about that, sir. I hope you don't take any offense."

They looked at me strangely and Russell said, "Red, you are just full of surprises. How did you know?"

"I overheard your conversation, sir, unintentional on my part I assure you. Let's just leave it at that," I said.

"No, no, sir," said Sir Richard. "You must show me just how you managed."

"Well, I hid until you passed by, and then I traveled as fast as I could to get here at the edge of the road that I assumed would intersect the other track. By the way, someone pissed on me while I was doggo in my hide. Quite unintentional I am sure, but still." Everyone laughed, especially Sir Richard.

"So you were actually underfoot!"

"Yes, Colonel, I was underfoot and almost underground."

"Get everyone loaded up; I am very interested in inspecting your hide. Then we shall have few drinks on me, and tonight you will all be our guests at the Mess for some local food. And afterward, we will get you all ready for the jungle tomorrow." So we filled the Lorries up and everyone talked about how they had been caught. How the Indian trackers saw through all the camouflage, no matter how good it was, and how they could track through any terrain. I had been lucky. The first group walking up to the log had covered my tracks, and they did not inspect the area because the whole group was standing there.

We arrived back at the starting point just as the rain stopped. It was just a short walk to where I had made my hide. The blanket of moss was still intact, and Sir Richard had quite a laugh. "Well, I'll be damned. I nearly stepped on you. Where did you learn to make this kind of hide?" he asked. "It is very clever, indeed."

"I am part Indian; maybe it is in my genes."

"You are, as Mr. Russell said, full of surprises," said Sir Richard.

"Yes, Mac here is always full of surprises, Sir Richard. You are quite right about him," said Russell with a curious smile.

Then we headed back to the barracks, where we cleaned up, changed into dry clothes, and walked to the Mess. I sat with the two British soldiers from the rally point, Nigel and David, and their mates. A meal of local delicacies was brought in and consumed with a great deal of camaraderie and a new local beer called Belikin, which was a real treat since we had had almost no beer during training. I enjoyed it all, especially being the hero of the day for not getting caught.

The next day we moved into the jungle. There was a base camp there, which consisted of some old tents, but we actually spent almost the entire time living rough in the jungle. This in itself was a daily lesson in survival.

• • •

At the time, I did not see any real use to most of the activities planned for us in British Honduras. Maybe the camouflage and silent moving through the bush was something to practice, but having a local farmer teach us how to survive on local plants wasn't going to be much help in Vietnam, and I didn't think I would be constructing any jungle shelters in Southeast Asia.

Training consisted of breaking up into our six-man teams and running field exercise challenges. Each of the several evolutions we ran were designed to teach and test different aspects of jungle warfare. Most of this was a rehash of our earlier training, only done in the real jungle.

The first evolution was moving through the bush silently. The six-man team moved single file with about three to ten meters between us. After ten minutes of slow, deliberate movement, travel stopped and we watched and listened for five to ten minutes. The first man was called the point man; he had to chart the course. This was not easy, since it involved map reading, estimating the distance by counting paces, and using the compass to maintain direction. Map reading in the bush with limited visibility was tough, and little things could make a big difference. Just determining distance and direction while having to zigzag through the bush and navigate around obstacles with multiple headings with good directional accuracy was really tough without having sight of any references like a mountain a hill or a big tree to use to take bearings from. For all of these reasons, we used offset bearings, which was basically adding a few degrees, up to ten, to ensure that we ended up a known direction from the intended point. So if you were aiming for a ford of a river, you'd make sure you were west of the point so you would know when you got to the river to turn east to find it. Otherwise you could end up walking in the wrong direction and having to backtrack all the way back to the starting point.

Determining distances traveled wasn't simple either—it couldn't be done with a measuring tape! The method we used was called pace counting by Americans or tally stepping in Brit speak. It simply involved counting the number of steps taken and converting this to distance. A device called a tally pace counter that consisted of two sets of beads strung onto some cord and separated by a knot. Every ten steps, the point man would move a bead on the lower set of nine beads, and when the hundredth step was taken, one of the beads above was moved and the process began again. Neither of these methods was highly accurate, but they were the best things we had. GPS was not even a glimmer in some research geek's eye at that point.

I need to be clear here, some people seemed to have an innate ability to accurately navigate and others no ability at all. I fell into the average group.

We went on many simulated missions, looking for the different teams and hiding from the teams. We learned a lot of woodcraft very quickly and learned how to wrap ourselves in the jungle to hide. We lived for a month on the infamous C rations or *rats,* as they were called, as well as some commercial products like corned beef. If you have never eaten breakfast, lunch, and dinner out of a can, then you do not really appreciate proper food. Some of these rations were really nasty. In my mind, the "mutton" stew was the worst. Pork and potatoes, ham and eggs, franks and beans, and ham and lima beans were all okay. My favorite thing was a fruitcake that most people despised It was easy to trade forsince they wanted to get rid of it and there was the occasional tropical chocolate bar. Needless to say, supplementing with food gathered in the forest became extremely important.

Of all the simulated missions we ran, the most challenging was a Snatch and Grab, where two six-man teams went into the bush and the first team was to navigate along a trail from the start to another location ten or twenty miles away. The second team was the Grab team, and their job was to capture a member of the first team and get him to another location.

We were paired with a six-man British team on our last Snatch and Grab. We were to grab one of the middle guys. He had a red cloth armband to identify himself. To be honest, the SAS were really the best of the best in this sort of stuff, but this particular team had very bad luck. We had set up an ambush along the trail in the perfect spot, right where our victim decided to take a leak. He stepped off the trail, electing to pee on a large tree Jarhead was standing behind. The rest of his team continued walking, and needless to say he was easily captured and they were sitting ducks when I triggered the ambush that "killed" the rest of the team. The SAS guys don't like losing much. We all came down onto the trail, and one of the guys, Norman Isherwood, couldn't control himself; he actually took a swing at me when I popped up and announced "Claymore you are all dead". My Aikido kicked in, since it was the last thing we had studied, and I easily put him on the ground and locked him up. This just added insult to injury, and he was really unhappy. I believe he may have had some significant money bet on the outcome of the exercise. Tough shit, Isherwood.

The final challenge was to spend three days in the bush with a machete, a liter of water, and little else. By that time, I was confident that I could do it. True, I had some concerns as I walked into the jungle, but my fear was quickly overcome. I found a small clearing and decided to make my camp there. Two saplings became the uprights for my lean-to. I used small lianas to make twine to tie supports in place. Fortunately, the local Palmetto palms grew in abundance. I cut palm leaves off one of the plants and made a roof by cutting them at the stem to make a hook, which held them onto the small cross sticks, enabling me to weave them together like shingles.

I was also lucky to find several banana trees at the edge of the clearing, probably left from someone's garden. I cut a banana trunk off about two feet from the ground and hollowed it out. It quickly filled with clear water, which I discarded, since the first fill was always bitter from tannins, and waited for the second fill for a nice drink. I carefully covered it with a banana leaf and went into the clearing to scout for wood. A few downed trees in a sunny spot provided some pretty dry wood, and the fibers from some of the wood helped me to build a "bird's nest" of tinder like

I had been trained. I did not have the materials for a fire drill, so I decided to try a fire plow, which is normally much harder than a fire drill, but if you get lucky with the wood it works. After some work, smoke began to coil up from the groove and the shavings I was making. I blew on the shavings, which were smoking, and dropped them into the bird's nest of dry shavings and tinder I had made earlier. Just a little breath until the smoke really started, and then it caught and I had fire! I carefully added small sticks and more tinder, then larger sticks, and finally a branch or two. I had water, fire, and a roof. There was a stand of bamboo not far down the path, and I cut several canes and used them to build an off-the-ground sleeping platform. I also cut some ferns to add some softness to the top layer. I kept the fire built up and placed wood around it to dry. Finally, I cut a few of the green bananas and ate one after roasting it in the fire. I had a good drink of banana water and was ready for the night.

I removed my boots and socks and hung them to dry by the fire. I positioned my feet so that they also got warmed and dry. Not bad for day one. I dozed but kept the fire stoked through the night. Toward morning, it began to rain lightly. I recovered my boots and socks before they got wet and put them on. Afterward, I added the last logs to the fire and, using bamboo chopsticks, I put some hot coals into a joint of bamboo filled with dry grass and tinder as an attempt to keep the fire available if the embers all got quenched by the rain. My shelter turned out to be very waterproof. As long as the wind didn't blow too much, it shed the water perfectly. I remained completely dry and warm, with water to drink and roasted green bananas to eat.

At the edge of the clearing was a "Bastard" tree (I later learned it was also called a Give and Take tree). It was covered with sharp thorns that inject a nasty toxin, and the only known antidote for the thorn's toxin was the sap of the tree. I gave it a wide berth—trees with spines all over the trunk and branches usually meant business. But close to this tree was a bank of canna lilies, related to the ones my mother had grown in our yard. They were edible; I dug up the roots, decided to bake them for a long time, and buried them in the ground wrapped in banana leaves, building my fire right above them. I drank more "banana water" and made a second cut just eight inches above the ground, cutting another hollow to get the banana to give me more juice. It obliged by filling the new bowl quickly. I decided to see if I could get some bamboo shoots, since I knew that they are good when eaten fresh and raw. I was not disappointed. I cut several very new shoots and was able to munch on them to keep hunger at bay.

While I was in the bamboo, I noticed two men walking toward my little camp and covering up their tracks as they went. I decided to go doggo and see what they had in mind. They proceeded to get close to my little lean-to and then hide, so when I arrived they would be in place for whatever they planned to do. Well, I figured three could play at that game. I had my knife and my secateurs in my pocket. I took my time, about two hours, to creep up on them. I thought one looked like my mate Nigel from the lorry. The other guy was a tracker. As I got closer, I could clearly see Nigel in his hide. The tracker was nowhere to be seen. Nigel's hide was almost open at the back, so I had an open back door. I happily obliged him by going in and silently crouching just behind him. Finally, he became aware of me and quietly asked how long had I been there.

"Quite a long while," I answered. "What are you and the tracker planning? A little surprise for me?"

"Well, actually we brought along a snake and thought we might give you a bit of a scare."

"Let's go wake up your tracker." We looked, but he appeared to be long gone. "You guys make too much noise for that, you know. What kind of snake did you bring?"

"It's a fer-de-lance," Nigel said.

"Was the plan to scare me or kill me?"

"Well, it's had its fangs removed, so…scare."

"Still, not what I would call a brilliant plan, you know."

"So tell me, how are you so quiet?" he said, changing the topic.

"I was well-trained by an Australian bloke, and I have had some Tai Chi; you know the very slow Chinese exercise? An old girlfriend taught me. It teaches you balance and deliberate slow action. Although I admit I am not too good at it—too soft, you know. But the slow careful foot placement is similar to silent walking.

"Well, it's getting dark; I guess you'll be spending the night," I said. "Let's harvest some bamboo shoots and bananas and get some water." I had the roasted Canna roots, which I dug out of the fire, and we put the bananas into the coals and let them cook while we ate the bamboo shoots. The next morning, Nigel and I made the hike back to the main camp. Nigel said, "I am supposed to rate your shelter and food. Don't worry, you passed with the highest marks."

Nigel's missing tracker was at the main camp; when he saw us he pointed and laughed at Nigel. "You get big scare, Nigel, big snake catch you. I see and go home, I not want big snake eat me too!"

This exercise ended the bush craft lessons. The rest of the training was about insertion and movement and was very intense. I learned a lot about the jungle. I completely changed my mind about the value of the training. I got much quieter and faster in my movements, and I also worked on being able to see into the jungle and know when something was out of place. But I never got used to the damn howler monkeys, and I knew I would never be like a native who had grown up in the jungle.

CHAPTER 5
Meeting the Team

• • •

I'd been told that true adventure requires putting your life at risk,
so I guess you could say the adventure had finally started for me.

MY FIRST MISSION WAS SIMPLE: become a member of an established team. To tell the truth, I was frightened by all the unknown things ahead. Could I really do this? Would the team accept me? Was my training good enough, or would I just be a fuck-up?

The morning after I arrived, Nash and I had breakfast, and he talked about the team I would join and my first mission. He said they were good, very good, and that I would like them. After breakfast, we took a company car and he drove us out the Air America Gate and to a tailor shop he knew, O.K. Tailor where I was measured for two new sets of tiger stripe fatigues and a set of rip-stop OD fatigues. When he had finished, the tailor said, "Ready after lunch, Mr. Nash."

Nash drove me around the area and we ate lunch at a Thai place in the city. We had the classic Thai Tom Yum soup with fiery hot chili oil floating on the surface and a Thai curry. It was all so blazingly hot it was painful to eat. Nash laughed as he watched me sweating over the spicy food. "You get used to it," he said smiling. "Unless it burns completely through your belly."

My flight to the secret base was by helicopter, due to leave at 15:00, and I was getting nervous. Nash picked up on my worry about the flight and said, "Don't worry about your ride; they can't leave without you. You're the cargo." We picked up the fatigues and headed back to the base. The Air America Gate was thick with what I guessed were prostitutes, and I had to ask. "Well, prostitutes, yes, but these girls are boys, so watch out. This isn't Kansas." I took a second look; they really looked like girls to me.

We stopped by the BX, where Nash bought me a Glycine Airman watch, which I still wear, for one hundred dollars, a lot of money at the time. This really impressed me, which was likely his intention. He also bought two bottles of Jack Daniels and one of Bacardi rum. "Give the rum to Mr. Mike when you get a chance; the Jack is for you."

"Why are you doing all this?" I asked.

"I am not doing this; SAT is doing this. We really want you to succeed, and you need this stuff for the missions you will be doing."

We stopped by the guest house, where I just made it to the bathroom in time. The curry I had eaten at lunch had decided to vacate the premises. Nash was laughing; he knew exactly what was happening. "Burned through your belly, Mac?" he asked.

"It looks that way, sir," I yelled through the door. I thought my ass was on fire.

When I came out of the bathroom, he handed me a chocolate bar and said, "I think this might help you. Don't worry, you'll develop a taste for it in a few weeks."

I picked up my duffel bag and he drove me to the flight line where the bird was waiting. He handed me two envelopes: one containing Thai baht and one with US dollars. "Marching money," he explained. "Don't lose it all gambling or spend it all in town on your first night." I soon learned that marching money was given to people who were traveling. We got some every month while in country, in addition to our salary.

"Remember, things here are cheap. Don't overpay and drive prices up. Stick with the team; they will help you." He sounded like my dad, terse and to the point. "If you need anything, let me know," he said. "I'll be out in a few days to see you." I walked to the waiting helicopter and loaded up in the bird for the flight. I thought about meeting the team as civilization receded behind me and we flew over an ocean of green. I didn't know a single person here. How was this going to go? I had survived the training. I was as ready as I could get. *Take a deep breath and grit your teeth—here we go.*

The helicopter pilot was tall and dark-haired and looked to be about eighteen years old. He introduced himself as Buzz. He flew at treetop level, mostly to try to scare me I thought, but then his name was Buzz after all. Well, I had done this a lot in training; I sat in the open door with my legs dangling, *knees in the breeze* just to prove I was not at all concerned. I also held the inside of the door in a death grip. Yes, knees in the breeze was the command to exit the helicopter and stand on the skids before an insertion using a free rappel. I had been scared shitless the first time I'd done it, but I got finally got used to it.

The copilot, a blond clone of the pilot, was named Fuzz. He looked back at me and yelled, "Take a seat. We don't want to lose you; it would require a bunch of paperwork!"

"Can I just stand on the skid for a little while?" I asked. "I like having my knees in the breeze."

"You guys are all fucking crazy—take a seat!" I settled into the nylon web strap seat across the back of the compartment. Fuzz put on his sunglasses and took the controls. We immediately gained altitude for a panoramic view of the countryside. It was strikingly beautiful, the fluorescent green of the rice paddies contrasting against the dark greens of the jungle with a few really giant trees standing above the canopy; jungle sentinels of some unknown purpose. The land there was remarkably beautiful; even the best photographs of it were only shadows of the amazing colors and forms. The sheer intensity of the green was overpowering. Even forty years later, landing in a tropical place like Brazil or even a runway surrounded by paddy fields in Taiwan still gives me the same feeling of amazement. I never saw the jungle as a Heart of Darkness—my jungle training in British Honduras saw to that, but it will kill you if give it a chance.

I thought about the upcoming mission. It was hardly a real mission, just a helicopter ride in and out—a milk run for my first time with the team. A bird had crashed with a new prototype multiplex receiver and retransmitter on board. We were to simply go in, remove the prototype, and go home. Why didn't we just get a Jolly Green heavy lift helicopter and lift it out? I had no idea, but it seemed not to be an option.

I took a peek at the marching money Nash had given me. There was one thousand US dollars in fifty and hundred dollar bills and several thousand Thai baht in the hundred baht red notes with the picture of the king. It was more than I could quickly count. This was a lot of money—enough to pay for a year of college. I wondered what I could possibly spend this on. I figured I'd be living in the jungle and eating C rations most of the time. I put it away and started some small talk with the "rotor heads" in the cockpit. I was about to meet the team my life would be bound up with, and I was nervous. I needed to make some friends. Fortunately, Buzz and Fuzz were pretty gregarious; I liked them immediately.

We landed at the base and I shouldered my duffel and clutched the envelope with my papers in it. I complimented Buzz and Fuzz on the flight as we walked from the landing pad to the bunkhouse, and I saw that I finally got my primitive. All the buildings were on two-foot stilts, with screen wire walls covered with ten-inch-wide corrugated tin and moveable "Venetian blind awnings" over them. We went to the bunkhouse. It was one large open room, just a series of double bunks with foot lockers at the foot of the bed and steel cabinets along the walls separating the bunks into bays. It was a lot like the training barracks, so I felt right at home. "Here, take this one," Buzz said as he indicated a rack. I dumped my bag into the empty locker.

"I guess I need to report in to Mr. Mike."

"Just across the main street," Buzz said. "I'll point you in the right direction." We shook hands and I started to head out.

"Don't worry, you'll fit right in. These guys are all crazy, just like you."

"How do you know I'm crazy?"

"You wouldn't be here if you weren't."

● ● ●

Mike, the team leader, sat behind a small, gray government desk that had seen better days and looked up at me with a dark-eyed stare so penetrating that it seemed like he was literally staring right through me. It did not help my feeling of being a stranger in a strange land at all. A large blond man sat near Mike; he was examining me as well. It felt like another goddamned interview. Mike introduced himself and indicated that the large guy was Moose. We shook hands. I gave him my papers and the rum. Mike was relatively short, maybe five foot eight, lean, and dark-skinned. He had a close buzz cut but with long buzz-cut sideburns and was dressed in an old A shirt and a pair of OD green boxer shorts, business casual for the jungle.

"You look pretty damn green to me, kid," he said in a thick Louisiana accent. "But the man says you are okay, so we will see. Just remember that as far as I'm concerned, you're just another FNG (fucking new guy). Try to stay out of the way, and thanks for the rum.

"You know the mission, I hope; it is all about device recovery. We go in and we put the Band-Aid on the chopper, check the devices, and Joe comes in and flies it out. If the bird won't fly, then we decide if we lift can the bird out or we take the device and hump it out...or, if necessary, blow the entire mess. In a day or two, we will have a map study and work out all the details before we launch. I expect you have all the info on the device we are looking for. If you are not ready, let me know now."

I had studied the device and seen how it was installed. I could take it apart and put it together, troubleshoot and repair it if necessary. The complete unit weighed about one hundred pounds, so packing it out a long distance would be a hitch, but with six of us we should be able to redistribute the essentials and lash it to a pack frame. Most of it was nonessential parts like the power supply, mother board, and the heavy metal case. I assumed we would chopper in and out as well if we could. We could also lash it to the frame and rope-extract it.

"I am ready whenever the team is, sir. Do you think you could put these in the safe for me?" I said, offering him most of the money and my papers.

"Sure, no problem; your passport needs to be in the safe any-way. Just don't sir me out here. This isn't the fucking Marines." Mike took my passport and an envelope with most of the mon-ey. I kept five hundred US and five thousand bhat, which was still a lot of cash.

"Okay, so the expectation is that you won't fuck up when we go in. I assume you can get into and out of a helicopter?"

"I have experience free rappelling."

"Okay, good. Look, I have a shit-pot full of paperwork to do now, so Moose here will go with you to issue you your stuff." Moose, a giant of a man, stood up from his chair and shook my hand. He was wearing green fatigues that had been cut off just below the thigh pockets to make jungle shorts and no shirt. Moose was huge, at least six foot three and 250 pounds, with no fat. He was built like a wall.

Mike continued, "Look, we launch out of Naked Fanny (Nakhon Phanom, or NKP) in three or four days, so if you want to go to town, now is the time. I will inspect you before we load up for Naked Fanny, so be ready, and Moose, it's your job to make sure he is."

• • •

Everyone had code names, call signs, or nicknames. Moose got his name by being large and coming from Canada. Being named Bruce probably had something to do with it as well. It seemed to me that he was the exact opposite of Mike. He was dirty blond, tall, and gregarious—always up for fun and games. As we walked to supply, he said, "So what do you go by other than FNG (Fucking New Guy)?"

"Well, I have been called a lot of things recently; I guess Mac will do."

"Just remember, Mike is an asshole motherfucker to everyone at first, so don't let it bother you. It gets better, but he brings everyone back alive, every time, so we all really like him, and trust me, he grows on you.

Supply was in a large Quonset hut, the most substantial structure on the little outpost, where I met Fredric Barbosa, the five-foot-tall, half French–half Cambodian supply clerk. Moose

introduced me as "the FNG who needs everything." Fredric proceeded to draw an assortment of equipment, including an M-16,
twenty-five magazines, a cleaning kit, bandoleers, thirty round
cardboard boxes of ammunition in ten-round stripper clips, baseball grenades, phosphorus grenades, white smoke, purple smoke,
Claymore mines with wire and clackers (triggers), four two-quart
collapsible canteens, a large ruck, a first-aid pack, BFI antiseptic
powder, orange marker panels, a signal mirror, a PRC-90 survival
radio, a spare battery for the PRC-77 main radio, and a long list
of other gear. I mentally added up the weight; the water alone was
almost twenty pounds. This was a lot of shit for a two-day hike.
Still, it didn't look like more than I had trained with, and I didn't
plan on any humping this around in the bush; this was to be an in
and out affair.

"You got bush clothes?" Moose asked.

"I've got two new pair of Tigers and two pair of Greens,
and one pair of British DPM that I wore in training in British
Honduras."

"Don't wear the DPM here, it just screams CIA. Got a
Boonie hat?"

"Yes—with my Tigers," I said.

"Does it have orange on the inside?"

"No, never heard of orange on the inside."

"Well, now you have. Give him a chapeau, Frederic," he said
to the supply clerk. "And sew some blaze orange in it for us."

A Tiger Boonie hat with a narrow brim and with a square
blaze orange panel appeared. "Sew it yourself Moose; you better
at sewing than I."

Moose slid, limbo fashion, under the counter door, dragging me behind him. I was impressed. He was really limber for someone so big. The place was a supermarket of all kinds of good stuff, and it was low key compared to the handling of weapons and ammunition I was accustomed to. Inside Supply was completely forbidden territory where I had come from. Fredric did not seem to mind at all. An ancient sewing machine with a wooden box for a chair sat against the wall. Moose sat down and with a pair of scissors from a drawer in the machine he quickly folded the panel and cut it into a perfect circle. Then, like a tailor, he rolled the edge under as he sewed it inside the top of the hat. That this giant was delicately sewing an orange panel into my hat was quite incongruous to me.

"If there's no orange inside, Mike will chew your ass and mine too, which he will probably do anyways. You got dog tags?" he asked. I pulled mine out. He looked at them and said, "No good. We'll make you a new set of tags." Moose sat down in front of a machine emblazoned with the name Graphotype, which looked exactly like what would happen if a 1940s typewriter had been bred with a band saw.

Moose turned it on, and it made a whirring sound as it came to life. Then he asked, "Name?" I called out my last name, first name, middle initial. "This ain't the army. First name first and how do you spell that?" I recited my information and he typed it into the keyboard. Then he asked for my social security number and my ID number. "Let's just camo up your weapon while we are here with the scissors," he said. "It's easier." He took olive drab "hundred mile an hour tape" and wrapped it skillfully around the black plastic of the stock of the weapon, creating a tiger stripe pattern. I now had a new Tiger Stripe CAR-15. We got a set of brown sheets, a brown towel, and a green poncho liner. "Brown is good. It don't show dirt or cum stains," he laughed.

You could hear the team was back before we got to the bunkhouse. The generator was running and "Riders on the Storm" by the Doors was blaring from a large reel-to-reel tape player and high-powered sound system. Moose and I piled most of my new stuff into footlockers, and he put the ordnance and my CAR into steel lockers along the wall. Moose introduced me to the three other guys on the team who had arrived and were playing spades. The oldest, and perhaps oddest, member was an Englishman named Campbell, known as Pipes. He was apparently a fine piper and an authentic jungle expert, having been in the Australian SAS in Vietnam. He was pushing twenty-nine years old, when twenty-five was considered old for the job. Occasionally, he was referred to as Old Man by the more senior members of the team...if they wanted to see a demonstration of his legendary grappling skills. I knew not to fuck with the old guy, and later we became mates and he taught me how to drink Scotch whisky properly.

Then there was Bloop, Lyndell Lafall Jr., an enormous six-foot-four-inch black man from South Dallas. Mostly, he was called Lyndell, but he was officially Bloop, because of his exceptional abilities with the M-79 grenade launcher and the distinctive sound it makes. He had removed the sights and cut down the stock to remove weight, but he was deadly accurate with what remained of it.

The last members of the team were Telephone, aka Booth Harris, a California surfer type, and the medic who was not officially on the team but was known as DD or Doctor Death. Buzz and Fuzz rounded out the team, but they were always out flying somewhere.

Moose and I took a stroll to the range to test fire the CAR. The range consisted of a small shack with a large berm about one hundred meters in front of it. Several distances had been marked off with posts, most of which were in pretty poor condition. Several guys were there, but they did not appear to have a range master. Eventually, it became clear that the helicopter pilots were having a competition with the fixed-wing guys. Everyone said hello to Moose, who seemed to be universally known, and he introduced me as the latest FNG.

After firing several hundred rounds in both single shot and full auto with Moose watching, I field stripped and cleaned the gun, and we headed back to the barracks. "You shoot good," Moose said. "Don't worry about anything. This is a walk in the park mission, in and out on the same day."

"Do I look that bad? I asked.

"Nah, it's just that Mike sometimes gets to people, you know." Considering I had lots of practice but nothing "real," this made me feel better about being able to execute my part of the mission. "Let's get back and get something to eat," he said.

We went back to the bunkhouse. As we walked in, DD said, "Line up and drop 'em, boys." I had done this exercise before. We formed up into a line and dropped our trousers to the deck. Shit, I was the only one wearing anything under them. I was out of uniform and didn't know it. It probably didn't help that I was wearing bright red jockey shorts, and my flaming red pubic hair didn't help matters any either.

"Well we all see now why they call you Red!" said Moose, and the entire team laughed. How did he know they called me Red? I had wanted to lose that name, so I had specifically avoided telling anyone about it, but it had made it over here before me!

DD proceeded to administer a shot to everyone in the line. I asked what the shot was for.

"Bicillin shot—we are going to town today," he replied.

Oh my goodness, what to say to that? I thought, *Well they are at least a careful lot of depraved maniacs.* I couldn't think of anything to say, so I just asked: "Who's going to give you yours?"

"You can since you asked." He loaded a syringe and handed it to me, dropped his trousers, and pointed to his butt cheek. I obliged and began to pump in the thick penicillin. He said, "Not bad for a Fucking New Guy. Okay FNG, you also need Gamma G and a Camolar shot as well. Are you taking Chloroquine?"

"Yes, I took a dose yesterday."

"Let's see." He dug around in a leather doctor's bag and pulled out two vials. "Okay, drop your pants again and remove your blouse."

"What the hell is Camolar?" I asked. DD responded that it was a new depot shot against malaria and proceeded to give me a shot of Gamma G in my butt for hepatitis and the Camolar in the shoulder. These painful marble sized globs of long acting juice became a painful knot on my butt cheek and one that really burned in my shoulder. These were now part of my standard onboard pharmacy. They hurt for days afterward.

• • •

We loaded eight people into Buzz's helicopter and headed off for Don Mueang Airport, which was called Bangkok International at the time. I looked at the helicopter more carefully this time and realized that it was not an AA or army bird. It was painted black and dark green, without any insignia at all. It was configured as a gunship, and I knew that with the extra guns and armor, eight fully armed men was a full load, but without packs or weapons, we were traveling light. We landed on the Air America ramp, and after securing the bird with the local guys, we called for three of Bangkok's ubiquitous Datsun Bluebird taxis and engaged them for the night.

From the airport, we went to Lucy's Tiger Den on Silom Road. It was a small expat watering hole with the usual cast of characters that included expats and spooks. We all wanted the turkey and dressing, but what we got was the infamous Hobo beans instead. The drinks were served by a grizzled old expat Tiger who owned the bar and was on a first-name basis with every spook and expat in Bangkok. He had the look of someone who had been around several times, and he may have been drinking his profits as well.

From there, we went on a whirlwind tour of the red light district, accompanied by copious amounts of beer. Around nine o'clock, we proceeded to a small, almost private brothel/hotel frequented by a variety of spooks. Air America probably owned it. We sat down in the parlor, and young ladies appeared. They were beautiful. A number of these ladies had regulars on the team, and at the end, three ladies were left. Moose and I, as the least senior men, had the double room, so we five headed upstairs to spend the night together. This was a first for me in so many ways. It was clear that I had fallen in with a rough crew, but everything seemed to be working, at least sort of. I felt like I fit in just fine so far. This team might have been a real challenge to anyone who was religious or conservative, but I was twenty-two and it was the most uninhibited of times in America.

• • •

I woke up to light streaming in through the windows, an old ceiling fan barely stirring the warm air. Sleeping curled up at my side was one of the girls. My mouth tasted of what must have been the remains of a bottle of Jack Daniels, and all my depo shots were burning. I sat up, cleared my eyes, and looked around. Across the room in a bed by the open window was Moose sleeping with a young lady. I then noticed that I was sharing the bed with not one, but two of the beautiful ladies I had fallen in love with last night! But then the beds were not large, and Moose took up a lot of room. The debauchery was all new to me, and I began to remember the high points of the evening. Those young ladies had taken advantage of my innocence several times. This was not only my first experience in a whorehouse but my first experience with somewhere between one and three girls. On a scale of one to ten, it was about a twelve.

But now I really needed to piss. Where was the bathroom? Just then, a girl opened the door and brought in a tray with several large mugs of steaming coffee. I took one of them. It was strong, sweet, and flavored with condensed milk and cinnamon: the perfect morning wakeup after a night of sin and debauchery. Jesus, I really needed to piss. I looked for a pot or a bucket, but no dice. I woke the girls and asked: *"Hong Nam?"* in my best Thai. There was no response from the girls except for giggles; I had probably used the wrong damn tone or just the wrong damn word. Okay, I figured, let's try French. Hell! I know some French, which ought to work: *"Où sont les toilettes?"* Again, no response. Having nothing left but German and Latin, I gave up and tried English. "Bathroom?" The girls just laughed at my communication attempts and started waking the Moose up.

Moose grunted and groaned as the laughing girls attempted to wake him. He finally rolled over and sat up, looked at me, and said, "Well, good morning, Sunshine." He surveyed the scene. "Must have been a hell of a good night as well."

"Bathroom?"

He stood up and said, "This way." We walked down the long hall together, both stark naked. Well, not really naked…I was still wearing my watch. I had absolutely no idea where my clothes or wallet were. Wandering the halls of a whorehouse in the nude was another first.

We carried the coffee with us and into a large tiled bathroom. It had been elegant at one point. This place had been some kind of French-style mansion. We stood next to each other pissing into an old-fashioned, fancy, porcelain trough-type urinal that smelled strongly like old piss. I realized that I needed more than a urinal and asked, "Commode?"

"Sorry, no commode, just the Oriental toilet," Moose answered and pointed to the corner. This was a large block of porcelain with two raised "footprints" for your feet and a strategically placed hole. Great, I thought. I had been told about Oriental toilets but had never actually used one. I mounted up and did my business. By now, I had absolutely no qualms about doing anything the rest of the world thought should be private. I was completely devoid of any expectations of privacy for anything: eating, sleeping, shitting, pissing, fucking, and bathing all seemed to be team activities. I cleaned up with the water hose and asked, "Shower?"

"You're not much of a conversationalist this morning, FNG."

"Sorry. I have a headache."

"Want some aspirin?"

"No. Wrong head, Moose."

He roared out a big Moose laugh. "Well, sorry, no showers here, just baths. Here, I'll show you." We crossed the hall to another tiled bathroom where there were several large tubs and several stools. "Here, sit down."

I took one of the teak stools and girls proceeded to lather me up with sponges and warm soapy water. *Damn*, I thought, *this is great.* Then the sponge was replaced by a warm, slick, soapy massage by naked girls, which led to a final encounter. I was now officially 100 percent spent, done, and finished. It was clear I would not be suffering from "blue balls" here in Thailand.

Magically, our clothes arrived, washed and pressed. As we dressed, the rest of the team, modestly dressed in robes like gentlemen, arrived for their turn. We just laughed at them, told them to enjoy their sloppy seconds, and headed downstairs to the parlor, where we drank coffee and polished off a plate of croissants. Mike came down the stairs first, followed by the rest of the team, and asked, "Everybody happy?"

We all smiled and answered, "Yes sir, very happy."

Mama-san appeared and said, "You got no bill, Mr. Mike, everything paid for by Mr. Nash. He says Mr. Mac win him a big bet with AA big boys and he want to say thanks." Everyone looked at me. I didn't know what to say, so I just shrugged my shoulders.

Mike looked at me, shook his head, and said, "Well, looks like Mr. Mac here must really be something to get Nash to part with any cash. Let's eat breakfast and find out what exactly Mr. Mac, I mean the FNG, did to win us a night out on Nash."

We walked down the street and turned into a sidewalk café; the air was heavy with the smell of fresh bread. We entered and took seats; more coffee, but no cinnamon this time, just lots of sugar and condensed milk. Some of the guys got it poured over ice. A cup of coffee a Thai would take an hour to drink we consumed in minutes. Bread and jam and *kai luak*, a soft boiled egg served in a shot glass, skewers of pork, and *patongo*, the Thai donut, all made their appearance at the table and disappeared as the team proved that they could really eat. I felt much more at home with the team now; I guess that was part of the twenty-four-hour, "instant male bonding" experience.

"Now, Mr. Mac, tell me: just what service did you provide to Nash?" Mike asked.

"Well," I said, "as soon as I set foot in the hangar at Udorn, two guys met me and announced that they were going to kick my ass, some sort of a twisted fuck's idea of a test. One was a big guy, some kind of Golden Gloves boxer, whatever that is; we didn't have them in Texas that I know of. It really wasn't much of a fight. It took less than a minute. I guess I passed the test. Nash must have bet on me kicking their asses, and a couple of white shirts named John and Bruce bet on the boxer, I guess. Mr. Nash's bet paid off really well."

"Well, John and Bruce are the big boys, and so is Nash. You seem to have been keeping pretty special company lately. You are still the FNG here, but if you keep it up, I might get to where I can just tolerate you. The last tech guy was a real turd, by the way. Mama-san could have kicked his ass. Can't remember what exactly happened, but he decided to go home rather suddenly. But I think we can stand to babysit you if we have to, at least for a while."

CHAPTER 6

My First Mission
Just a Milk Run

• • •

*I must not fear. Fear is the mind-killer. Fear is the little-
death that brings total obliteration. I will face my fear. I will
permit it to pass over me and through me. And when it has
gone past, I will turn the inner eye to see its path. Where the
fear has gone there will be nothing. Only I will remain.*

— FRANK HERBERT, *DUNE*

WE PREPARED TO MAKE THE trip to Nakhon Phanom, known universally as NKP or Naked Fanny. It was sort of a semisecret base on the Mekong River bordering Laos. People there called it the "end of the line at the edge of the world." It was semisecret since everyone knew about the base and the electronic monitoring and covert actions that were conducted from there. Well, not all the electronic stuff done was actually done from NKP; a lot was at

Camp Ramasun,[1] just down the road. They had two IBM 3650s (cutting edge, state of the art, "Big Iron" computers) located in the boonies of Thailand, behind two razor wire–topped fences. This was more computer power than most American universities had at the time.

In the early days, when it was originally built with PSP (pierced steel plate) runways, it must have been pretty primitive. But by the '70s, the idea that it was the end of line and the edge of the world was just bullshit. They had food and water, a gym, a swimming pool, a bowling alley, and a theater.

In preparation for the launch, we had a map study, where we looked at the map carefully, marked important things and then waterproofed the maps with a silicone oil. Soon, everyone was putting together their packs. I laid out the equipment on my rack so I could see it all. To give you a rough idea of what we carried, I had collapsible canteens of water (sixteen pounds), my CAR-15 (seven pounds), a five-pocket bandoleer with a hundred rounds of 5.56 for my rifle in cardboard boxes of stripper clips (six pounds) and two regular canteen covers, each with five-by-twenty-round magazines, (seven pounds), two Claymore mines with wire and clackers, (five pounds), two phosphorous grenades (four pounds), four HE frag grenade (six pounds), six 40 mm grenades for the bloop gun (M-79; three pounds), spare battery for the PRC-77 (two pounds), PRC-90 (three pounds), one brick of C-4, blasting cap, wire, and a lot more assorted shit. I counted at least sixty or seventy pounds. Moose took a look and said, "Pretty heavy; you

---

1 *Ramasun* is a Thai god of lightning.

are loaded for bear, but it's okay. Mike won't be happy unless he cuts it down some anyway."

As it turned out, Mike didn't bother to make the inspection, and I went overloaded and armed to the teeth. Everything was packed, and the packs were given the shake test to make sure nothing rattled or squeaked. We all ate lunch and then loaded up on Buzz's bird and flew to NKP. NKP sat on the Mekong River bordering Laos. From the air, the Mekong River was a massive brown snake moving through the green jungle. It reminded me of the Mississippi River in Louisiana, a true force of nature. When we landed, we were picked up by a box truck to keep us out of sight as much as possible. It took us to Tiger Village, a kind of barracks arranged for us by Nash. Everyone crashed. We would launch at first light. I did not sleep well. Before dawn, I got up, went across to the latrine, and made sure I had emptied both bowels and bladder. I did not want to piss myself or shit my pants on my first mission, a real possibility, I had heard. Soon, the team was up and moving. It was paint up time, and each person had his own favorite pattern. I used the paint sticks to make my head and neck dark green, I lightened the eye sockets with Sandy Loam and added a tan *U* on my forehead where I have natural creases. Then I darkened my nose and chin. The general rules are: if it sticks out it is dark, if it is recessed it gets a lighter color, and a few dark tiger stripes just for the hell of it.

We walked out to the transport chopper. Mike was there with a Montagnard priest, who proceeded to bless the chopper and us. Mike then asked, "Is everybody happy?" We all growled an affirmative. It was not far, so we all took our rope sections and tied up Swiss seats for the short rappel. A Swiss seat was the original mountaineer's harness for rappelling. To tie it, you took about a twelve-foot section of rope and ran it around your waist and then under your legs and back around the waist. You clipped in with a snap link, or a carabiner in mountain-climbing parlance. This snap link connected the harness to the rappelling rope. When you tied the Swiss seat, it was very important to carefully place the lines that went under the legs so they didn't crush your nuts or dick. We all gave our Swiss seats a couple of good test pulls to make sure everything was good to go. Once that was done, we loaded up and sat in middle of the helicopter back-to-back, facing the doors.

The copilot was a guy named Joe; he had been the pilot of the crashed chopper, so he knew where it was. Off we flew into the morning darkness. Three lengths of black kernmantle rappelling rope, not the shitty army "green line" the military used, were fixed to each side of the helicopter, since we would probably have to rappel in. One of the C-130 Specter gunships had made passes over the area looking around with FLIR[2] and had not seen anything. We were the first ship in a line of five helicopters that flew at treetop level following the contour of the forest tops. We approached a small clearing, and the line of helicopters slowed. Out onto the skid I went, holding the line hooked up with a steel snap link to my Swiss seat. I had done this many times before, but I still felt the butterflies in my stomach big time. We dropped out of the line of birds and went into

2   FLIR: forward-looking infrared.

hover; we tossed out the rope coils, pushed off, and rappelled down the short distance to the ground, just to the edge of the bomb crater. I had to break hard as I was going way too fast from being so heavily loaded, but I managed to slow just before I landed. It was as perfect a rappel as I ever did (and ever would do, for that matter). The other helicopters "hopped around us," our helicopter going from the first to the last in the line. The idea was that, to an observer, the line of helicopters appeared to continue without the pause for insertion.

As I was the first to touch down, I immediately cleared my weapon for action and looked at the downed bird. This LZ (landing zone) must have been a result of large bomb; it had a meter-wide swimming pool at the center and it had blown down and apart trees around it for a distance of fifty meters. It was a miracle this was not a complete crash; the pilot had made it to the edge of the crater, but the skids had disappeared into the soft clay soil that now anchored it solidly to the ground. We quickly scanned the area around the site and saw nothing. I moved over to the downed chopper. It was in really bad shape. It had been sprayed with pretty high-caliber weapons, probably a Dushka heavy machine gun and the Russian equivalent of the US fifty caliber. As we got closer, the damage became even more obvious. The rotor blades had taken several bad hits and were not flyable even if the engine had been good, and the engine was shot to shit as well. This could not have happened in the air; it had been hit with bullets here where it sat. There was no fixing this junk heap. Now we needed to check whether or not the receiver was intact. This was the high tech kit we had come to get. It was a prototype, designed to read the new sensors. The receiver had not been removed, but it had taken a hit from a Russian fifty-one-caliber bullet, which had basically exploded it. I pulled as many boards as I could, stuffed them in my pack, and reported that our work here was done unless we wanted to blow the thing, and that was unnecessary in my opinion. There was no reason to even think about lifting this heap of junk out and back home. There wouldn't be a big fat bonus for this job.

Mike said, "No problem, let's go—this is a really hot area these days." He got Telephone to raise the extraction team, and the decision was made to head to the alternate LZ as a PZ (pick-up zone). This way we would avoid a string extraction, in which we would be lifted out with a rope. "We will have to bushwhack a bit to get to a trail to take us to the PZ," Mike said.

We made it to the trail and headed toward the pick up zone (PZ) as fast as we could. The PRC 77 crackled to life in Telephone's earpiece. "There are NVA on the trail headed your direction." Mike called for a Parthian Shot[3] to give us time on the outbound. It was ambush time, us on them.

Mike decided on an L-type ambush, set up where the trail curved sharply around a steep hill. He would be at the end of the L with the Stoner 63, a light machine gun, and two Claymore antipersonnel mines would be set against the hillside to take the back blast as much as possible. These mines, when detonated, produced a blast wave and together spray fourteen

---

3 A Parthian shot is a term meaning you turn and attack the enemy while you are fleeing.

hundred one-eighth-inch steel balls, which cut through the enemy like the great sword they were named for. The remaining team would be in two elements, Lyndell at the opposite end of the L with the M-79 and Moose. I was in the long element with Telephone and Pipes. There was probably some concern as to whether I would really be able to fight. We quickly dug the mines into the hillside with overlapping kill zones against a small rocky outcrop covered with jungle growth. The rest of the team moved into cover as quickly as possible and camouflaged the entire site. This took all of ten minutes; I discovered that we could dig really fast when we needed to.

I crawled down into a little hollow, arranged my camo plants, and felt the damp ground beneath me. My heart was pounding. Fear clutched at me; blood rushed so loudly through my ears that I worried the entire world could hear it. Then, through the brush, there was movement. I slowed my breathing and ignored the insects buzzing and biting, and then amazingly, the fear left and a strange calm arrived. Time slowed to a painful crawl, as the hair on my neck tingled but my stomach relaxed, my fear replaced by focus. They began to enter the kill zone, but there were too many—way too many. At least twenty-five men were spread along the trail. Their point man slowed, almost stopping just outside the kill zone. Behind him, the long line of soldiers began to bunch into a tighter formation because the trail was narrow on the steep hillside and they had to step off the trail and onto the hill. They were almost in the center of the kill zone.

Now! Mike triggered the Claymores. The blast wave and shot from the two mines swept down the slope, devastating most of the group and blowing some of them off the trail and down the hill. The back blast passed upslope and my ears started to ring. I was up and firing as the team began sweeping up the remainder of the trail with gunfire. Lyndell fired three rounds with the bloop gun as the team swept down the slope and back along the trail, mopping up the remainder of the NVA.

It was over in an instant, but I could still feel the adrenaline and hear my heart pounding in my ears. I was still ready to fight. Mike began calling for immediate extraction—the bird was twenty minutes out. Cleanup began; we quickly looked for any Intel in the packs. Since I was the FNG, Mike assigned me to check for any signs of life or Intel among the enemy who had been blown downhill by the Claymores. It was, naturally, a really nasty job. The smell of blood, death, and burned powder hung in the air as I tried to keep myself from gagging. I picked my way through the mangled bodies as quickly as I could, looking for any papers or maps and using my Tanto knife to methodically open the carotid at the neck just be sure. *What the fuck am I doing here? I should have gone to Canada!* There was a sudden movement; somehow one of the NVA had survived the blast. He had begun trying to stand up and was attempting to pull an AK up from the tangle and turn upslope to target the team. No one saw him except me.

The sudden movement caused me to snap back up, and as I did, I lost my footing and slipped on the bloody ground. I slid down an inch or two and then spun as my foot slipped and then caught. Basically, I fell on top of him as he was turning and trying to stand. Trying to regain my balance, I had swept my arms around and down like a spinning back fist. In doing this, the chisel point of my knife, with all my weight behind it, struck him in the back of the neck. The blade went through his neck, between the axis vertebra and the third cervical vertebra, causing him to expire instantly and giving me just enough resistance to regain my balance. I stood up, regained my footing, and went back to the task at hand without a word. I was embarrassed by falling like a complete idiot, and now I was covered with blood and gore as well. The entire team had seen me fall. Shit, I thought to myself, *what a fuck-up!*

As it happened, however, the team had seen my mistake as a purposeful spinning leap down, striking the man cleanly before he could fire his weapon at them. Moose laughed and said, "Well the FNG isn't much of a conversationalist, but he sure gets the job done, not like the last tech guy at all." I heard Flaubert ringing in my ears: "There is no Truth, only perception." I know I am a fuck-up, and this poor bastard was the victim of me being a goddamn klutz. My first blood, my first kill, was the result of a fucking circus act tumble. I did not have time to even think about the strike, it had occurred just as Sykes had said it would back in training:

"The perfect strike must come naturally like snow
falling from a bamboo leaf, without thought".

I thought to myself, *this couldn't have been what he meant, could it? Nope, this was just a massive fuck-up. I was not snow, and I did not fall from a bamboo leaf. This could only have been improved with clown shoes and a banana peel. I remember that it is better to be lucky than to be good—it takes no effort.*

I could have been in a normal army line unit; I could have run away from my responsibility and gone to Canada. But I didn't. I was here, and it was now: do or die. Sherman was right, war is hell. Oh, dear God, I am just such a fuck-up!

Later, after I had had some time to consider the events of that day, I realized that in war, morality is suspended. If I had let him kill someone on the team, then I would have been responsible for his death. It turned out that all that honor, duty, loyalty, and responsibility that had been beaten into us our whole lives was just a load of crap. Maybe I was lucky; my first blood did not require a conscious decision. It happened quickly and without any mental debate, but the final, cold, steely-eyed analysis is that the decision is either kill us or kill them, and everyone will always vote to kill them. I did what I had to do, what I was trained to do, and what I was expected to do, although in this case, I did it by accident. I felt like a total fuck-up at the time, of course, and did not say anything to the team about my feelings.

• • •

"Did anyone else notice this guy wasn't a gook but is whiter than me?" Mike looked and said, "Probably another fucking Russian bastard. Look at the stainless dental work; Westerners always use gold." It seemed there were Russian Special Forces "volunteers" fighting against us. Why was I so surprised? It was a great training opportunity for their Special Forces and probably their pilots.

There were several shoulder bags of Chinese and Vietnamese papers among the bodies. I collected them quickly and got over to the rest of the team, who were getting ready to move. Out of the corner of my eye, I saw Mike looking across at me with his goddamned intense gaze. The son of a bitch could stare holes through you. If he only knew...*The FNG is really a fuck-up but a lucky fuck-up* is what he would think. Maybe he *did* know. Reality intruded again. The smell of death was just awful; I felt like puking again, but I didn't.

We heard the incoming slicks and moved as quickly as possible toward the PZ, with no attempt to be silent, about two miles farther down the trail. The pilot radioed that there was more movement down the trail behind us. Mike pulled little disc-shaped "toe popper" mines from his pack and planted a couple on the trail and one ten meters down the trail but off to the side. Mike, with the Stoner-63, and Lyndell, with the M-79 grenade launcher, pulled off into some thick cover. I gave Lyndell my 40-mm grenades and bandoleer and handed Mike a Claymore with a phosphorous grenade taped to the front. "You carried two Claymores? Shit!"

Was he complaining? "Always be prepared, you know."

"Thanks." He grabbed the mine and quickly placed it in a location backed up to a tree to reduce the back blast and camouflaged it with loose leaf litter and dirt. I took his pack and Moose and I carried it between us. DD and Campbell grabbed

Lyndell's pack and we headed off as fast as we could to the extraction site. Just as we got to the clearing, we heard a small explosion. "Probably the toe popper," said DD. Shortly afterward, the Claymore, the bloop gun, and Stoner all opened up, and then we broke out of the jungle into a clearing and ran toward the center, where we popped purple smoke, flipped our hats inside out so the orange panel pointed up to the sky, and waved at them. Within a minute the extraction bird came in, hot and flared, reducing both vertical and horizontal speed to allow a near zero-speed touchdown. Mike and Lyndell were sprinting across the clearing and into the helicopter. Up we went, and then the pilot gave the all clear to the gunships that came in and plastered the area from the clearing to where the white smoke from the phosphorous grenade drifted up marking the location.

I was now "blooded," as they say. The short trip back to NKP was uneventful; I actually fell asleep in the helicopter, wedged between Moose and Lyndell. Moose woke me up after we landed. "Damn it, Red, you slept the whole way back."

"Did I miss anything?" I asked.

"No, not really." I was really tired; must have been the adrenaline wearing off.

"I just really needed a nap, I didn't sleep well with my first mission with you guys coming up", I said. Everyone seemed to be looking at me as we walked over to the chief's office to drop off the Intel and the boards I pulled and to brief Nash that the bird was 100 percent a loss, while Buzz fueled up the bird.

Mr. Nash looked at me and asked, "Whose blood is all over you, Mac?"

I remembered how I must look and replied, "Not mine, just some guys we met while we were on a walk."

Nash smiled and shook his head. "Looks like you just went completely berserk on some unfortunate bastards. They told me you were aggressive and Sykes's attack dog, but Jesus, Mac, you are covered with blood and gore and you really stink. Just try to keep a little bit lower profile, okay? Even the Air America guys will be asking questions. You all look pretty damn suspicious."

Sykes' attack dog? What the fuck was that about? So I was Sykes' attack dog? Really?

So my first mission was pretty much a complete failure. We didn't recover the complete box, we made contact with the enemy, and I came back covered in blood and guts. Of course, it could have been worse. We were all back in good shape and the bad guys got a pretty good bloody nose for their efforts. I did not give a shit; we were in and out and alive, and I got all the important circuit boards. They were damaged, yes, but *we had them.* I'd take failure like that any day. But this was supposed to be a milk run mission with no excitement. If this was a milk run, I didn't want to know what happened during a *real* mission. I was more than a bit concerned.

We headed back to our own little base camp, satisfied at having completed the mission and living to tell the tale. I was completely filthy, covered in gore. I should have taken a shower at NKP, but I was still in shock and not thinking about keeping a low profile. I headed for the showers, which, as luck would have it, were empty. Every time I wanted to shower, they were empty, but it seemed like we always had really clean Marine guards.

So there was no warm water, and no water at all until the water truck came. The solution to my dilemma was literally heaven-sent: it rained. This was a really common shower method during the rainy season. The storms were amazing; sometimes you could see the curtain of water moving toward you, and all you had to do was stand still. I stood outside on a wooden pallet, stripped off my clothes and began to scrub myself with a bar of soap. I was soon joined by the rest of the team, carrying beers.

Nash handed me a beer, and I said thanks and handed him the soap. He and rest of the team proceeded to dump their beers on me in what was affectionately known as the beer baptism, making me an official member of the team. Nash then announced my new name. "I thought a lot about this one and decided Snake fits you pretty well. I was told you were full of surprises, and you seem to be damn fine for a tech guy." *Well at least it wasn't Red,* I thought. It could have been worse, although as it turned out Snake didn't stick for long anyway.

The rain slowed and then stopped. We got dressed and gave our dirty clothes to the local laundress. I gave her an extra two green notes (about forty baht) due to the condition of my fatigues, and Mike said, "Let's go to town." We piled seven people into the team vehicle, an old Citroen DS that had been made into a convertible of sorts. The car literally sat on the ground; its air suspension was tired and leaky from years of brutal service and neglect. Mike started the beast, and it rose up like a magic carpet. We proceeded to a local restaurant where I ate the best pad Thai I had ever had and then to a local bar where the Jack Daniels tasted better than it ever would again. We moved from the bar to the bathhouse and soaked in the hot water. There was one more thing we wanted, and that was available here as well. I would have time to think about my first mission after we got home.

CHAPTER 7

Getting to Know the Guys

• • •

And once you are awake, you shall remain awake eternally.

—— FRIEDRICH NIETZSCHE, *THUS SPOKE ZARATHUSTRA*

GETTING TO KNOW MYSELF WAS harder than getting to know the guys. I woke up in a soft bed with a beautiful Thai woman. What did I think about? Well, my first mission. It is not easy to describe my feelings and emotions during or just after my first firefight. I am not sure it is really possible, and it is probably different for different people anyway. A firefight, for me at least, is similar to sex—it starts with a rush of hormones and heightened sensitivity and ends with deep relaxation and tiredness and sleep. There is that initial waiting period, and the adrenaline really builds before the fight starts; the hair stands up on the back of your neck and your arms. Your blood pounds and the "battle high" comes. Time really slows, seconds seem like minutes, colors seem more saturated, and smell is more acute. During the fight, the smell of blood and powder smoke seem to fuel a growing feeling of primal rage. I attempt to control the adrenaline-fueled power with patterned breathing and meditation to center the mind until the action starts. Everything happens quickly, but it also seems to happen in slow motion and high definition. I just have to go with the natural flow of the fight; I don't think you can really control it, although I tried to let my Lao Tzu mantra run through my mind: "The best warrior is not violent. The best fighter is not angry." But it does not work. It occurred to me Mr. Tzu was never in a firefight.

Maybe uncontrolled rage is what berserkers feel; I don't really know, but I do know how "having your blood up" can lead to crazy heroic actions. It is important to be cool and not let fear or anger get complete control. Once the fight is over, I quickly settle down and amazingly, I feel strangely relaxed and sleepy, just like after sex. I fell into a deep sleep in the bird on the home. A more mellow high follows for a long while afterward, which is probably the result of residual adrenaline in the system and surviving a near-death experience.

● ● ●

My serene morning was disturbed by the Moose, as he woke everyone up by singing, "Nothing could be finer than to be *Indochiner* in the morning."

We got up, ate breakfast, and headed back to the nest in the old Citroen. I really liked that damned old car; what an interesting life it must have had. Our next mission would be in a week or two, and we needed to plan and prepare. I felt like a good long run to clear my mind and sweat out the alcohol. I slung my rifle over my back and ran an out and back for about an hour in boots and fatigues. The next day, Moose, Telephone, and DD joined me; they said they did not want me to get lost. The team really liked to work out together, and so did I. I was beginning to feel more like a team member. I knew I had passed the first real test, but I was still uneasy and wondering if maybe I had cheated. If I had killed the NVA on purpose, I could have been proud of having done the right thing, but while I did kill him, it had not been a conscious decision. Appearances were important out there, and I wanted to be a hardass, not a pussy or a fuck-up. I guess I was a fuck-up.

Mike cornered me when we got back and said, "I was told you were full of surprises. You are just too good with that damn knife to be a tech guy, but you need to know that you can just shoot the next motherfucker if you want. We don't count the ammunition out here. It's all free." I started to say something like: it was a mistake...but he cut me off with, "No, it was good; I have never seen a spinning technique like that. Just don't take any chances you don't have to. You will have to tell me about your training later." So I did sort of try to tell him the truth, but perhaps total honesty is overrated.

● ● ●

So now we were between missions, and we played a lot of cards. Partner spades was the game of choice, and since we knew sign language, cheating by sneaking in a sign without getting caught was part of the game. One evening, we were playing cards and drinking rum when Mike placed his cards on the table and looked at me. "Snake, my friend, it is time to tell us about your training—all of it. Tech guys don't know how to rappel or use a knife the way you do. Where else were you in combat? Are you ex-military? Your papers say no but your actions say different, so I want the whole story, and don't leave anything out, okay?"

"Really, it wasn't—"

Buzz and Fuzz interrupted and told the team they had been tipped off and had watched my fight in the hangar. "The boxer was really a huge guy, and he hit the deck in about thirty seconds."

"Just a lucky kick," I said.

"Yeah sure, brother, we saw the fight, remember?" said Buzz.

"And I saw the flying knife trick whack the bastard on the trail," said Moose. "Come on, what the fuck are you?"

The more I denied it, the more of a badass I became. Now I had lots of undeserved credibility, the more I denied it the more I got. I looked across at Mike, and he just smiled and shook his head. "It has been established that you aren't too much of a conversationalist, at least so far. So we want everything; we seem to have lots of time. Take a day or two if you want."

Telephone leaned over and refilled my glass. "So what do you want to know?" I asked.

"Everything."

"Everything?"

"Yes, we want all the details."

I was starting to feel a little drunk. We had started drinking just after breakfast, and my glass was always full. Maybe they were trying to lubricate my tongue. "Not much to tell that's interesting. My draft number was forty-nine. It was this or the army. My training was in Austin. I spent my first night in a hotel, a round, drum-looking building close to the river. Is this too much detail?"

"It's fine, but what did you do before that? The short version of that, please."

"Oh, I was in school. I got a degree in chemistry with minors in physics and math. I moonlighted in labs and in a hospital ER. I had a girlfriend and I played tennis and handball. I studied Tang Soo Do and Shotokan, is that important?"

"Yes, but get back to the training."

"The day after I arrived, the recruits met with Southern Air representatives. Mr. Nash was one of them. My instructors were Mr. Russell and Mr. Sykes."

Mike interrupted. "Sykes and Russell were the instructors?"

"Yes, they were. Do you know them?"

He nodded his head yes and said, "Well that explains a lot. Continue with the story." He refilled my glass. I realized I was definitely pretty damn drunk. My head spun. *How can I tell this story? It is too long and I am too drunk.*

"How do you know them?"

"We can talk about that later; now is your time to tell your story."

"Well, we did a lot of PT and combatives. We really beat the shit out of each other. Half the people left. I beat the Bear. So that was my training." Everyone was looking at me and wanting more. Oh, and I kicked Norman Isherwood's ass in British

Honduras too. The room was really spinning. I felt like vomiting. No, I didn't feel like it, I was going to vomit, and before I could get up I puked all over the table on my way to the floor.

"Shit. We gave him too much rum!"

"Who the fuck is Norman Isherwood?"

Mike propped me up and said, "Snake, my friend, my very, very drunk friend, let me tell you about the last tech guy from Austin. He couldn't eat the food, didn't fuck the women, and wouldn't carry a weapon or rappel from a helicopter. Did I mention he did not drink? I put him on a plane out of here after the first week. Nash put you up for the job, and I will have to say you eat the food, fuck the women, kill without hesitation, and can get the fuck out of a bird. A vast improvement. Oh, and I forgot, you fired your weapon in the general direction of the enemy."

But I didn't want to fire my weapon, I wanted to give it a good performance review and promote it. I want to promote everyone! *Wasn't that funny? Didn't want to fire it wanted to promote it?* I stood up and puked again then sat down on the floor.

"This is very funny but that garbled "promote it" shit isn't funny at all," said Mike. "So I really hope you can handle electronics better than you handle your liquor."

I made it back into the chair. "I have a minor in physics. I took courses in digital electronics and I passed the training for electronics in Dallas, so I guess so. When do you guys tell me about your history?" I demanded.

There was a chorus of *fucking never, not going to do that,* and *it will take more than a bottle of Jack to get that out of me.* At that point, with

Moose and DD carrying me, I exited the bunk house and promptly vomited on the way to the latrine for a bout of whisky diarrhea. What are friends for? You have to have good friends who will carry you to the outhouse and hose you down afterward. But then, they were the people who had gotten me blind drunk to start with.

The next morning, I woke up wrapped in a poncho liner on my rack with a massive hangover.

• • •

After the whiskey interrogation, there was a noticeable change in my attitude and in the team's attitude toward me. I guess I was accepted as a real member of the group. True, Mr. Nash had "greased the skids" for me by paying for a night on the town before the first mission. It is possible he just didn't want to lose another tech guy. My ability to fire a weapon "in the general direction of the enemy" and in particular my brilliant spinning knife technique seemed to seal the deal. Being the first man on the ground from the helicopter didn't hurt either.

I had been pretty quiet so far and didn't talk too much. I had thought it might just prove I was a geek. But as I became more at home, I began to open up with the guys a little. Telephone and Moose were kindred spirits, young and tech savvy. I soon realized the team didn't really need another tech guy; they had two capable guys already. But I had had the "special" training, which would have taken about a week to teach them.

At first, I thought the Moose was just another big dumb jock. He certainly was big and he was a jock, but he was not dumb. He spoke English and French perfectly and had passable Thai, which is not an easy language to learn. He was a math whiz and had been a math major in college. I had a minor in math, but I had struggled with it the whole time, and my Thai was horrible. I just could never hear or "sing" the tones right. Fortunately, I was told my shitty Thai sounded like Lao! I tried to improve my Thai, but it was pretty much a failure.[4] Yes there is a difference in Thai between tee shirt and tiger but I had trouble with it and then there is the issue of kao, kao, kao, kao, and kao.

All the guys were amazing in their own ways. I walked by Mike's rack one day and he was reading fucking Friedrich Nietzsche's *Beyond Good and Evil*. I was shocked. There was more to him and everyone else there than met the eye. I thought I was the Lone Ranger of educated school boys who read Nietzsche.

Mike was always an enigma. He never spoke of his training, really, but it was clear he was an expert jungle fighter. He had been in the military, but I did not feel close enough to really question him about it much, and he did not volunteer much information. Still, I did learn that he had been on a team with Sykes and Russell.

---

4 Many years later, in Houston, Moose came to take me to lunch. We met at the front desk. He said something nasty to me in Thai, and I replied with something equally vile. We had a laugh and left for lunch. Our receptionist that day had been replaced by Kathy, the assistant HR director. Kathy was a real, *fresh from the ranch* kind of Texan, as down home as you can imagine. When I came back from lunch, she called me over to the reception desk and said, "When were you in Thailand? I didn't see that on your resume. And by the way, it should be *kop* not *ka*; you must have learned that from a woman." I felt my face heating up as I turned scarlet. It turned out that Kathy had been in the Peace Corps, not far from our secret base, teaching English in a small Thai school. You can't judge a book by its cover.

Lyndell was really interesting. He came from South Dallas, which was a pretty rough neighborhood. He had spent time in the Marines in a long-range reconnaissance patrol (LRRP) and was tough as nails. He had a degree in biology and was thinking about medical school when he returned to the world.[5] He and DD occasionally studied anatomy together in their spare time.

Pipes began his career in the British SAS. When he had the chance to move to the Australian SAS and fight in Vietnam, he immediately took the job. In 1971, they were pulled from Vietnam and Pipes ended up with us. He came from the upper crust of British society—his father was a physician and his mother was in the Foreign Service. I think they were appalled by his choice of occupation. We met in London on a return trip and spent a few days of rest and recuperation with Pipes and his younger brother, as well as a few days with his parents. The morning after a particularly difficult night of drinking, I remember his mother proudly presenting us with a traditional English breakfast of fried kippers with a fried egg resting on top of the fish. His dad ate this with incredible relish, saying his wife only made kippers for guests. The smell of the fish nearly triggered me to vomit. A cup of tea and some toast saved the day, and I managed to eat the thing without giving offense.

• • •

There was little time to be bored with this team; someone was always thinking of something to do or a prank to play. As the

---

5 Lyndell actually became a dentist.

newest team member, I was often in the thick of things, usually as the butt of a joke.

Moose and Lyndell both seemed to have natural muscles that needed little exercise to maintain. The rest of us exercised every day and were lean in the extreme. There were lots of wrestling matches, planned and extemporaneous. Pipes was a grappling expert with a lot of experience in joint locks. I learned a lot from him, and I don't think anyone ever beat him. It was like wrestling a python; he was just bone-crushingly strong.

Moose was in one of his wild moods after my first mission and decided to play with Telephone, who was sleeping peacefully in his rack. Moose just reached over and grabbed him, lifting him out of his rack, and stood him up on the floor like his latest Moose toy. By the time he was upright, Telephone was mostly awake and pretty pissed. Moose stood in front of him just laughing. Telephone then punched Moose in the gut, which didn't faze Moose at all; he just continued laughing.

Poor Telephone gave up and went back to bed.

Since Telephone wouldn't play, I became the next target. Moose leaned over me, grabbed my shoulders and started to pick me up. I responded with a palm heel strike to Moose's chin. It seemed Moose had a glass jaw, and he collapsed on top of me; 250 pounds of Moose pinning me to my rack vividly illustrated the rule of unintended consequences. The rest of the team, who were all sitting around watching, started roaring with laughter. I squirmed out of from under Moose before he completely came around and jumped into his rack under a poncho liner. He noticed that I was gone, but he didn't understand exactly what had happened and why everyone was laughing. "Where is the fucking new guy?" he asked. Lyndell thought this was the funniest thing ever, and even Mike laughed.

Telephone was a real joker. The Marines had set up a latrine over the klong that flowed past their end of the camp. It was a primitive L-shaped walkway, the long end of which had a board to sit on and hang your posterior out over the klong that flowed underneath. Telephone created a little boat with a piece of wood and nailed a tennis ball to the top of the board. He assembled the team and told us to watch this. He soaked the ball with lighter fluid, lit it, and then launched it from upstream and sailed it under the three Marines who were sitting on the improvised latrine. The first one felt the heat and jumped up yelling, then the second one, and then the last guy just stood up to avoid the "Fire Boat." They instantly realized who had done this to them and proceeded to chase Telephone around the camp. He ran up to me, begging me to help him. I said sure. The Marines caught him, dragged him to the klong, and threw him in. He came back to the camp and walked right up to me, saying, "I thought you were going to help me."

I said, "I am, Telephone, I'm pumping water into the barrels for you to take a shower with," and I handed him some soap.

If the individuals were unique, then as a team we were unique squared. We were tough, aggressive, and hard to handle, both in the bush and in the bar. Mr. Nash never really trusted us unsupervised; he tried his best to keep us out of trouble and on a short leash. As long as we had plenty of missions, this was not a problem, but when we had a lull in the business, boredom became the cause of many adventures and misadventures.

CHAPTER 8

A Blue Interlude An Idle Mind Is the Devil's Workshop

• • •

You only live once, but if you do it right, once is enough.

— MAE WEST

WE NEEDED A LITTLE DOWNTIME after the close calls we'd had at the downed helicopter. Two firefights during a milk run mission was two too many. We were not supposed to even make contact with the enemy. It looked like they had had a watcher on the site and planned to use the helicopter as bait to take down a team. That place was getting to be real "Indian Country," too hot to run any missions in.

Our next mission had not been set, so it was decided to go on a "training mission" to the local restaurant, bar, laundry, tailor shop, and bath. This was one of the team's main hangouts, and I was interested to see just what it was. I had really enjoyed the last team hangout, especially the coffee and the pre-coffee exercises. We all loaded up with our Swiss seats and rappelling lines and took the quick flight over. We rappelled down and Buzz sat the helicopter down in a clearing not far away and walked over. That counted as training.

The "town" was a tailor shop, a laundry, and a bar/bathhouse, all located in one long building. I had the marching money I had been given and asked Moose if he would help negotiate a price for a couple of new sets of Tigers, with the shirt pockets being slash and not straight and a few extra pockets for things like a compass. He said sure, so we started at the tailor shop. The price was low, and I saw what Nash meant about things being cheap here. Afterward, we went to the bar to have a little fun.

We drank a significant amount of Black Jack, and we were having a great time. I was listening to some team stories, which were numerous and humorous. Pipes was sorry for not bringing his bagpipes along, and in a nationalistic fervor he started drinking a quart of Cutty Sark Scots Whisky. I still remember the yellow label and the fact that it was advertised as Scots Whisky, not Scotch whisky. I decided to help him with this, and we proceeded along quite well.

We were in the back bar, a room almost as large as the main bar that, in addition to tables, had a number of large wooden tubs that could be filled with hot water for bathing. As the night rolled along, the team began to sing, and I was amazed at how good we sounded; they were amazed that I could sing harmony. We sang bawdy songs, none of which I knew the words to, but I followed along pretty well, at least well enough for a room full of drunks. Pipes provided a stirring rendition of "The Minstrel Boy" on the old piano, and it was decided that we should enter the Air America singing contest in Taiwan next month...if we didn't get killed before then, which was always a possibility.

The tubs were filled with hot water from the laundry next door, and we hopped in for a nice long soak. The water was too hot at first, and we ended up sitting on the edge of the tubs with only our feet and legs in the water as it cooled. Pipes noticed a bar of a dark blue substance in a small tray. I assumed this was bluing of some sort for the attached laundry. Pipes recalled that the ancient Scots would paint themselves blue with a blue dye called woad to make them wild-looking and as a protective amulet. He suggested that we should follow the custom. We were all drunk enough to agree, and before long we all had wild blue stripes and swirls painted everywhere, including Lyndell, who opposed being converted from a black man into a blue man. Ultimately, the dye colored the bath water in the tubs as well, and everyone, including several of the bar girls, were tinted a nice shade of blue.

The time had come to get on with the night's entertainment; however, the blue was not like laundry bluing we were familiar with; it was apparently permanent. Despite lots of soap and lots of scrubbing, and rinsing with vodka and even lighter fluid, we all retained a decidedly azure tint. Buzz still had discernable blue wings drawn on his back, and Pipes and I had crude "Book of Kells" designs coiling over our entire bodies. There may have been a snake as well. There was nothing for it but to enjoy the night, and I fell in love with a sweet blue barmaid.

The next morning, just before the ritual of coffee and condensed milk, Mike asked, "Everybody happy?" and we all replied in the affirmative (except the bar owner, who was not impressed with his new blue bar girls). Then he said, "Well, you all look a little blue to me." There was a collective groan. Mike might have been human after all.

After breakfast, I picked up my new team Tigers and we hopped aboard the bird and went home to the nest. When we touched down, Mr. Nash walked out to greet us. When he saw seven decidedly blue men exit the helicopter and walk in his direction, he pressed his hands to his ears, shook his head, and said, "Please do not tell me. I don't even want to know, I might not be able to take it," and then he muttered something about keeping a low profile as we headed to the briefing hut.

It turned out he was with several members of the Thai Special Forces, men known as the Queen's Cobras. These guys were, to be blunt, a bunch of tough motherfuckers. Unlike Nash, they were favorably impressed with our paint jobs, as it was well known in Thailand that shadows are not black or grey but dark midnight blue. In their opinion, we had just taken camouflage a step further than most, proving we were serious soldiers. Or maybe they just appreciated people who knew how to party.

• • •

Nai Daeng (Boss Red) was a Thai Communist leader who had been trying to get a Communist insurgency going in Thailand. He had been infiltrating men and equipment into Thailand from along the Thai-Cambodian border for a few years. He was becoming bolder, and his most recent exploit had involved moving in with about five hundred of his followers. He did not expect the Thais' response, which was to send fifteen thousand troops to the border area. They hunted the Communists down like rats and killed all of them, including Nai Daeng. This was a setback but not an end to the Communist insurgency problem.

The real issue was that Thailand had ethnic minorities, especially the hill tribes or Montagnards and ethnic Chinese who had not been assimilated into the Thai mainstream. These minorities were the targets of the Communists, who were attempting start a Communist insurgency by infiltrating the hill tribes with a cadre of Thai, Cambodian, or Lao converts. This had begun to really concern the Thai government, and they wanted to see if we could help them stop this.

Since we were "guests" of the Thai government, we were ready to do everything we could to help them and prevent another of "Kissinger's Dominos" from falling to the Communists. This probably meant a cost-plus contract project for the company and lots of goodwill from the Thai government.

We were ready to do anything we could, so we would soon be building an electronic fence along the Thai border and into Cambodia, or at least providing the Thais with the training and materials to build it. American companies were always willing to help, since the profits were large and the contracts often cost-plus.

We would run some joint missions with the Cobras to work on a small sensor net and see if it would be useful in stopping the Communists' infiltration of the hill tribes. Soon Kamon, Klahan, Chanchai, Wirat, Ram, and Punyaa were our boon companions. They had been chosen because they all spoke some English; in fact, Kamon, the leader, had excellent command of the language.

The plan was that we would form a twelve-man team for a couple of sensor-planting missions on the Thai side of the border. Then we would split into two six-man teams for a few missions (still on the Thai side of the border) before we crossed into Cambodia and Laos. The border between Thailand and Cambodia has a natural geographic barrier, the Dangrek mountain range. These are not high mountains, only two to three thousand feet tall and not very steep, but they are forested and the terrain is often rough jungle.

The Cardamom Mountains demarcate the border between Cambodia and southern Thailand. And we knew the Communists had used the Cambodian border town of Paillin to cross into southern Thailand before. This area was rough and sparsely populated, and many of the local people were of Burmese (Shan) extraction rather than Thai or Khmer. This area was a hotbed of the Communist Khmer Rouge activity and one of the first places they controlled. This area would be considered later if our northern sensor fence proved to be useful.

The first several missions with the Cobras went off without any problems, and we planted a small sensor fence along probable infiltration routes on the Thai side of the border. The missions were all the same, select a site, and conduct a short map study, then insert, plant, and exit. These were what my first mission should have been, in and out in a day. We made it look like we were looking for Communists, not planting sensors.

Even though most of the action in Cambodia was along the Vietnamese border, we thought the missions into Cambodia needed more stealth, so we enlisted Koobs and his oldest son Koost. Koobs didn't like the Thais very much, but he *really* hated the Communists, and especially the Vietnamese, so he agreed to help us. This made two seven-man teams, just a man over our normal six. We carried full combat loads and we were "loaded for bear" for every mission just to be sure.

The Cobras were tough guys, battle hardened from fighting in Vietnam and Laos and at home in the bush. Kamon gave us a real compliment: he said that we were silent and invisible in the bush, not like the Americans in Vietnam who talked and smoked cigarettes on patrol. They named us Blue Smoke, since we could disappear off the trail in an instant. He said they were happy to fight with us and "our" Montagnards.

We ran several missions in Cambodia where we had enemy contact, but none were bad except one. The split team with Kamon in command and Lyndell, Koobs, and Moose as the technical guy ran into a group of twelve Khmer Rouge guerrillas on the trail. They set up an ambush and eliminated all of them without as much as a scratch.

● ● ●

We decided to take a little R&R and go to Bangkok for some shopping, eating, drinking, and other amusements. We wore our green fatigues with big red "Sat Cong" (Kill Commies) pocket patches. The first thing we did was find a tailor shop and bought dark blue silk jackets with a Tiger embroidered on the front and back and Dragons down both the arms. Buzz and Fuzz got a large bird, probably a phoenix, on theirs. We then went to the Atlanta Hotel, an old art deco hotel with a large swimming pool, one of the few pools in Bangkok at the time. There were rules and regulations, so everyone purchased proper swimming suits at the hotel and we went down to the pool wearing bright Hawaiian shirts and swimsuits, looking like a bunch of tourists with really short haircuts.

Silk Tiger Jacket

I knew this was going to be difficult for me, since swimming was not my thing, but I thought I could just catch a few rays and drink something with an umbrella stuck in it. Naturally, Moose tossed me in, but I managed not to drown. It was great to be able to unwind for a bit. We had a real Western-style meal, a few drinks, and a great sleep in a soft bed—in a room without bugs, bats, or snakes.

We were all up early and took our time at breakfast, the orange juice and coffee made it feel like being home for a few minutes. The jackets we had ordered were delivered, and we all put them on. Now, we thought—no, we *knew*—we looked really fucking good.

We all looked like crazy foreigners I think. Keeping a low profile was forgotten, and since we had no official insignia anyway, we felt free to use everyone else's with impunity. We were often army or Marines depending on the day and never the same thing twice. Our laundry lady was great with patches, and she had a real collection, but today were had our own insignia, we were all Tigers in Tiger Jackets. We met up with some of the Thai guys (the Queen's Cobras) that we had entertained at the base after the infamous blue incident and had worked with for a few weeks. We had some of the silk jackets made up for them as well, with a cobra coiling around the torso and looking at you over the shoulder. In return, they found us a nice small bar and threw everyone else out. This was now a bar for Cobras and Tigers only for the night, and we were officially christened as Tigers by the Cobras, because of the jackets and tigerstripe camo we wore and maybe our attitude as well. Anyone who did not leave voluntarily was physically ejected by the Cobras. One of the "ejected" Thais complained to the Thai police. They came into the bar with the guy, and when they saw who was there, the police took turns slapping the protestor around and then threw him back out onto the street. It seemed the Cobras had real clout. The locals called them "the men who piss anywhere they want."

That made it our bar for the evening. The owner was fine with the arrangement, since we paid him more than he could possibly make in a night under normal circumstances. We had a really great time. The Cobras told us about a battle against the NVA in Laos and a lot of other entertaining stories. We ordered out for food and ate, drank, and were merry. The bar had a couple of girls who could sing American rock and roll songs with absolutely no accent, except when they sang Tammy Wynette. The beds had clean sheets and good companionship.

The only dark spot was when one of the Cobras said he thought we were being followed. He had seen a guy trailing us down the block, and now the guy was sitting outside and watching us. Two of the Cobras left out the back door and in a few minutes they had the man in custody. Apparently, someone at the hotel had paid him to keep an eye on us. That was pretty curious to us—why on earth would anyone care? I thought it was probably Nash. The gentleman in question decided to spend the night with us tied up in the corner. We sent him on his way after breakfast with a message to his friend to never to be seen again and that the Cobras would be watching for him and his kind, and the Cobras don't usually take prisoners.

CHAPTER 9

Out of the Fire and Into Hell

• • •

To live is to suffer, to survive is to find some meaning in the suffering.

— FRIEDRICH NIETZSCHE

OUR BRAND-NEW SUPER SENSORS, OUR technological marvels, were dying. And we didn't know why. Had the bad guys figured how to detect and remove them, or were they just going bad? The problem was becoming serious, to the point where the program and the product was close to being declared a complete failure. We needed to fix this and quickly. It was decided by someone that we needed to recover some of the dead sensors. This meant that a mission must go to the trail, find a dead sensor, and retrieve it. This was more difficult than it sounds, because even under the best conditions there was traffic on the trail: NVA troops both day and night, especially at night, and teams with dogs looking for groups like us. The only reason to risk it at all was that Koobs, who had planted many of the sensors, was going to accompany us. Koobs was an expert Hmong tracker.

Just a word or two about the Hmong: they are the indigenous people of the northern part of Laos. Like Native Americans, they lived relatively primitive lives, but they were excellent at bush craft and really hated the Vietnamese. They also hated the indigenous people of southern Laos, the Lao, but less than they hated the Vietnamese. So they especially loved helping us kill the Vietnamese. If the stories were true, Koobs had near-magical abilities in the bush, and he figured he could find and remove the devices—assuming they were still there.

But Koobs was busy with other things and could not make it for at least two weeks, so we just hung around the base eating canned rations, playing spades, and listening to DD's collection of tapes. He had a thing for the Doors and the Rolling Stones, but otherwise, he had a broad collection. I was pretty illiterate in the area of pop music, but I got an education in a hut in Thailand. Occasionally, to the delight of many and the consternation of some, Pipes would play the bagpipes. He was really good, but my favorite was Lyndell and his jazz harmonica—he was a master of the blues. The most unusual thing was that our group sang together. Just like in training, it became a real bonding experience. We had decided to enter the Air America singing contest in Taiwan, so we practiced a few good songs and did our best to get ready while we had down time. I continued to do calisthenics and run daily. The rest of the team thought this was really abnormal behavior, but they came along with me anyway, just to humor me.

After the blue episode, we were not exactly welcome at the local bar, but Nash sent us a case of Jack Daniels and a couple coolers of frozen steaks, complete with a residual amount of dry ice. We loaded up several bottles of Jack, a cooler full of steaks, and a bag of charcoal and paid a social call on the Marine barracks at the opposite end of the camp. While the steaks thawed, we had a little partner spades game in their bunker. No one mentioned that we all knew sign language. This wasn't really cheating, just taking the high ground...okay, it was pretty much blatant cheating. But we donated all the money to their party fund, and everyone had a good time.

• • •

Koobs arrived on the weekly supply truck. He was short, like all the hill tribesmen, with bright eyes and dark, wrinkled skin. I was glad to see him again. We drank some beer and they told stories. Koobs, who was a shaman, gave us each a silver spirit lock. It was a Montagnard good luck charm to wear around the neck, generally at the back where a clasp would be. It prevents the spirit from leaving the body, and I, for one, was glad to keep my spirit inside where it belonged.

Spirit Locks and an Elephant Hair Bracelet

We went to town and ate some of the local food for a few days, knowing Koobs would enjoy it. We also wanted to get past the full moon so the nights would not be quite so bright. This was planned to be a three-day mission, so we packed de-hydrated LRP rations and Koobs packed rice balls. This mission needed exceptional stealth to be successful. I was still not as silent I wanted to be in the bush, and I hoped Koobs could help me with some training. We loaded up and Mike asked, "Everybody happy?"

"Yes, sir!" we replied and then got to the bird with Buzz and moved out at first light.

The LZ was a large, grass-filled area. This was a single ship insertion, and we just hopped out into the tall grass and headed for the perimeter, following Koobs. We moved quickly toward the spot where Koobs thought he had planted the sensors. The terrain was hilly and rough. The jungle seemed to have only two directions: uphill and downhill. Everything was out to get you. If it was a bug, it bit and stung, the plants all had razor sharp leaves or hellacious thorns. It might be beautiful to look at from a plane, but it was hell to walk through.

We avoided any large trails, as the chance of running into NVA traffic was too high. We proceeded in a pattern: we moved as quietly as possible for ten minutes, listened for at least five, then repeated. It made for slow progress. We moved close to a well-worn trail, and since it was getting late, we decided to laager up (find a defensible position) and lie doggo (still and quiet). We were close to some thick jungle around a small hill. Once we made it to the top, we set out Claymores to protect the approaches and formed up in a circle with our feet pointing to the center and dug in as best as we could. From this position, we could easily watch the area below and not be observed. A number of loaded bicycles in a large group passed by and we just lay in our laager and watched. It was beginning to get dark, so we pulled out our dehydrated rations and Koobs ate a couple of rice balls. I got pork with scalloped potatoes. We did not have any way to heat the water, so we just added the water and allowed them to sit for longer than normal. This tactic worked on everything but the infamous "Chili con Carne," which had rock-like dehydrated beans that even hot water couldn't soften.

We saw it coming—a black storm with lightning playing across it. We watched as it swept up the valley toward us. It was like being in the street and watching a truck coming at you. But we had to stay where we were; we had no alternative. Since we were traveling light, we had no ponchos, just three sleeping silks for the entire team. These were basically silk or rayon sleeping bags with no fill, just a single layer of fabric, which had a more or less waterproof bottom and a net upper half to keep bugs out. Rolling over when you were asleep could make a lot of noise, but the sleeping silk reduced it a lot. We took them out and put them over our packs in an attempt to keep them dry and got ready to hunker down for the storm.

What a storm it was! The rain came down in hard sheets, and the wind howled and blew from what seemed like every direction at once. But the lightning was especially frightening, and we were in a high spot. Telephone and I crawled out to disarm the Claymores; we pulled the blasting caps out and inserted the transport plugs. We left them where they were and left the blasting caps outside our position as well. We did not want the lightning setting them off in our vicinity. By this time, we were all soaked. Being wet and in the wind, I was so cold I started to shiver involuntarily; it was a miserable night for us all. A lightning strike came in very close to us, so loud my ears rang. It was a near miss. Finally, morning came. It was warmer, but we were still wet. We reapplied our face paint and continued to travel through the bush for several hours. Koobs recognized the area, and amazingly, it took him very little time to find the sensor. We quickly removed it and "sanitized" the area before melting back into the jungle.

The team proceeded, with Mike as the point and Koobs as the drag, since he was the best at sanitizing the trail we made. It was getting late, and we needed to find a good place to lie doggo for a while. A spot in thick bush not far from the ridgeline was chosen for this purpose, and we all circled up in the center of the bushes under a spreading tree. Almost as soon as we settled down, Koobs motioned for complete silence, and we froze where we were. A large party of NVA walked right by us; there were somewhere between twenty and thirty of them, and they were all carrying weapons. They were clearly silhouetted against the setting sun. We didn't even dare to breathe until they were out of sight.

Then Mike put the antenna onto the PRC-77 and attempted to contact Sky King, a circling radio relay plane. We failed to raise anyone. We decided to wait an hour and try again. Koobs made his way in the semidarkness to check out the trail on the ridgeline.

This was not a normal place for a trail since it was exposed to attack from the air, but Koobs reported it as heavily used. Night was falling, and while we really didn't want to remain so close to a trail, we had no good choice; we would be unable to see very soon. And so, another long night began. No one really slept. Mike finally raised the Banshee, a C-130 gunship purpose-built "off the books" by AA in Taiwan. Armed with Vulcan cannons and a 105-millimeter cannon in the tail, it was the only gun support we could expect. It flew mostly at night, since it was too large of a target during the day. It had Forward Looking Infrared (FLIR), Low Light-level Television (LLTV), and other sensors that made it a real night killer, even from twenty thousand feet. The Banshee relayed our request for pick up. We told them about the traffic on the trail and they searched but didn't find anything. They decided to put a few 105 rounds in the tree-covered area where the trail had disappeared into the jungle. There were a lot of secondary explosions, it looked like they must have hit an ammo dump.

The Banshee headed home before first light, and we waited in the small hide, hoping our run for the pickup zone would be fast and event-free. When the choppers were fifteen minutes out from the PZ, we exited the hide and ran. It took us about ten minutes to get there. Mike waited another two minutes and then popped purple smoke while we flipped our hats to show the orange lining. We all made it into the helicopter as quickly as possible. The bird cranked up and we were on the way home, the mission completed.

Everyone was really happy, laughing and smiles all around. We had made it in and out without contact. I was ready for a shower, some supper, and a trip to town. Then, from out of the tree line, came a shot. We couldn't tell if was well aimed or just lucky, but the bullet struck Telephone just behind the ear. It went through his skull and left a large hole on the left side. He was killed instantly. Since I was sitting next to Telephone, I got much of the splatter: his blood, bone fragments, and brains were all over me. We laid his body on the floor of the helicopter. I took out a canteen and washed as much of the blood and brains off my face as I could. I felt really sick and barely managed to avoid being sick.

I sat still and began the precombat breathing and meditation drill I had been practicing. Slowly, I calmed myself, but I kept coming back to the death of Telephone. In a fight, it wouldn't have been so bad, but we had been out of harm's way, done with the mission, and on the way home.

We landed at Naked Fanny. No one said a word; it was one of the most painful experiences I have ever had. We always knew there was a high degree of risk in what we were doing, but Telephone's death brought it all front and center. We didn't know what to do. We carried his body from the helicopter in a sleeping silk. Nash was there and found a proper body bag for him. The team decided to accompany the body to the morgue in Udorn. A company DC-3 was ordered. We looked like shit and felt that way too. It didn't seem real. We had been 100 percent one second and completely fucked the next.

We went to the showers, and I just walked under the water in my Tigers and cried like a baby. I watched the blood color the water as it came off of me and went toward the drain. I was washing my dead friend's blood off me. When I took off my blouse, I found a leech on my arm. I pulled out a bottle of bug juice and drowned the bastard. It fell off and I crushed it. We all checked each other for more, but I was the only lucky guy that day. The leach bite continued to leak blood for quite a while. I put a bandage on it, but it became saturated with blood that ran down my arm and onto my hand. I didn't care.

Nash's aide brought us our green fatigues. We changed, went to the bar, and tossed back several large shots of Jack Daniels. Once the plane was ready, we loaded up and took Telephone's body to the morgue in Udorn. The mood was beyond somber. We had been "out," without any real enemy contact, and then a single shot had ended it. Nash had been through this before, as had the other members of the team. It was my first time, but it would not be my last.

The problem was that as time progressed, the enemy became more sophisticated and stronger in numbers. Maybe that shot hadn't been an accident but had come from a well-trained sniper. The numbers game put us at a great disadvantage, and that disadvantage was growing. They now used teams with dogs to hunt us and had people watching all the good landing sites. On our side, we officially turned on and off the bombing and played political games. The question in my mind of why were we here doing this was never really answered; we just assumed the guys at the top knew what they were doing. I assumed they used our intelligence to know the volume of infiltration from the north. I knew a few good B-52 strikes could really help us even the score, but they simply had not come.

We said our last goodbyes, and there were tears from everyone. We discussed whether we should accompany the body back to the states. That would present difficulties, since you would have a hard time not telling the truth about the cause and place of death. Nash said that he had recruited Telephone and he would travel back with him. We each donated $500, a lot of money at the time, and gave it to Nash for Telephone's family. We all planned to write letters as well, when we found the time. Nash said that the company held a lot of insurance on us, so we shouldn't worry about his family. We worried anyway, and we still had to clean up his belongings in the nest. In the real army war, I know people went through much more of this, but it doesn't make a difference, dead friends are dead friends. It was not easy for me to adapt to Telephone being gone.

The team was physically and emotionally spent. We went to the hotel and ate Thai food and then to the bar where we all drank heavily. I don't remember much about that night. We drank a lot of Jack and toasted Telephone's memory, and everyone who knew him well told funny stories.

The next day, we returned to the nest. I carefully washed the mud off the sensor, dried it with towels, and set about disassembling it. As soon as I cracked it open, the problem was obvious: it was full of water. Electronics do not like to be wet. The clamshell was missing a gasket. Some idiot had left out the gaskets and killed the sensors, and in my mind killed Telephone as well. I wrote a short note back to David Snow in the assembly department describing the problem and told them that this had cost us more than a few sensors. I wanted the people responsible for final assembly and QC to know that their stupidity had cost us a life.

My response to stress was sleep. I slept for almost twelve hours. Wisely, the team left me alone. When I finally got up, I was starving and ate a pad Thai made by the bartender at our club hut. Then I decided I wanted a shower and Moose helped me pump the water from the water truck up into the barrels that served as a heater. We had just about completed this when the usual afternoon tropical rainstorm started. We were soaked in an instant, so we just stripped off the green boxers we normally wore in camp and lathered up with a bottle of shampoo. In a minute, the rest of the team came over and got up on the pallets we used as duckboards. Someone started to sing the antiwar anthem by Country Joe and the Fish, and everyone joined in:

Hell no we won't go!
And it's 1, 2, 3—what are we fighting for?
Don't ask me, I don't give a damn!
Next stop is Viet Nam.
And it's 5, 6, 7; so open up them pearly gates.
There ain't no time
To wonder why
Whoopee!
We're all gonna die.

The rest of the base just watched us; we were cheap entertainment for the Marines. They were pretty sure we were fucking crazy, and this concert certainly helped cement our reputation as a bunch of mad, bad, crazy motherfuckers—well, at least the crazy part. Nietzsche again: "And those who were seen dancing were thought to be insane by those who could not hear the music." We were hearing the music for sure.

Then, suddenly, we began to sing "Amazing Grace." It was beautiful, and we needed a little beauty at that time, so we made it for ourselves. Lyndell had a magnificent, deep, resonant voice, and I amazed everyone by singing natural harmony.

Even though I had only been with them a short time, I felt closely bonded to the team. I had had close friends before, but never a brother. My brothers in arms filled this void for me, I guess. I really enjoyed being with the team. I missed Telephone; he and I had really hit it off in just a short time, and I would never forget us pulling the blasting caps out of the Claymore mines during the storm. His death brought home that this was reality, not a training mission or a game.

The call went out that we now needed an RTO (radioman), to replace Telephone. About a week or so later we got an Australian, Bobbie, who had been in Bay 6 during my training. Training seemed to have been years ago, now. It was like old home week as I welcomed him and I now was absolutely no longer the FNG! I thought it was going to be hard for Bobbie to replace Telephone. To my surprise, Bobbie was so gregarious that he quickly fit into the group. He did not replace Telephone, but just seemed to naturally fit in with everyone. He called me Red and I didn't care and he told everyone the story about me fighting a giant guy called the Bear in training, a story which he added a lot to for increased entertainment value.

"Listen, what you guys don't know is that Red here was Sykes' attack dog. When we had combative training Sykes loved to put him against anyone no matter how big they were. He gets this wild look in his eyes and then just goes crazy kicking and punching and throwing people down on the mat. When he gets "the look" he does not seem to feel anything or just does not give a shit and becomes a real wild man. People thought he was just plain crazy.

On the first day of training I watched him beat the shit out of the Bear and four or five other guys in a row, and the Bear is a giant, six foot four and built like a bear, tough as they come. And then there is the knife, he was Sykes' best student there as well. Got his arm cut and didn't even seem to mind as he finished the entire two man form bleeding everywhere. And then in the jungle in Honduras he managed to hide from the local Indian trackers..."

That was not how I remembered it at all. The 'wild look' was just plain old fear and since I did not have prior military experience. Sykes was trying to get rid of me by sending me against the biggest guys in the program. I had heard people occasionally call me Red Dog but I did not think anything of it. It was just a nick name.

CHAPTER 10

Into the Breach Once More

• • •

But when the blast of war blows in our ears,

Then imitate the action of the tiger:

Stiffen the sinews, summon up the blood.

— SHAKESPEARE, *HENRY V*

WE HAD COMPLETED ANOTHER ROUTINE road watch mission and were all loaded up and on the way home once more. I was tired, hungry, and glad we were out. As usual, I caught a few minutes of sleep on the way home sitting between Moose and Lyndell. Instantly, I was so far gone that I didn't wake up when someone painted me up with pig's blood. They just laid blood-soaked shop towels on me while I slept. Probably Buzz and Fuzz were implicated as usual. Making sure I was a bloody mess was becoming a goddamed team ritual.

My wonderful deep sleep was interrupted by the Blue Cheer album *Vincibus Eruptum* at full volume. Buzz and Fuzz hadn't wasted their time while we were on the mission. They had modified their beloved helicopter with an improvised sound system. They had hooked up a Psychological Operations loudspeaker system with two horn-type speakers, an amplifier, and an eight-track player. As a finale, we came in and made an orbit low and slow around our "secret" base with Steppenwolf blaring "Born to Be Wild":

Get your motor runnin'
Head out on the highway
Lookin' for adventure
And whatever comes our way
Yeah Darlin' go make it happen
Take the world in a love embrace
Fire all of your guns at once
And explode into space

I like smoke and lightning
Heavy metal thunder
Racin' with the wind
And the feelin' that I'm under
Yeah Darlin' go make it happen
Take the world in a love embrace
Fire all of your guns at once
And explode into space

Like a true nature's child
We were born, born to be wild

We can climb so high
I never wanna die

Born to be wild
Born to be wild

This got the attention of the Marines and anyone else within a half mile. Good thing Mr. Nash wasn't meeting us, I thought, this was quite the theatrical entrance, not exactly "low profile." We landed on the pad and humped our gear back to the bunk house. Just as we got there, Nash surprised us by walking out of the briefing hut and asking, "Who selected today's theme music?"

Then he saw me. "Jesus Christ, Mac, I thought you guys made no contact!"

"I'm sorry, sir, I work with a bunch of jokers." Immediately the entire team started to howl like dogs and chant "Red Dog, Red Dog, Kill! Kill! Kill! Red Dog, Red Dog, Kill!, Kill! Kill!"

"And to think I was worried you might not fit in with the team."

• • •

We lazed around for a week and ran a few missions to some of the other bases but nothing for real. It was June, and the weather was beginning to get unsettled and rainy. The monsoon was a bit early that year. The monsoon was not a constant rain but was made up of periods of intense rain that lasted up to several hours. It also seemed that the higher altitudes got more rain than the flats, but maybe this was just because we were outside in the mountains and inside in the flats. We only had time for one or two more missions before the season really set in.

Enemy activity had increased with some 37 mm (1.45 inch) antiaircraft guns. The ZSU-23, which was a four-barreled radar-controlled gun, was especially deadly because the radar could not be evaded by going "stealthy mode" at night. This artillery made flying much more dangerous than the occasional 7.6 mm AK small arms fire, and that was bad enough already.

Koobs was back from a visit with his wives. He had apparently heard of my spinning knife exploit and asked me through Moose if I would allow him to bless my knife, which would give it the ability to cut through spirits as well as flesh. Naturally, I jumped at the chance. To bless the knife, Koobs built a small fire using a flint and steel. The team sat in a circle and Koobs took my Tanto knife and passed it through the fire. Then he cut his little finger and dripped blood on the blade, passed the blade back to me, and asked me to do the same. I bleed like a stuck pig, so there was a lot of blood on the blade. Koobs took the knife back, opened a small pouch, and sprinkled some gray powder onto the blade, mixing it with the blood. He then asked that I wash the blade by pissing on it. This I proceeded to do, and then I passed the blade back over the fire to Koobs. He pissed on it too, and then he asked the team to put the fire out by pissing on it, which they did. Next, he washed the blade with whisky, which he sprayed from his mouth, and then with water. Now the blade would cut spirits as well as the living.

After the ritual, we focused on getting ready. We would be looking for the main training camp in the last area we had been in. FLIR and other intelligence suggested where it might be, but we needed a better position to do anything about it. This was a difficult and dangerous event to consider. Close to the base camp meant that the enemy strength would be at maximum and the potential to be discovered high. If we were discovered, the potential to be overrun was also high. So we would have to get in and out undetected and without going into the normal open landing zones, since they were probably all watched. This was a tall order, but getting rid of this camp might make life a lot better for us, so it was decided that we should make an attempt. This mission would also secure our reputation for being completely crazy.

Rather than going in just before dawn, we would go in just before night. Moving at night through the bush was exceedingly difficult, since the vegetation was very thick and night was very dark. The use of flashlights was not possible, since the light would mark your position from a long way off, so we had a bit of technology to help us see in the dark. The AN PVS-4 night vision scope had already become available. We obtained one of these but with a modification of the technology: night vision goggles. The SU49/PAS 5 NVG would give us the edge at night. Mike gave up his Stoner and decided on H&K MP5 with a silencer.

The goggles were not light, the images were not very clear, and they ate batteries quickly, but we hoped they would allow us to get in and move some at night without much moonlight.

And in we went, looking for trouble in trouble's backyard but confident that we owned the night this time…or at least had taken out a lease.

Mike, Moose, Koobs, DD, Bobby the FNG, and I made the final six. We loaded up after a nice meal at NKP. We turned over our tags, wallets, and "If I am dead" letters to Nash before we left. Rather than Buzz's normal "slick," we managed to get a loaner from the guys at NKP, a state of the art Sikorski Pave Low helicopter equipped with Forward Looking Infrared (FLIR) and Low Light Telivision (LLTV) to allow you to see in the dark. This was an upgrade of the normal Pave Low and had the latest optics, terrain-following radar, and countermeasures including chaff and thermal decoys. Like the old Pave Low, it had three 7.62 (.308) Vulcan miniguns (made by GE—*We Bring Good Things to Life…and Death*) and a fifty caliber in back. Not only could it see at night, but it also had quite a bite. We borrowed a pilot with experience and Buzz acted as copilot. The rest of the crew was on loan as well. They loved to shoot the miniguns. Nothing was on the FLIR or LLTV, and it was a go. I liked running joint missions; it just felt good to think you might have some backup if you needed it.

We inserted at the top of a small, brush-covered hill by rappelling down from the bird. No skids on this one, it was just out the ass and down. When we hit the ground, Mike, with his night vision goggles and illuminator, took the lead while the rest of us followed. It really was *can't see your hand in front of your face* dark. Every man had a small British tritium adjustable map-reading device with a clamp to hook it onto our pack that we had adjusted to shine a very, very, small pinprick of light. This enabled us to move as a team, with each member able to see the dot on the man in front of him. Mike used the night vision as Point to pick the trail and Koobs used night vision as Drag to cover it. Holding to the pack in front of you and trying to move together was impossible. We had practiced with just a little moon, and it was possible, but in the bush, with no real moon or stars, it just did not work. The rest of the team had the goggles, but we wanted to preserve some normal night vision since the image screen killed normal night vision. We put the goggles on and did our best with the two illuminators to move quickly and quietly.

When we hit the trail, we made quick time for about an hour, and then, still in the almost pitch-black dark, we left the trail and headed up a steep incline toward a ridge. The ridge looked across a steep valley. Straddling the ridge was a small grove of trees and thick brush; we worked our way carefully into this thicket and found a natural depression where a large tree had been blown down. Carefully, snipping some additional foliage, we camouflaged this completely. We circled up, feet inward, eyes outward, and waited for dawn to come. I ate a slice of fruitcake and drank some water and felt better as the sugar surged through my system. It was really hot and really wet, without a breath of wind. Sweat poured off me even as I sat still in the hide. The temperature rose with the sun, and we could see that the entire valley was engulfed in a thick mist. It reminded me of a line from Beowulf: "The dragon's breath lay thick upon the land," and indeed it did almost every morning.

Although the mist lay like a layer of water in the valley, it was possible to see pillars of smoke rising slowly through the fog, which indicted the cooking fires of the enemy camp. From here, we could get all the Intel we needed. This was a real stroke of luck. If the fog cleared, we could just lay doggo during the day, carefully observing the goings on in the camp below. At mid-morning, the fog finally did clear, and we could see several large structures that were probably sleeping quarters and a covered truck park with about thirty trucks. This place was huge and easily covered an area the size of a football field. The steep ridge sheltering it meant you would have to fly directly over it to really see it in the thick bush. NVA soldiers stood in formation and then marched off into the bush and then along the wide trail, following a small convoy of trucks. Occasionally, a patrol of two men would walk the trail just along the ridgeline. We just held our breath, lay doggo, and prayed they didn't see us.

Mike carefully shot several azimuths with his compass to pinpoint this place on the map, but mostly we just watched and sweated all day. Night fell, and we waited until early morning when it was still completely dark to leave the hide and work our way back down to the high-speed trail. We traveled as fast as possible to make sure we didn't run into a convoy of trucks or NVA soldiers. Dawn was just beginning to color the sky when we turned off the trail and headed for the PZ. We climbed the hills silently but quickly. Then Mike stopped and signed for Koobs to come up. There were fresh tracks.

Koobs looked at the tracks and followed them carefully up the hill by the PZ. Across the little valley and about one hundred meters ahead, well concealed from us, was the sniper. With Koobs pointing him out, I looked through the binoculars and saw him. Koobs leans over and whispers Soo Aha in my ear. Soo Aha that is Tee Shirt in Thai I think.   Mike decided to get in close and use the silenced MP5. The sniper was not Asian. He was blond and white, maybe a fucking Russian. He had set up very well, but he wasn't really in his hide yet. He stood up and turned around, and then from out of nowhere I saw a flash of color as a tiger took him. I could see it clearly through the binoculars. It only took an instant. The tiger held him by the back of the neck and shook him like a cat with a mouse, and then it dropped the body and disappeared into the bush. *There are fucking tigers in here! Goddamn man-eating fucking tigers!* I knew I would never sleep at night in the bush again; having the VC and NVA chasing us was bad enough, but tigers!

At least this one seemed to be on our side. Koobs now points and says Soo Aha again.   Well it turns out that the Thai for Tiger and Tee Shirt are only different in tone, which I could not differentiate.

He led us up, and when we got close it was easy to see the man was dead. There were long claw marks gouged deep into his flesh, blood everywhere, and a crushed neck. I walked up to where the tiger tracks started; a leap of at least twenty feet from the body. The footprints were huge; at least four inches across. Koobs motioned me back. Disturbing the scene as little as possible, I took the sniper rifle and a canvas bag and walked backward, careful to stay on a log to hide my tracks as much as possible. Then, like a complete klutz, I slipped and fell flat on top of the body. *Shit, just like my goddamn first mission.* Koobs was pointing and laughing whit his hand over his mouth. Hey, at least I got him to laugh! I carefully backed up and left the area of the sniper's hide. We turned back to the trail, with Koobs as drag, sanitizing our trail except for the few big footprints I had made in the sniper's hide. We learned much later from Koobs that another Montagnard tracker, forced to work for the NVA, had tried to convince the NVA that our team could become tigers at will and that we had, in the form of a tiger, killed the sniper because of the death of one of our team. As proof, he carefully showed them my footprints changing to tiger paws and the mauled corpse that had not been eaten, just killed. He warned them that we could appear out of thin air because we could take any animal shape, even birds or dragons. And this explanation worked pretty well—our team mascot was the tiger, after all. I don't think the NVA bought the story, except maybe the tiger part, which they had some pretty good evidence of. I was now keenly aware that we were not the only deadly predators in the jungle those damn tee shirts were out there as well.

It was just too hot of an area with too many bad guys. We needed to get out before we ended up in a firefight we might not be able to win. Mike immediately called for Evac and moved to the top of a nearby hill that had a few small trees and lots of low brush cover but no really large trees. We all got low in the bushes and tied our Swiss seats and waited. When the bird was five minutes out, we popped purple smoke and prepared to exit via a rope that had large loops every few feet where you could hook your snap link and stand in the one below that. The bird came in, dropped the rope lines, and we all hooked up. I was on the bottom of the rope and Koobs was just above me. We went up quickly and the rope started to slowly spin. I held out a hand in an attempt to correct the spin and failed. We were moving really fast now—it felt like over one hundred miles per hour—and I needed that hand to hold the rope. The spin slowed some, but the rush of the wind just sucked the heat from my body; I was freezing and, as usual, I started to shiver. When Buzz slowed down the spin got really bad again, made worse by a heavy pack plus a sniper rifle. The Swiss seat ropes cut into my groin and hurt and also cut off the blood flow to my legs. *Next time, please let's use the rope ladder,* I thought. Buzz finally went into a hover over a large open space covered with tall grass. He slowly descended and allowed us to unhook. Once everyone was off the string, we clambered on board and headed for Naked Fanny, but not before I vomited because of the spinning. I could barely walk, my head was spinning so badly; it was worse than being drunk. Even so, I was very happy to be inside the helicopter as opposed to hanging on to the rope for dear life.

When we landed at Naked Fanny, Nash came out to meet us. "Okay, Mac, whose blood is it this time?"

I looked down and the blood from where I fell on the sniper had mixed with my own puke and pretty much covered my blouse and trousers. "Oh, just some Russian sniper's blood. Tiger got him. It was pretty messy, but thanks for asking. Don't worry, I'm just fine."

He shook his head and everyone else laughed, knowing how it got there. "Why don't you guys get cleaned up before the debriefing? Especially you, Mac. As usual, you really stink," he said.

We showered in a real shower room. Well, it wasn't a real room—it was a hooch made into a shower room; they also had latrine hooches. We changed into our greens, and then we went for food and beer before the debriefing with Nash. Nash had brought a carton of steaks, and when we offered them to the small contingent of Marines at the base, they organized a barbecue. The steaks were first class, and we ate a lot of meat and a few somewhat warm beers. We made a bunch of Marines happy that day.

Nash asked about what we found and we said barracks for at least a hundred or more and a truck park for at least thirty and maybe up to a hundred trucks. Mike said our air assets were presently nil, and a B-52 strike was not possible as a result of politics, so we would have to decide what to do with the limited resources we had. We did not have enough forces to consider a ground attack. We had a Spectre or two and some World War II–vintage ground attack planes, but this was not an easy strike any longer because of the possibility of radar-controlled 23 mm antiaircraft guns, which were very effective weapons. He said that we might be able to "borrow" the MH-53 Pave Lows since they were currently completely idle due to politics.

The possibility of using a "Daisy Cutter" bomb dropped from a C-130 was discussed, but getting one was going to be a problem. "Okay," Nash said. "Mac, you are a chemist, make us some napalm. We will drop it from a C-130."

Okay, I thought, *we have empty barrels and pallets. We have thermite grenades, regular grenades, and phosphorous grenades. If we can get some napalm thickener powder we are home free. If not, we can get lots of Styrofoam from coolers and packing. We have diesel fuel and gasoline, coconut oil, and a drum of toluene as a cleaner. We dissolve the Styrofoam into the toluene mixed with diesel fuel. We dissolve Lux soap flakes in water and add an Epsom salt solution; the greasy precipitate is another potential thickener. I think I can do this. Then you band the drums together on a pallet and strap a regular "baseball" grenade, a thermite grenade and phosphorus grenade to each drum. It will take a while to get the Styrofoam and enough Epsom salt, but it might work. Do it like a resupply drop, with parachutes to retard the pallets for a few seconds. Use a C-130 with Ro-Ros (the bed of wheels for moving cargo out of the cargo hold) and push the pallets out the back, just like a supply drop. Some of the pilots are very accurate at this. Wires could be used to pull the grenade pins as the pallets exit the plane. It might work. Not as good as a Daisy Cutter, but then what is?*

• • •

To make the napalm, we needed supplies, so we decided to go to the home base AA in Udorn. We convinced Buzz to get the guys in the Pave Low to fly us and have a little R&R for their help. This was not difficult, since they were temporarily grounded from missions (except for helping us). So off we went to Udorn. We had our five and the Pave Low had five, so we had ten people total. We landed at Udorn close to where the Pave Low's cousins, the Jolly Greens, were. We were dressed in our Tigers with no insignia, and the crew and pilot Captain Scott were in their normal "sanitized" greens, which they wore when they worked with us. At Nakon Phenom, we fit in fine. At Udorn, we were a little out of place, since most of the people were air force. The ground crews were mostly shirtless in the tropical heat as they loitered around with little to do, but everyone else gave us the eye. The idea was to talk to General Andrew Evans, the Chief of Special Operations, and see what we could get to help us. Nash had paved the way with a phone call, so we expected no real problems.

As we made our way to the general's office, a spit-and-polish lieutenant decided to take it upon himself to admonish us regarding our uniforms and the lack of insignia. He obviously did not know who he was dealing with, which can be a fatal mistake. In a particularly dumb move, he decided to ask who was in charge and then give Captain Scott shit. I guess he thought we were all AA personnel, and if that was the case he could harass us with impunity. Captain Scott simply identified himself as Captain Scott, and the lieutenant assumed he was an AA captain and told him he needed to know the names of all the non–air force personnel…meaning us. Mike pulled out his "Get Out of Jail Free Card" and said, "As you can see, you are interfering with people operating under the direct orders of the president of the United States. You have detained me and questioned me, which you are clearly forbidden to do. You are a puffed up junior grade officer who has never seen a day of combat, and you are about to get an ass chewing, which will be legendary, if I recall General Evans."

Mike then said, "I would like you to accompany us to our meeting with General Evans, not only for a proper ass chewing, but I think you might be perfect for an upcoming ground mission into Cambodia." The lieutenant visibly paled.

"I have duties here," he said.

"Nothing the general can't fix for us, Lieutenant," Mike said. We all proceeded to the general's office and were immediately sent in. All the air force guys saluted the general. The rest of us did not, following the Marine protocol of never saluting any-one indoors, and hell, we were civilians anyway. Mike then dismissed the lieutenant: "Thank you for showing us the way to General Evans' office, Lieutenant. I am sure you have other more important duties to attend to." This was definitely a learn-ing moment for the young lieutenant. Everyone smiled as he made a quick exit, and the general thought we were all very happy to see him.

General Evans asked us to eat with him at Angel's Truck Stop, the officers' club at Udorn, named for the Angel who ran the place, I guess. It was pretty new, a low wooden building like a lot of the construction on the base. It was pretty nice, actually, with a bar and tables. There was food and drink available and large number of bored and somewhat drunk pilots. There was an interesting red paint blotch on the ceiling in the shape of a ladies derriere…Angel's, I assume.

When the general walked in, there was a significant reduc-tion in the noise level, which then picked back up a bit. We sat at a round table, and everyone ordered drinks. I decided on rum and Coke, which you could not get out in the bush…since there was no Coke and no ice. The general ordered Scotch and water, and everyone else got beer. The general then asked if I was in the navy.

"No, sir, just thought I would have something I can't get in the bush."

He laughed and said, "Let's order something to eat; you guys look hungry."

After lunch, the general said, "Okay, gentlemen, what can I do to help you?"

"A B-52 strike would be perfect, but I know that is not possible at the moment, due to the politics," said Mike.

"I will not elaborate, but we are in total stand-down mode for a while" said the General. We discussed our crazy plan and the NVA base, and the general listened intently and said"his is important Intel. I will have to speak to Nash about it".

"So, who is brewing up your napalm? And I know nothing about this at all, gentlemen. Unfortunately, I can't provide even the napalm powder; the munition auditors have really been on my ass lately. You can do whatever you want to do, but I can't *officially* assist you with planes or munitions."

"The brewer would be me, sir," I said.

"What can I do to help?"

"If we can't get the thickening powder, the most important things for our plan B are polystyrene and an aromatic solvent like toluene, which we can use as the thickener. Maybe some alum if we can find it."

"Well, I think I can help with the solvent, possibly, but polystyrene and alum I don't know."

I said, "Lots of things are made of polystyrene; we should be able to find beer coolers or something like that in the city or in Bangkok. We have the AA guys looking for us as well. Maybe the Royal Lao Air Force has some thickening powder they would share."

"Well, let's see, I will ask John, my sergeant, to find you some toluene and polystyrene. He is really good at such things, but it might take a few days to get the stuff. Do you guys need housing?"

Mike replied, "No, we have reservations at the AA guest-house, and we need to go to Bangkok for a few days."

The general flashed a knowing smile and said, "Well, stay out of trouble, gentlemen. I will let Mr. Nash know if we find your toluene and polystyrene so you can just give him a call for the details. I've got to go now, but if you need anything on base, just let me know." The general was a real *let's get it done,* bottom line—oriented guy. I heard he had lot of problems with the paper pushers and the jet set.

After the general left, we called Club Rendezvous (the AA Club) and asked them to send the minibus over for us and our gear. Mr. Nash had arranged for five of us to be members of the club and the five air force boys to be our guests. We had five rooms and an expense account at the club. You can't do better than that.

We were just finishing our drinks when the lieutenant from our earlier encounter came over and asked to join us. "Sure, why not?" we said.

"I am sorry about this morning," he said, "but it is hard to keep discipline with the airmen when everyone is walking around in odd or no uniforms."

"That is why they call it Special Forces, Lieutenant," said Moose.

"Well, I just want to thank you for not telling the general I was acting like an ass."

Moose said, "Lieutenant, until now we were pretty sure you were not acting. But if there is a next time, I will requisition your underwear and your trousers and leave you naked on the flight line." That made us all laugh, even the lieutenant.

"What are you guys here for, anyway, if you can say?" he asked.

"We are here for toluene and polystyrene."

"Well, I can't help you much directly, but these new bean bag chairs are just full of the stuff, you know, little polystyrene beads that is? How much do you need? I bought one in Bangkok about a week ago. You can have it if you need it. They are pretty cheap."

The lieutenant had just solved our polystyrene problem.

• • •

We had thought we could take the Pave LOW to Bangkok, but in the end we decided that a DC-3 would be better transport, as it might be hard to explain a Pave Low sitting at the Bangkok airport. Again, AA came through for us, and we had a flight out the next morning at 10:00 a.m.

We decided to spend the rest of the day at the pool and have a nice American supper. Some of the guys didn't have proper swimsuits, so they went to the base BX while the rest of us went on to the pool. While they were gone, a bevy of AA stewardesses arrived. Moose immediately started up a conversation with them. That was the nice thing about hanging out with Moose—he could really speak to women. They love the blond surfer look, I guess, even with a very short crew cut. We bought them some drinks and were having a great time, but when the boys came back from the BX my odds for a date got worse. We all decided to have supper at the club, and we went and got changed into our best clothes. The air force guys had real civilian clothes, slacks, and Hawaiian shirts, so we were definitely outclassed. I had my grays but opted for Tigers to fit with the rest of the team, and we all had our silk jackets. To beret or not to beret? That was the question. No beret was the answer; I looked enough like a fool without a fucking silly beret. There were just too many dicks at this party now anyway, and I didn't think anyone was going to get anything out of this except a good time in the platonic sense, regardless of how great we looked. Well, except for Moose. He was really a ladies man, and could apparently charm anything with tits.

Soon we were sitting around tables in a nice restaurant, eating off Air America china, complete with the AA wings logo, with four nice-looking, young American women having polite conversation. It was like being back home, but we were still in Thailand and the wild side of the red light district was about to prove we certainly weren't in Kansas.

Several AA pilots from the stewardesses' crew came by and asked if we wanted to hit some of the local clubs with them. We decided why not? I wished I had opted for greens. Still, our tiger jackets didn't look any worse than the air force pukes in their Hawaiian shirts, so off we went. We hit the Wolverine Bar first, since one of the AA guys was from Michigan and the wolverine was the University of Michigan's mascot. It was a go-go bar with a central stage and what looked to be strippers/ladies for hire dancing in various stages of undress. The stewardesses were not looking very happy. Unfortunately, most of the nearby places looked, well, not exactly ladylike.

Rosie the redhead looked at me and said, "We said we wanted to see a real den of iniquity. Johnnie said he would take us to one; so I guess this is it."

"Oh, no," said Johnnie (one of the AA guys). "The one across the street is the real thing."

"Well, since we're here, let's go then," said Rosie. We walked across the street and walked directly into the club, since the door (if there was one) stood wide open. It was very dark inside. The stage lights were the only lights in the place. I could have used my night vision goggles. We were seated at two adjacent tables. My eyes began to adjust, and I could see a large number of tables close to the stage. The stage lights came up and there were dancers on the stage in skimpy costumes; some were topless. Someone ordered a round of Singha beers. Two of the dancers pulled a very drunk airman onto the stage. They were all over him—not that he was objecting. They took his shirt off and his buddies howled. The stewardesses were watching intently. I thought, "Oh my God. What is about to happen might kill someone with a religious upbringing." Pretty soon, they had his pants around his ankles, and the girls were providing oral stimulation. His buddies stood up and howled some more. In a minute, he was down on all fours, pounding one of the girls. With every stroke, she was slipping across the stage, and he had to pursue her. Fortunately, the act didn't last long because *he* didn't last long; as he pulled out and stood up, his buddies cheered.

"Okay! Well this certainly is a real den of iniquity," said Rosie.

"No, not so!" said Johnnie. "The real den of iniquity is next door, but you have to pay to get in." But this was quite enough for Rosie, who said, "Let's find a nice quiet bar. I think I have had enough of the 'den of iniquity' scene."

"Sure, but you girls didn't walk out when you had the chance," said Johnnie. The red of them blushing was visible even in the dark. I may have even blushed for them. Audience participation was a little new to me. I knew I had hit yet another level of degeneracy. Were all Air America pilots like this? That would have offended the sensibilities of a whore.

Moose said, "Hell! I could have done better than that. That guy was a real amateur." I wondered just what, exactly, was next door.

We found a "real American bar" in the Paradise Hotel and proceeded to have several more drinks. Thanks to Johnnie the pilot's "den of iniquity tour," I was pretty sure nobody was going to make any time with these ladies tonight. If Johnnie had thought they would get all hot and bothered by the live sex show, he was half right: they were bothered.

It was nearly two o'clock in the morning when we got back to the guesthouse. We were leaving for Bangkok at 10:00 a.m. God alone knew what we would find there, but the last trip had been very relaxing. I went to sleep, and about an hour later someone started pounding on the door. It was Johnnie the pilot. He was drunk (as were we all).

"Can I sleep here?" he asked. "Moose threw me out of Rosie's room. Didn't want to share Rosie, I guess, and there are no other rooms available." Well, score one for Moose, that dog.

"Sure, there is a bed. Have at it."

"Thanks. I need to get undressed. I can't sleep in these shoes and clothes. You wouldn't have an extra set of PJs, would you?"

"Not only do I not have an extra set; I don't even have a set."

"Is that why you are naked?" Johnnie asked.

"Well, yes I guess so. Okay, Johnnie, good night, and please turn out the light."

Johnnie piled his clothes on the bed and lay down like a dead man. I couldn't help but notice the AA wings tattooed on his ass as I went to turn off the lights. Johnnie was a class act: low class. I went back to sleep. *Bam! Bam! Bam!* Someone was knocking on the door again?! I staggered to the door and opened it. It was Moose.

"Do you have a rubber?" he asked.

"A rubber what?" I replied.

"You know, a condom."

"Well, actually no, I forgot to pack any. I might have a Claymore. Maybe Johnnie has one." Moose shook Johnnie awake and asked him, "Johnnie, got a condom?"

"In my pants pocket maybe; you can look." He did, and Moose left. I went back to sleep.

Bam! Bam! Bam! For Christ's sake! "Who is it?"

"It's me, Moose, man. I need another one. Well, I don't think Rosie would fuck us both or I would invite you over. She is pretty conservative. Well, until she gets drunk, that is."

"That's okay, Moose. I just want to get some sleep." I went back to bed. Before I got to sleep, Johnnie started banging around, trying to find the bathroom. I aimed him toward the toilet and he proceeded to offer the toilet gods a large volume of vomit. I gave him a glass of water, which he drank and then immediately threw up.

"Man, we are in a spin," he said. "I think I am going to crash." He had the dry heaves.

"Okay, back to bed, Johnnie." I said as I aimed him in the general direction of the bed. He crawled in and collapsed. When I finally got back to bed, it was fucking 5:00 a.m. I slept through till 7:30. Johnnie was up and in the shower. I went in to take a piss and told him to hurry; we had a plane to catch.

"Don't worry. The pilot is still a bit drunk, takeoff may be delayed until after breakfast," he replied. Just the news I had been waiting for: Johnnie was our pilot. A perfect fit, since it seemed he was crazy too.

After I showered and shaved, we went down to breakfast, and there were Moose and Rosie. "Greetings," I said and ordered bacon, eggs, and pancakes. Everyone looked like hammered dog shit except for Moose and Rosie. Somehow, they managed to look fine. The rest of the dining room was staring at us like they were expecting a show.

After breakfast, I sat quietly enjoying my coffee and watching rain pound down. "So, does the pilot think we will leave today?" I asked Johnnie.

"Not in this rain," he said. "Postponed until this afternoon or tomorrow."

"Good," I went back to bed.

• • •

In Bangkok, we obtained about a hundred beanbag chairs filled with polystyrene and arranged for them to be delivered by truck in two days. This was more than we needed, but we wanted something to sit on. We also found a large cardboard barrel of alum, which is mined somewhere in Thailand. The general located drums of xylene for us, and we were ready to go.

The formula was simple: Into one oil drum pour the contents of a large beanbag chair, cover with xylene, and add three shovelfuls of precipitated aluminum soap. Stir and let sit for twenty-four hours. Then stir in diesel until the drum is three-quarters full. This produces a thick jelly. Secure the lids and, using steel bands, place four drums on each pallet. Using the steel banding, attach a fragmentation grenade, a thermite grenade, and a phosphorous grenade to each drum, as well as a small retarding parachute to the top. Take one C-130 with one very experienced loadmaster with a lot of experience kicking loads onto runways, camps, and other places, four experienced kickers, and an intrepid pilot or two, and you are ready to rock and roll.

The pallets were loaded and secured with ropes to stabilize the cargo, which would not be cut until the very final approach. The firing pins on the grenades were all wired together to be pulled upon exiting the plane. Again, the final connections were not made until the very final approach. Likewise, the parachutes were adjusted to deploy on exit to slow the descent.

Then, on a dark and moonless night, we infiltrated the area and placed three strobes in tennis ball cans along the ridge. That way no light could escape any way but up, and they would act as markers. The Pave Low, followed by the C-130, made a single pass, and the kickers pushed out the pallets. They separated into individual drums and then the grenades ignited and provided a dispersing explosion. The resulting fireball of napalm covered the camp; incinerating everything on the ground to smoking ashes. There was nothing left except some secondary explosions as things "cooked off."

CHAPTER 11

Planting the Sensor Garden

• • •

Do one thing every day that scares you.

— ELEANOR ROOSEVELT

WE HAD ANOTHER SENSOR-PLANTING MISSION scheduled. Getting ready for a mission was never fun for me. There was always some stress just because we were going in. I followed a certain ritual to prepare myself. I ate and drank high-energy, low-fiber foods like chocolate and meat for a day or two, avoiding fiber. I always made a visit to the toilet just before launch to make sure I was leaving on "empty."

We humped our packs, which were particularly heavy since we carried the prototype sensors to plant, out to the bird and stood on the tarmac ready to launch. I was used to the procedure by now, but this was not going to be an in-and-out mission, it was an overnight or maybe two overnights for sure. Mike, a creature of habit, came out and asked his favorite question: "Everybody happy?" In unison, we all replied we were very happy sir. Mike then had the local shaman bless the bird and then us. Since the rucks were heavy, we helped each other into Buzz's old bird, not his new Pave Low.

We made a number of false insertions just to make sure we caused as much trouble as possible. We would actually enter and immediately exit an LZ. Soon, one team of new guys would be working here, and before long we could have three new teams working the field, something we had never done before. To be honest, we had a tight team and we did not relish working with two FNG teams for the first time, even if they were well-trained and led by experienced people. There is a camaraderie that occurs in a team that is hard to explain. When you live in such close quarters, risk life and limb together, eat, drink, and party together, it really bonds you tightly and quickly. But working with others was better than the suggestion that they break us up and scatter us into the other teams. I trusted Mike and the team, and I can say with certainty that no one wanted to be split up. Also, no one wanted to be the leader of a bunch of newbies. Hell, no one felt good enough to lead except Mike. It looked as if we would just be running as an independent team without much change, which was good for us. The other teams might even locate elsewhere, as we had little spare room.

• • •

So we were all aboard the bird, and we launched into the darkness of the early morning. We arrived at the LZ at first light, and as the helicopter flew slowly over the tall grass, the downdraft from the blades caused the grass to ripple like water. When we were within six feet of the ground, the helicopter settled into a hover and we moved out to the skids and swung down to the ground from there.

The grass was tall and so thick it was difficult to walk. The edges of the blades of grass were sharp—they really were blades. I wore a pair of thin handball gloves to avoid getting cuts or scrapes. Cuts in the jungle were bad, because they almost always became infected. Any time I got a cut, I took one of the iodine tablets we used to purify water and dissolved it in as small an amount of water as I could. Then I would put the concentrated iodine on the cut, which helped prevent infections.

As we reached the tree line, the grass thinned out and movement became easier. There were bamboo thickets to our left. We avoided them because travel through them was almost impossible anyway, and at best it was slow and noisy. We would lose time going around them, but it was the lesser of two evils. It had rained the previous day; the ground was still soft and the humidity was 100 percent. We were all sweating and overheating, partly because of the temperature but mostly because of the humidity. After a few kilometers, we took a water break and stood with the sweat pouring off us. We decided it was time to go into "silent mode." We began to move slowly through the bush, placing every foot deliberately to avoid making any unnecessary sounds. We would move for ten minutes and then listen for five. We continued with this routine until we could see a trail snaking down the hill below us. At this point, we decided to find a hide and go doggo for a few minutes while we watched for any traffic on the trail.

We had just gone into hiding when two NVA soldiers came down the trail, seemingly without a care in the world, talking and laughing. They continued past us and down the trail until we could hear them no longer. We knew we were in "Indian Territory" now, and we knew that we had to maintain complete stealth. If we were discovered, getting out would be very difficult indeed. Mike and I whispered to each other, trying to decide if this would be a good place to implant the new sensor. We decided this trail was too small and we needed something larger. We left the hide and carefully moved down to the trail, crossing it on a rocky part so as not to leave any footprints. We made our way up the hill on the other side of the trail, trying to make sure we did not disturb the plants or leave any sign of our passage. We moved as quickly as we could while maintaining stealth, trying to get into the bush so we would not be visible from the trail. It was so hot and so humid that we had to rest. We found an area of thick plants and did our best to disappear into the foliage. Even sitting still, the sweat poured off of me. My fatigues were completely wet, almost as if I had been standing in the rain. After fifteen minutes rest, we pushed on to the top of the hill. We approached the ridge carefully. Mike moved out first, reconnoitering the way ahead so we could maintain our stealth as much as possible. Crossing the ridge was dangerous, because we could not see what was below. The cover was much thinner on the downslope. If anyone was on the hills across or below our position, they might easily spot us.

It was beginning to get dark; we had to find a good hide for the night. The terrain past the ridge was pretty steep, and since there was no cover we decided to find somewhere on the reverse slope to spend the night. We moved to a small high spot that had a thicket of small trees and worked our way into the thickest brush, using clippers to remove and reposition some of the smaller trees and brush. We arranged ourselves into a wagon-wheel formation with our legs pointing inward. It was almost dark. We took turns trying to sleep: three men sleeping, and three sentries. The temperature began to drop, and the wind began to pick up. Another series of thunderstorms rolled up the valley and over the ridge. The rain came down in sheets. After the storms rolled away, the air was noticeably cooler, but we were all completely soaked. It was a cold and miserable night.

When morning finally came, we were starving. I had my usual canned fruitcake and water, making sure I had squeezed all the air from the collapsible canteen so it wouldn't slosh and make noise when I moved. We moved into the brush at the top of the ridgeline. Below, we could see a high-speed trail wide enough for trucks where the hill reached the valley floor. But there was no clear way to get to the bottom without being seen; the cover was very sparse. We decided to continue moving in the jungle since it kept us from being seen. We hoped to find a gentler slope with some cover so we could make it down to the trail undetected. We moved in "deep stealth mode," moving for ten minutes and then watching and listening for ten. The trail was actually a series of switchbacks; we found a position midway up the hill between two tight turns that offered us just what we needed. We could set sentries at the turns, while the section between the turns would be perfect to set up the sonic sensor. The trees and brush were thick enough that it was impossible to be seen from the surrounding hills, and the jungle provided more hiding places if needed. Mike took one end as sentry and DD took the other. The rest of the team worked to dig the trench needed to bury the sensor and the cabling. This particular sensor had three parts: two sensing units that were cabled into a third central unit. While this provided better data than a single unit, it made the installation difficult and time-consuming. The unit contained very little metal to make detection using metal detectors more difficult, but that also meant it was more fragile.

Many methods had been tried to put sensors along the trail; chief among these were air-implanted sensors. Unfortunately, many of the air-implanted sensors were failures. Stuck in the ground, they were easy to spot, even when they were made to look like plastic plants, dog shit, or pieces of wood. All of these were used, and all of them suffered from a short battery life of only a few weeks.

In an attempt to render metal detectors less useful, we salted the trail with metal fragments and pieces of wire, as though a bomb had detonated in the general area. We did the same thing thirty meters away in both directions on the trail. We assumed the plastic sensors would be more fragile, so we were careful to bury them in a narrow portion of the trail where the truck wheels would not be directly on top of them.

We dug and covered them as quickly as possible since we felt vulnerable and exposed on the trail. Just as we completed the final camouflaging, Mike came running toward us, signing for us to get into hiding. The team disappeared into the thick jungle on the upslope side of the hill. I ran up the trail to alert DD. When he saw me coming he immediately moved into the jungle. I joined him, and we went into silent mode hiding. We could hear the trucks coming. Everyone was locked and loaded as we waited for the convoy to pass. When the last truck passed, we could see it was carrying troops and dogs. This was not good news. It meant the NVA had a hunter team ready to go with dogs, and dogs were always a problem. The convoy passed without detecting us, and we all breathed a sigh of relief. We had more than halfway completed the mission, now the trick would be getting out undetected.

We formed up and moved out, trying to put as much distance between us and the sensor that we had planted as quickly and quietly as we could. The PZ was more than two miles away, and the terrain was very difficult. It would take many hours, since we were moving in stealth mode. Night would fall before we got there, so we needed to find a good hide for the night where we would be able to eat and maybe get some sleep.

We were away from the trails, which meant the going would be tough, but the chances of meeting up with the NVA would be lower. Mike found a steep hill, and we moved to the top of it. We were able to circle up at the top, so we could see almost 360 degrees but could not be seen ourselves. We repeated the wagon-wheel formation of the night before. We were all wet with sweat and the night seemed cold, but when it was my turn to sleep I immediately went under.

I only slept for an hour, but I felt much colder. I was stiff and hurt everywhere, so I decided to employ some of our chemistry, which we used routinely when in the bush. I signed drugs to DD and he offered me two Motrin, a 200 mg caffeine pill, and a 5 mg Benzedrine.[6] I considered the Benzedrine for a minute, and then I thought *why the fuck not?* and I took it. For good measure, I took 200 mg of Butazolidin, the "nothing hurts, everything feels great" drug. Just an exercise in better living through chemistry. I had another hour of sleep; I was thinking maybe I could sleep some before the drugs kicked in. As soon as the sun came out, we were up and on our way to the PZ. About halfway there, Mike used the PRC-77 to contact Buzz, and the rendezvous was set. We picked up the pace, choosing speed over stealth. As soon as we got to the top of the hill, we unrolled marker panels, hoping not to have to pop purple smoke to signal Buzz, since it signaled everyone else, and they had mortars and snipers, so smoke was just asking for it. We had been very lucky so far, and we wanted to keep it that way. I felt great, probably because of the handful of pills I'd taken, but also because I hadn't gotten my ass shot off so far.

Buzz's old Huey came over the top of the hill. I was glad to see the helicopter headed in our direction. Buzz flew over us and then, seeing the marker panels, looped around. He went into a low hover, one skid at the edge of the hill. We clambered on board in less than a minute and were off toward home. It felt great to get that goddamn heavy ruck off my back. We were

---

6 Benzedrine is the trade name of the racemic mixture of amphetamine (*dl*-amphetamine). The drug was often referred to as *bennies* by users and in literature.

in and out without incident, and to quote Mike, everyone was happy.

On the way back to NKP, Buzz passed a thermos to Moose, who asked me, "Want some?"

I thought, *great, we have coffee* and I answered, "Hell yes!" Moose took the top off and poured the big lid full of liquid and then tossed it on me. It was pig's blood!

"Hey, man. We can't break your record with Nash, it would be bad juju. We need good juju." Everyone laughed, including me. After all, what could I say? I did my best to get as much blood on everyone else as possible. When we landed, Nash came out to meet us, and I was still dripping with pig's blood. Nash looked at me, shook his head, and said, "I am not even going to ask but at least you smell better than most times"

"Sorry, sir, and thanks for not asking. I don't want to talk about it either. It does not belong to anyone on the team, but possibly some of their family members." Everyone laughed again, and we headed for the showers.

The locals knew something was going on since strange helicopters like the Pave Low and strange planes like the Pilatus Porter or C-7 without markings kept showing up. And a few rough-looking, not in normal uniform guys in desperate need of a bath would come and go. We were not the only ones working the trail, and the other teams that occasionally passed through NKP looked just as bad as us, I'm sure.

I had planned on going to town to see if I could get something good to eat and maybe fall in love with a bar girl before the Benzedrine, caffeine, and adrenalin wore off. I didn't even make it past the Charon Hotel. We ate in the restaurant, and I was asleep within five minutes of obtaining a horizontal position on a real bed. I slept like a stone until morning. Staying in a hotel named for the guy who ferried people across the Styx river into hell seemed somehow appropriate.

CHAPTER 12

Playing with the Marines

• • •

They're misconstruing horseplay as something improper.

—— CHRISTOPHER PLOURD

BOREDOM. LACK OF ENTERTAINMENT AND excitement. It was slowly creeping over us, since we had not had a mission for over a week. Something political was happening, and we were supposed to lie low...low and bored to tears. Inventing games is always fun. With time on our hands and only so much shooting and grappling before they get old, games were always a nice break. We played a lot of partner spades and poker, but the entire team played chess. I will admit I was an average player. My friend Steve at school had handed my ass to me every time we'd played, but still I liked the game. I was not the worst player on the team, but I was not the best either. Lyndell was really good, and Fuzz was only a little behind him, but even that little bit meant Lyndell pretty much won every game. So to even things out, we invented "team chess." It required an even number of players: six or eight worked pretty well. Players on each side alternated moves, player one on white played first, then player one for black, then player two for white, and player two for black, and so on. This let everyone play and created some interesting situations, since each side generally had a master as well as a bonehead or two.

There was also the drinking version of team chess, in which every time a piece was taken everyone drank a shot. This added to the complexity of the play. By this point, my liver had accustomed itself to lots of alcohol, and I had a lot more tolerance than even a few months before.

Then Buzz and Fuzz returned from one of their trips with two boxes of frozen steaks and four cases of 33 beer (a local brew) came with them. This was definitely a party in a box. Since the steaks were thawed but still cold, today was the day. DD and I had been out on a run, and we heard about the party and decided to take a quick shower while the guys organized the event with the Marines, who had both the grill and the cook. DD and I would bring the last cases of the beer when we were done.

All cleaned up, DD and I picked up the last three boxes of beer and carried them down the short walk to the Marines' bunker. When we arrived, the drinking had already begun and a debate was going strong. The Marines had the idea to do some betting on a wrestling match, one of theirs versus one of ours. It seemed they had a new guy, Charlie, who was a star high school wrestler, and he had been pinning all the other Marines in impromptu matches. The Marines were constantly wrestling and fighting with each other; it was a form of training after all, but to tell the truth they just enjoyed the competition of it all, and given the fact that most of them were under twenty years old, it mostly amounted to roughhousing without adult supervision and having great fun. The "old guys" of over twenty-two were relatively calm in demeanor—we were spooks, after all, and we had a reputation to uphold.

They had rejected Moose because, well, because he was a big moose. Pipes and Mike were out since they were too old and too mean. I expect they had seen Pipes in action before and knew he was pretty much unbeatable, having demonstrated his joint-lock techniques for the Marines already. The list of candidates was getting shorter all the time. Since Bobby had a cut and bandaged hand, he was out. Lyndell was slightly larger than Moose, so they rejected him too. This was the point when DD and I walked up and into the conversation. DD was immediately the target of the Marines until Mike asked, "So you want one of your guys to wrestle our Doc? Man, you guys are really Whisky Deltas." Whisky is *W* and Delta is *D,* so he meant WDs, short for weak dicks. That left me standing there, and naturally I was chosen for this little exhibition. The team was quite happy to have a demonstration of my stuff, even if they lost their bets.

The rules were no punching or kicking and first man on the ground lost. Mike and the guys immediately agreed this was fine with them, but it wasn't with me—I generally needed to be able to land a quick kick to win. Regardless, the match was on. The Marine came out, pulled off his fatigues, and stood there in a pair of white briefs. They expected me to do the same thing.

Sorry guys, I can't wrestle—I'm not wearing any underwear! Guess you'll have to pick someone else.

Fuzz chimed in,"No problem; I'll get you a pair." He turned and ran back to the bunk house. Great. How much more fun could this be? Five minutes later, what a surprise, Fuzz returned with my bright red jockey shorts, I knew I should have gone myself. I stripped and put them on, and everyone else formed a large fighting circle.

So how am I going to beat this guy? I wondered. He was better at wrestling and was very muscular. I figured he was probably stronger than I was. I didn't have much in my bag of tricks, except for the fact that I knew he was a wrestler and would probably immediately grab me first thing, which would give me one good chance.

We shook hands and started. As expected, he immediately stepped up and grabbed me on the shoulder. Speed was now required to get him before he got a good second hold on me. This was a perfect setup for the Aikido technique Ikkyo. Rather than going against his strength, I pulled him in just a bit and used my opposite hand to slide down the grasping arm and force it down while I grasped the knife edge of his hand. Then I turned the hips while my hand trapped his wrist and locked it, using the other hand to control his elbow. Then I stepped through and down. Now he was no longer aggressively attacking but on the ground and under my control. This entire action took less than two seconds. Aikido, when it works, is just amazing, it really looks like magic.

There was sort of a gasp from the audience, and I released him and left him lying on the ground. Mike gave me a little knowing look and slight head shake with a big smile. Standing beside Mike was a new arrival: Mr. Nash smiling a big grin at me.

Then the audience started yelling, "Do it again! Do it again—we didn't see what you did. Did you Judo him? That ain't fair."

"Why not?" I asked. "I didn't hit him, not even once."

Charlie got up from the ground and shook himself off, appearing clueless as to what had happened. Charlie then said, "What the fuck? We didn't even wrestle at all. You just put me on the ground."

"Wasn't that the idea? First guy off his feet loses?" I asked.

"Well, yes, but it was too fast, way too fast. It wasn't even a match."

"Shit, I'm sorry. No one told me was I supposed to win slowly. You made the first move and I put you on the ground without breaking anything or hurting you too much. Can I have a beer now, please?" DD handed me a beer. Wow! It was a cold beer; I wasn't expecting that. I drank my beer and officially retired from the ring, my unbroken series of wins—one in a row—intact.

"Hey, we wanted to watch a real fight. This wasn't a fight at all. Look, Charlie is too small—your guy is four inches taller than him," the Marines complained.

"You picked Charlie and you picked Snake—the whole thing wasn't my idea," said Mike. "What do you want now?"

"How about a real fight, no holds barred? Our biggest guy and your biggest guy?"

Well, I guess, but Lyndell might not want to fight. He is a very quiet sort and he is always afraid of really hurting people, and for good reason: he only has one speed, and that's *kill*. How about your biggest guy against our smallest guy? That would be fair, right?"

"Who's your smallest guy?"

"That would be me," Mike said.

"Oh, well I would like to see that that," Robert the young Marine lieutenant said. "Johansen, get over here." A very large, shirtless, almost white blond Viking who had just arrived to the party stepped forward. "Eric, would you like to fight Mike here?"

"No, sir," said Eric, "he is too short and too little. Give me Moose, please, sir, he is my size and we are neighbors, I'm from Minnesota and he is a Canuck."

"Well, could you try Mike here first for me and then you can have the Moose?"

"Sure, but it just wouldn't be fair for the little guy."

Ace, DD, and I were listening to this conversation. We three looked at each other and smiled, knowing Eric was right: it wouldn't be a fair fight. Mike would crush him like a bug. But it might be fun to watch, and we needed to get good seats fast since it would probably only last for a few seconds.

So the ring formed again, with Ace, DD, and I standing next to Mr. Nash in a prime location so we could see both Mike and Eric, who towered over him like a giant over a dwarf. The signal to start was given, and Mike instantly became a blur of action. Eric was up off the ground, his feet going up, up, up, and then he was coming down, down, down, finally landing on his ass. Mike had his arm and had reversed the joints, and Eric was just howling with pain.

"Who is too little now, Eric?" Mike asked.

Eric continued to howl in pain, and we began to howl in laughter. Even the Marines started laughing. The whole thing happened so quickly that even I wasn't sure what Mike had done, and I was really looking for the technique. Mike was blindingly fast. Finally, Eric found the right words and said, "Not you, sir, not you. You are tall and you are mean!"

Eric was finally released and said, "Jesus, Mike, you 'Judoed' me just like Snake did Charlie."

"No, Eric, I did not use Judo on you. I used Hapkido, which is a Korean martial art that is much more aggressive than the Japanese style Aikido, which Snake applied to Charlie. But then they all seem to work, don't they? Anyway, I think we need to stop before someone really gets hurt, don't you?"

"Yes, sir, I agree we can't fight that stuff with just wrestling, and—Jesus Christ—my arm really hurts, I mean *bad*."

Robert asked Mike, "Could you guys teach us some of that stuff?"

"Well, it takes a lot of time, but we might try as long as we are not too busy with work," Mike said. So having finished the preliminary manly "whose is bigger" contests, we settled down to a feast of steaks and beer, which we had Nash to thank for, and potatoes, which the Marines had. Their cook had decided to boil the potatoes whole, which was kind of like baking them, and the meat was grilled on a large, home-made grill. These steaks were just amazing. They were from a company called Kansas City Steaks, and they just tasted like home. The beer was good and cold, thanks to a large tub and a huge chunk of ice delivered by the local ice man, insulated in rice hulls and then chipped into small shards by an ice pick. Cold beer was really a treat out here, since ice deliveries were infrequent.

Everyone had a great time, and before long the party wound down, and then it was over. Everyone was full of steak, potatoes, and cold beer. But Nash was here, which could only mean we were on deck for a new mission, and he and Mike had already gone back up to our end of the camp together. I figured they were probably in the little briefing hut talking about it.

As it turned out, Nash had brought us a new mission. We were all ready for another routine "road watch" monitoring mission. The sensors had been planted for twenty days when we left the base. I completed my premission toilet break, ate some fried rice with chicken for breakfast, and then we all painted up and loaded up. We had spent the night at NKP, rode out in the box truck, and loaded up before dawn into Buzz's insertion helicopter. There were six of us: Mike, Moose, DD, Pipes, Lyndell, and me. Bobby stayed back to operate the radio and communicate with us.

The insertion was to be a fresh bomb crater close to the trail. This was not our normal routine. On a normal mission, we would be several days' walk from the target area. This was because a lot of the LZs close to the trail were watched by the bad guys and the insertion bird was an advertisement to our presence. Our gunships had worked the area over the previous night. The flight was about 150 klicks (km) from NKP. This was well within the 500 klick range of the Huey.

It was a standard drop-in insertion: three ropes on each side of the helicopter and a rapid rappel down to the ground. Now we had a couple of days of hiking to get into position. We would monitor the trail while the sensors were monitored in order to correlate the traffic to the data from the sensors. We had to move in full stealth mode. It was a long hike timewise, but it was not that far in terms of distance. We used the secateurs only when necessary to open a way. We moved for almost seven hours and finally found a good hide to spend a few days in. Moose and I checked the planted sensors and relay equipment. Everything looked good; then we had to go doggo for a while and listen and watch to make sure we were alone before we made it back to the hide. It was a good thing, since a company of about twenty-five soldiers came down the trail. In the thick bush, I was sure we were invisible, but it still provided more than a little adrenalin shot. No one liked paying multiple visits to the same site, but to get the data we wanted there was no alternative. The good news was that the site we had planted sensors on really looked to be active. The ten days we had received data was correct: there was a lot of traffic on the trail headed into South Vietnam.

What we did not know was that earlier that year during the dry season, November until April, there had been a big offensive by the Vietnamese up north at Long Tieng against General Vang Pao's mercenary army. Well, nobody ever told us anything. This battle caused a temporary reversal in the flow to provide more reserves for this battle. We won that battle, by the way, and it really kicked the NVA in the teeth for a while. I learned much later that it required lots of air power to overcome the 130 mm

NVA artillery, which was really hammering us. After failing to take Long Tieng after over a hundred days of fighting, they gave up and were redirected into the offensive into South Vietnam. This was the battle at Long Tieng where the Cobras and other Thai volunteers had fought.

We maintained a close watch for five days and then silently packed up and headed for the PZ. The entire mission had been uneventful in terms of no real contact with the enemy, so this was a "perfect mission." The extract was done by ladders into a Pave Low, and we were whisked back to NKP. Nash met us and we did a short debrief before showering and a longer one immediately after showering and changing from Tiger Stripe fatigues into OD green fatigues. He noticed I was clean this time, but he didn't comment on it. Then it was off to the Charon Hotel, where we headed for the hotel bar, had several drinks, and immediately went to bed. Despite using lots of Columbia Medicated Powder to dust my neither regions, I was developing a case of Jungle Jock Rot. This was no fun at all. DD had me drop my pants and painted the area with his bright purple Gentian Violet. Then he gave me some anti-fungal cream, which I applied four times a day. Just another occupational hazard of working in the tropics. Hey, at least I finally got the purple badge of courage.

I began to realize that we really were "pack animals," like dogs or wolves, and it was burned into our subconscious. I'm not sure women feel these bonds the same way as men; perhaps it is fueled by aggression and testosterone as well. Joining the team was like joining a pack. We relied on each other and the team. We became comfortable together and with the team in the bush.

But there was change in the wind. The actual war in Vietnam was changing. Politics ruled the day, antiwar demonstrations back home were growing. The United States was pulling men out as fast as we could, "Vietnamizing" the fighting at a rapid pace. Unfortunately, it happened so quickly that it had to fail, and we allowed the NVA to move. We continued to bomb the hell out of Laos and Cambodia.

But when Congress became directly involved by stopped the funds and preventing the use of air power like B-52 strikes, our job changed from helping win the war to working to provide "a decent interval" between the US pullout and the fall of Saigon. This was so America did not completely lose face with our allies and look like we had just cut and run on the Vietnamese. We cut and ran. We "Vietnamized" the war but in the end the Vietnamese were missing a few things like logistics to get ammunition and fuel where it needed to be. Both the American Ambassador and some of the Vietnamese were in denial until the bitter end.

CHAPTER 13

Things Begin to Really Heat Up

• • •

Chipmunks have the best instinct: run and hide.

—— MARTY RUBIN

THE INSERTION WAS FINE, BUT we were in trouble almost before we let go of the ropes. We figured they must have had watchers on the LZ. We took a few rounds of AK from the far edge of the LZ and decided it was a good idea to get the hell out of Dodge. We headed along a nearby trail while Mike had Bobby call for immediate extraction. The Pave Low was close, so we hoped it would not be long in coming.

We were pretty sure were being pursued. We were trying to open the distance from the LZ, but it just was not happening fast enough with our heavy packs. If anything, we were probably losing ground. Mike looked at me and said, "Got another special Claymore, Snake?"

I did, but the question was where to put it? There was not a good place for a kill zone. The trail ahead ran up and then down into a valley between two small hills. I stopped to pull the Claymore out of my pack and then ran to catch up to the team. I handed the Claymore to Mike. Moose and I took his pack between us while he sprinted ahead. When we caught up, Mike was planting the Claymore upslope of the trail against a large stone. He ran the wire behind a group of large boulders some distance away. If we were lucky, these boulders would stop the blast, direct it forward, and give us cover. I never understood why there were occasional big rocks in the middle of the jungle, but there were.

We set up behind the rocks, and Mike sent the FNG Bobby ahead to the chosen PZ to pop purple smoke and to get us the bird ASAP. The patrol chasing us came down the trail just in time to see Bobby as he made the turn. They smelled blood and started to run. They entered the kill zone and Mike triggered the Claymore. We didn't stop to check the damage but continued as quickly as possible to the top of a small hill. A second platoon of at least twenty-five NVA were hot on our trail. Making it up the slope was difficult, but we were motivated to make the best possible speed. We finally got to the top and spread out marker panels. We did not want to pop smoke and show our position. We set up as best we could and began to take long shots at the NVA, which slowed them down some. We saw the Pave Low; it made one orbit with the miniguns blazing for a full thirty seconds. This effectively suppressed all the small arms fire, and they were able to come into a low hover. We clambered aboard.

Just as we were lifting off, a mortar round landed on the hill and sprayed the Pave Low with fragments. Some impacted the airframe and splintered into smaller fragments. The ramp was still down, and Moose and I were the last onboard and were firing at the bad guys out the back. I got a small piece in the left hand, just at the base of the thumb, and a few very small fragments in my chest and left arm. Moose got a larger piece in his shoulder, a deep cut that was several inches long. I took a bandage from my pack and pressed it against his wound, using the pressure to stop the bleeding from my own hand at the same time. DD came over and told me to lie down and hold my hand up. I did as he said while DD took over caring for Moose's shoulder. The bandage on my hand was saturated with blood and had started dripping on me. So had the blood from Moose's wounded shoulder.

"Goddamn, fuck, Moose! Stop bleeding on me!" I noticed my left arm was also dripping a bit, the blood running down my arm. Eventually, DD stopped Moose's bleeding and I started clotting pretty well, only dripping a little.

Mike moved over and said, "Snake, you're covered with blood again. Man, it seems like every time you go out it is just buckets of blood all over you! What are you going to tell Nash? 'Look, just blood no guts this time'?"

"Fuck! It wasn't my fault. I was just standing there and the next thing I know goddamn Moose and I are blood brothers. Does that mean I can't fuck his sister?"

"I hear his sister is bigger than Moose. Would you really want to fuck her?" asked DD.

Moose just looked at us and said, "She is married with three kids, you flaming assholes!"

"Okay, so that would be a no, I guess, but if you bleed to death, as your blood brother I get all your stuff right, Moose?"

"Hell no," said DD, "We have rules on how to do the split. Besides, I just saved both your lives. Nobody is dying today, but you both owe me big time."

"That settles it then. Give me your knife, Dog, we'll make DD our blood brother too so we won't owe him anything."

DD took another look at my hand, arm, and chest and decided I would live. "We need to clean both of you up before I sew you up."

"Great, just one more fucking thing to look forward to." I tried to button up my blouse one-handed. I got about halfway through before I looked down. "I really am pretty bloody, I guess. The small holes bled pretty good, and my arm and that damn Moose dripped on me, but they are clotted pretty well now."

We made it to Naked Fanny and got out of the helicopter, and as usual, Nash met us. He took one look at me and started laughing. "I'm sorry, Mac. I know I shouldn't laugh, but you, well, you are the technical guy and you just come back looking like a fucking butcher every goddamn time I see you. Well, except when you turn up blue, that is. I think you have the worst case of bloodlust I can ever remember. You're going to need another trip to OK Tailor at Udorn; want me to call ahead for you?"

"Hey, that would be really great but it's *really* not my fault this time. These clothes just don't last very well in this climate, what with the shrapnel and bullets that keep putting holes in them." Then, looking at Moose, I said, "And then there is everybody just going out of their way to gush blood on me. I admit I occasionally fall down, but if you don't mind, I want the slash pockets not straight and the compass pocket on the sleeve at the shoulder."

He laughed again. "Well, they have your measurements, so I'm sure it wil be fine. You and Moose both need to stop by Tony Tik's, the jewelry shop next to OK Tailor's. I'll have something waiting there for you both."

Well, no one was hurt really bad, but this was getting to be a lot less fun. If the aggressiveness and sheer numbers on the part of the NVA continued, we would have hell getting anything done without getting killed. But with no B-52 or Spectre gunship missions, we started to wonder why we should even bother.

DD said, "Let's get to the infirmary so I can sew you guys up." We got into the box truck and rode to the infirmary.

We walked into the base infirmary. A medic and doctor from the Air Force greeted us and invited us in; it had been a really slow week. "Okay, Red Dog, you and Moose take your blouses off. Actually, since they have a shower here, just get in and wash up with this surgical scrub."

Moose went in first and got scrubbed down and sent for an X-ray. I followed his example of scrubbing up, being pretty careful with my chest and arm. The tiny half-inch cut on my hand started to bleed again. It was pretty deep. They brought out the peroxide and washed it out. The doc arrived amd came over introduced himself and then took over the exam. He probed my hand a bit and pulled out a small bent-up piece of metal. "Must have been a ricochet from something," he said. For good measure, DD poured peroxide across my chest and it fizzed and burned. The doctor said, "No peroxide, it doesn't work worth a shit; just use the surgical scrub." No local anesthesia was offered or really expected. My chest had several small wounds, and the doctor probed them and pulled out several small metal fragments. Then, to my complete astonishment, he called for a water pick and a styptic pencil. He plugged in a water pick toothbrush, put in saline with a dose of the surgical scrub, and proceeded to clean out each wound with the pulsing water jet.

"This thing really works great," he explained. I started bleeding again. He used the styptic pencil to stop the bleeding and announced, "I may have to debride a few of these and maybe put in a stitch or two just for fun. I may need the electrocautery unit." I just tried my best to lie still and went to my happy place while he and the corpsman worked on me.

Moose was back from X-ray, and DD walked in with the lidocaine I was supposed to get. "Oops," the doctor said. "I guess we forgot the anesthetic. I thought you were ready for this. Well, you didn't complain, so I didn't know, and you did real well without it."

Maybe it looked that way from out there, but not so much from in here, I thought. "Give it to the Moose; he needs it more than me," I said.

"I am going to finish you first," he said. He explained that he normally didn't apply a topical antiseptic, but he decided to put some Silvadine on the cuts and holes and then close them with

"Stitch" Band-Aids. There were a lot of Band-Aids. "Don't take these off for two days, and then come back and let me look at them. Just to be sure, I want an X-ray of you as well." So off I went to X-ray after the fact.

While I was in X-ray, the doctor water-picked Moose and sutured his shoulder back together. His was a larger piece of shrapnel but really a nice clean cut. We got the mandatory tetanus and bicillin shots. Finally, Mike brought us clean clothes. The blouse I got was at least an XXL and had the arms ripped off. My boots were such a bloody, muddy mess that rather than clean them now, I decided to just buy another pair. Someone handed me a pair of flip-flops, and we went to the BX to buy a new pair of jungle boots and some socks. I needed a second pair of boots anyway. I must have looked really good: tiger stripe trousers, a monster-sized blouse with no sleeves, and a chest covered with Band-Aids. We went to the club for beer and something to eat. I had the Khao Pad Moo,[7] and I don't know if it was really excellent or I was starving—or both—but it was great. Somehow, both food and sex are both significantly better after a near-death experience. Actually, pretty much anything is improved by not getting killed.

Nash had us booked into the NKP Hotel, which was a nondescript three-story white building with two marvelous features: real air conditioning and a Western restaurant. This was luxury compared to a hot hooch in Tiger Village. Since Moose and I needed to get checked out by the Doc, we were there for

---

7 Pork Fried Rice

two days. While we were there, we decided to see what the town had to offer. The NKP had pretty good security, a large vegetation-free zone, and lots of wire in multiple rings and base security including "gun trucks" and military dogs. A few rounds were occasionally fired at the base just to keep everyone on their toes. There were several bars and clubs in town. The first night, we visited King Cobra, the Mustang, and finally the House of the Rising Sun, where we fell in love with some of the local girls, but we still made it back to the hotel for a night with clean sheets, not drinkable but running water, and air conditioning.

The next morning, we slept late and met at the hotel restaurant for breakfast. I was feeling strange. I had no appetite and was generally unwell. Then the chills and fever started, and suddenly I was one very sick puppy. The boys took Moose and me back to the doctor at NKP. He looked at the wounds and said, "Your wounds look fine, but you have a temperature of 103," he said. "I'll have some blood drawn, but I don't think it's your wounds. I think it is dengue (break bone) fever. You'll be sick for a week. Everyone gets dengue eventually; it's just a question of when."

"Today is your lucky day," said Mike. "Nothing to do but suffer until you get well."

They put me a hospital bed, and Nash paid two Thai nurses to stay with me on twelve-hour shifts and take care of me day and night—not that there was much to do but wait it out. I was delirious with fever for a few days, during which the nurses gave me aspirin, cold sponge baths, and cold wet towels. My recall of this time is poor. I do remember that I hated it when

I was freezing with chills and they slapped cold wet towels on me. With dengue, the entire body aches and the joints really hurt; I was in constant motion and couldn't find a position that was comfortable for more than a few minutes. It was like influenza times ten. There were two beds in the room, and one of the team stayed with me most of time, just in case I needed anything.

About four days and several bottles of saline later, I began to feel human again. I had lost a lot of the weight, which really hurt since I had worked so hard to put it on. Despite, or perhaps because of, the fever, all of my wounds had mostly healed, but the doctor put the Band-Aids back on. The doctor required me to stay in bed for another two to three days. I objected to no effect. Nash and Mike both said it was bed for me. But they changed my nurse with another one who was much younger. I thought, *Well at least sponge bath time might be more fun.* I eventually found out that this new "nurse" came from Mama-san's. If you have to spend forty-eight hours in bed, I can't think of a better way. I felt well enough to require a couple of sponge baths. I think one of Nash's rules was to never let the guys get horny; they just get into trouble.

On the second day, they decided I was well enough for company and moved in a Marine named Joe who had somehow burned both his hands on a rope and had to have them bandaged. He seemed like a nice guy; I had met him at one of the barbecues. When my "nurse" arrived for the evening sponge bath and took care of me; I asked Joe if he needed a sponge bath too. He turned out not to be shy, and she took care of him as well. Just as she left, the doctor made his rounds and remarked on how upbeat we were. We both laughed, and I said, "It's all about attitude doc. We will be out soon." I still had no appetite, had lost a lot of weight, and was generally in a pretty weakened condition. I needed some rest and relaxation time.

In a few days, my appetite finally came back and I was ravenously hungry, but the orders were to start eating slowly with bland food. Bland food in Thailand meant rice or farang (foreign) food from the club or the base. I was craving spice. "Just a bowl of Tom Yum Cai—it's just chicken soup," I pleaded, but I only got rice with a mix of soy and fish sauce and some fresh bread and chicken broth. I think I ate the whole loaf; it was so good.

When we finally made it back to the nest, I just lay around for a couple of days. The boys and I played cards and drank Jack with the Marines. DD took off the Band-Aids and inspected the scars. "Not too bad," he said. "They've all healed up pretty well." Then DD had his weekly foot inspection: we all lined up and had our toes and feet checked for any signs of fungus. Keeping your feet in good shape was very important in the tropics, where fungal infections could run rampant. We did everything we could to keep this stuff under control. Any place that could get hot and sweaty, and any place that would encounter friction, like feet in boots, was susceptible. That is why we didn't wear underwear; that second layer of cloth was just an invitation to excess humidity, which made for a fungal party for sure. I quickly learned the use of medicated powder, especially Columbia Medicated Powder and Bismoline Powder. These were applied to feet, crotch, armpits, and the inside of the elbows. Allowing yourself to completely dry out was a good idea as well. "Sun showers," which was what we called getting a little sunshine on your feet and crotch, were helpful too.

After inspection, DD announced, "Well, FNG Bobby has won the prize." DD then sang his "You Got the FUNGUS and I Got the Cure" song. He pulled out a bottle of Gentian violet and painted Bobby's toes purple, and then he told Bobby to drop his pants. Sure enough, the pesky little fungus had found its way to his crotch. By then, Bobby had figured out that he was being hazed, and the rest of the guys had to hold him down while DD shaved him and gave him quite the purple paint job. They took a look at me but thought the better of it. They should have done it while I was an FNG, it was too late now.

Having properly hazed Bobby, it was time for the naming ceremony. "Since you operate a PRC-77 known to everyone as the PRICK-77, we originally decided to call you Prick. But then we noticed that you play cards pretty well, so we changed it to Ace. But keep in mind Prick is still available if you want it." Then we carried him to shower for the traditional beer bath. The newly minted Ace scrubbed his purple privates with soap and discovered what we already knew: it was permanent and would take weeks to wear off. He didn't need to worry. The bar girls didn't mind; they had seen the prank before.

• • •

I still questioned why we turned the bombing on and off and why we bothered with sensors if we weren't going to do anything but count trucks going into South Vietnam. Congress was getting more directly involved in the war. There were problems fighting in Cambodia and Laos where the trail was. They wanted to increase the amount of covert operatives since they were decreasing the overt. Nixon was getting his ass into a crack about using a group of Cubans and people on the White House staff to break into the Democratic National Committee's offices. These were exciting times, and we were finally getting reinforcements.

Twenty-four newbies were about to come over, and some of them were guys I had trained with. The number of blond Cambodian and Laotian pilots seemed to be increasing a lot as well. It didn't come close to making up for the Special Forces teams they pulled out, and when they stopped bombing the North, the bastards shifted all the AAA down to protect the trail. Getting in and out was becoming a lot more dangerous. We were only supposed to be working on the prototypes, but we seemed to be doing a lot more. We might have an AC-130 or two, but it wasn't the same as having AC-130s, AC-119s, a B-52, and lots of ground attack birds. I was pretty sure we were becoming the rear guard or maybe Spartans standing in the pass to provide a politically acceptable time interval between the US withdrawal and the inevitable fall of Vietnam. Neither scenario appealed to me.

I was looking forward to seeing the guys from training, and I sat around all day waiting for the plane with DD and Moose. The rest of the team went into town. Finally, a C-130 with the group arrived and was about to land. I was watching when three mortar rounds impacted on the runway, quickly followed by three more. One of these landed almost on the center of the plane, and it exploded in a fireball. Immediately, the firefighters and mechanics responded with the fire truck and jeeps.

But DD, Moose, Buzz, and I responded by grabbing weapons and ammo and heading for the chopper. We didn't have time to pack; we just grabbed what was at hand. Buzz was screaming, "We need the new Pave Low wound up and in the air before it gets mortared!"

We were ready to kill something, and we saw the boats trying to make it to the Laotian side of the river. They began shooting at us with AK-47s; we returned fire with the miniguns as Buzz orbited them. It wasn't a fair fight; they were ground up completely, except for one boat that made it to bank, and they run for the cover of the jungle. One of the NVA turned and fired an RPG at the helicopter. Buzz, a bit perturbed, swooped in for the kill, and Moose, on the port side minigun, obliged him by literally blowing the NVA to pieces. Six or eight got away, and we wondered what to do now. We wanted to go after them, but we didn't really have everything we needed. I had a half-packed ruck with a Claymore, a phosphorous grenade, and five fragmentation grenades; my knife bag; and a few sundry items like face paint. I vowed that this would never happen again. From now on, I would always have a second ruck full to the brim and ready to go.

Buzz had a small stash of five twenty-round clips of 5.56 in the bird, and I had ten clips plus one in my weapon. Moose had his machete and his weapon with one magazine and bandoleer with one hundred rounds in cardboard boxes, and DD had his weapon with one magazine and his med kit. Together, we had about a hundred rounds apiece but no compass or map. "Well, the air force or Thai Force Protection team should be on the way, and we took care of two-thirds of the attackers from the air. Maybe they can mop up the rest of this mess?"

Then the call came over the radio that no one else was coming. The air force would not enter Laos without permission.

"Put us down up the trail and we will wait for the bastards." We painted up on the way. I had my big ten-inch Tanto blade and gave Moose my real knife with a six-inch blade and DD my Sykes knife. I gave Moose all the grenades, since he was better at chucking them long distance and short distance was not helpful. I gave DD the Claymore, and I kept the PRC-90, a small survival radio. We were ready now. Buzz went down like a rock and hovered over a stream, the only wide opening in the trees, and we jumped out. He was to go get some more people, if we had any, that is. Our goal was to infiltrate and set up an ambush before dark.

We moved up the trail as quickly as we could and then I saw something ahead. I signaled to the others to take cover. Moose was on one side of the trail and DD and I were on the other. I signaled that I was going to take a look and moved slowly and quietly through the bush. It looked like our NVA friends had friends of their own: there were more than twenty men and a 12.7 mm (fifty caliber) machine gun that they had dug in on my side of the trail. They expected to be followed, and they planned to put it on anyone who did. But they were not expecting an attack from the rear, so it was our lucky day.

Well just how crazy are we, three against twenty? They probably have traps and mines set as well. I know what we have to do: kill them all. But just how to do that has not come to me yet. Moose was on the other side of the trail. We signed back and forth for five minutes, barely able to see in the dim light. I tried to call in on the radio, but I got nothing. This was not good at all. We decided to wait for full night to see what we could do. It got dark quickly, and soon a quarter moon came out. Even so, the jungle soaked up most of the light. Our NVA friends probably thought they hadn't been followed, but they still decided not to try to move off at night. Even with a trail, moving at night without lights would be difficult. With lights, you would be a target for aircraft.

They dug in a bit and sent two sentries down the trail. They took up positions on either side of the trail, and I was in the bushes close to the guy on the right side of the trail. Getting behind him was going to be a trick. Finally, my guy decided to take a piss. This was a big mistake, since as he turned away to piss on a tree I caught him with his pants down. Perhaps it was just bad feng shui: never leave your back unprotected. I silently stepped out behind him directly into jōdan-no-kamae stance, pointed the blade to heaven, and just as I had trained ten thousand times to do, I quickly and silently, with a single strike of the knife, sent him to hell. Moose eliminated the second guy, not as silently as I had, but quickly. We recovered some water, two AKs, and one hundred rounds of AK ammunition from the bodies. We also found four RGD-5 Chinese grenades. The ChiCom grenades were pretty powerful and much more reliable than the older stick type, but they still really sucked compared to ours. We carried the bodies to the center of the trail and sat them back-to-back. The idea was to set the Claymore up in this area with the dead NVA as bait.

We couldn't see them clearly, but Moose and DD moved in close, about forty meters from the NVA perimeter, and unleashed several grenades, throwing them as far down the trail in the direction of the NVA as possible and running like hell into the bushes and behind the large trees. This was not a safe maneuver even during the day, but at night in the bush, the possibility of hitting a branch or tree and bouncing the damn thing back into your lap was significant. Big balls, those two. Two almost simultaneous explosions lit up the night with a flash. With grenades, you see no muzzle flashes, so in the dark there was no good way to know where they were coming from. There wasn't a massive amount of smoke and flames like in the movies either, just a very large bang and a flash. The NVA opened up the Dushka fifty-cal and aimed it directly down the trail in our direction. It was loud, and several bullets impacted the bodies we had sat on the trail, literally blowing them to pieces. Coming under fire from this weapon was really frightening; it could literally cut down small trees.

From out of nowhere, Moose, who had been a pitcher in high school, threw an M-61 "lemon" grenade at the muzzle flashes, and the explosion silenced the gun. I judged it was at least fifty meters, and he got a direct hit on the muzzle flash. Well, it might not have been exactly a bull's-eye but it had to be close, because the kill radius was only ten to fifteen meters. This either demoralized the remaining NVA or killed the commander, because the remaining guys decided to make a run for it. Or maybe they were really pissed; in any event, they ran straight up the trail into our waiting arms. It was still pretty dark and it was hard to see, just muzzle flashes coming toward me. At this point, Moose threw a WP grenade into what he thought was the middle of the charging NVA. The Willie Peter does not make a really strong explosion and concussive sound, it's more like a muffled pop, but we saw a flash and then eerie light and smoke from the burning phosphorous. This really took the wind out of their sails, so to speak, and we opened up and moved toward them, spraying the entire area with 5.56. We each expended about two or three twenty-round clips very quickly, and then we moved back into the bush. On the way, Moose gave them two more of the ChiCom grenades.

We decided to wait until morning to see the results. We did a silent recon after dawn, and the trail area was a real mess. The WP and 5.56 as well as the other grenades had decimated the NVA running down the trail toward us. Most of those who had been hit had bled out during the night. The well-placed ChiCom and U.S. grenades had also been very effective, and we had been very lucky indeed in having two high school pitchers on our team. We still had the unused Claymore. There had been no good place to put it before the Moose unleashed the barrage of grenades. This was a real mistake. This should have been the "break the back of the charge" device, not WP and 5.56. We were probably lucky to be alive and we amazingly we were unscathed as well, but this was really poorly executed fire fight, and I knew it was mostly my fault for not finding a good place for the claymore.

Then, just after daybreak, the cavalry arrived, having finally gotten permission from God himself in Washington, D.C., for *hot,* though by now it was cold, pursuit. We saw them as they cautiously moved up the trail. When they got close, we called out to them and identified ourselves then we cautiously came out of the bush. We had done a pretty good number on these guys; only one or two were still alive, and they were not in good condition. They counted twenty-six down. It was so dark that some of them may have shot each other. I told the captain who led the team that we were done here and were going home.

He looked at me and said, "Aren't you going to clean up your fucking mess, boys? Where is the rest of your fucking team?"

Boys. He called us boys, and I looked as old as he did. I lost it. "Well, let me tell you, we three MEN are the entire team and probably the meanest motherfuckers you have ever come across. As I see it, we *did* clean up the mess that was caused by the lack of base protection that let these guys get in and really fuck us good in our "safe" base. Your Thai boys need to do more than drive around in their armored cars looking mean. Our people in the C-130 died as a result of these bastards, so don't give me your arrogant fucking 'clean up this mess.' We are done, and there is nothing left for you BOYS to do here but the counting. Now I don't want to seem like an ass, which I am by the way, but I want to see what damage these dead motherfuckers caused to our friends in the plane they mortared, which was on fire when we left in a real hurry to get these bastards. We have had our payback from these guys. We are now officially out of here, so if you don't like it, I'm sorry, but as you know, we are not under your command. And just to be completely clear, *I don't give a shit about this mess.* It can stay where it is as a warning of what you get for fucking with us."

He just looked at me and said nothing.

I glared back at him and then I finally said: "You can claim the kills if it makes you happy; we couldn't care less about the numbers. And you can deal with the Dushka and the ZPU as well. Count yourselves lucky you were not on the receiving end of those babies. Oh, and if you want, I would love to meet with you and General Jones next time he is by. I am pretty sure I know how that meeting would play out. Did I mention General Jones taught me how to spit shine shoes? So I accept your apology. Now, is everybody here happy?"

Moose and DD were amazed, having never seen me explode and give anyone shit like this before. As we walked down the trail, Moose chuckled and said, "Well, you certainly explained it to him. Do you think we should requisition his trousers?"

Moose had already contacted Buzz on the PRC-90 and he was inbound with the Pave Low. There was no place to land, so he went into a hover and threw out a rope ladder that we climbed up to the bird. Mike, Pipes, and Ace were all ready to go and seemed happy to see us but asked, "Why didn't you wait for us?"

"Well, it was getting dark fast and you guys weren't back yet, so we decided to launch before nightfall, and we didn't want the Pave Low mortared by waiting around on the tarmac," I said.

Buzz followed the trail deeper into the jungle, even though only patches of it were visible. Suddenly, there was a ZIL-150 truck lumbering along the trail toward the Force Protection guys.

Where were all the "friendly" Lao troops when you needed them? The truck heard us and pulled off the track as fast as they could. Our miniguns followed them with a hellish spray of 7.62, which chewed up the truck and the men in it before they could escape. Buzz then headed for the base; our work was done. On the way home, we alerted the base to the presence of the truck and troops and they contacted the captain I had chastised. These NVA were way out of their safe zone, and I felt sure there were more trucks out there. I expect that *Banshee* and *Thor*, our good old AC-130 Spectre gunships, would be on the hunt tonight.

We returned to the base, where Nash met us, as was his custom. At least I wasn't bloody this time. He just smiled. Moose announced, "We got 'em Nash, all twenty-six of them." I had carried the body of the sentry, and as a result I had just a bit of a stain that I had forgotten about, but it was certainly no worse than Moose's. Nash just looked at me and smiled. "Every time, Mac, I mean Red Dog—absolutely every fucking time."

"Well, regardless, we all made it back in one piece. Oh, and by the way, fuck the air force, especially their captain who is a dog shit dumb ass motherfucker". Nash looked surprised and said, "Well, he speaks highly of you, Mac. Told me on the radio you three wasted twenty-six of the bad guys in the bush, eighteen more at the river, and a truck-full down the trail. Only left three or four to interrogate."

"Well, we got no fucking help from those guys, and he wanted us to 'clean up our mess.' If we hadn't *made* a mess they would have been eating commie fifty-cal rounds from the Dushka the NVA had on the trail, not to mention the ZPM. They were planning on hitting us with AAA, and I'm pretty sure that a 14.5 mm (fifty-seven caliber) ZPM shell will just eat a bird. Hell, it is a lot bigger than a Ma Deuce fifty-cal. So what happened to our men in the plane?"

Nash said, "It was pretty bad. Ten were killed outright; the rest were all hurt in one way or another. Two or three were not too badly hurt, but the fire was really bad. They are all over in the hospital, except some of the really bad burns. We have moved them to a special burn unit in Japan."

I had decided to see them before I did anything else, but Nash told us to get cleaned up and get something to eat. He said he could go see the guys after the debriefing.

Suddenly, I felt amazingly tired. I had been awake a long time, and the adrenalin had been running very high for a very long time. *Yes, sir, see you in a couple of hours.*

We went to the hotel, and I scrubbed up in a hot shower and changed into greens. I told the guys to let me sleep for twenty minutes and then I would be good for the debriefing. Moose and DD followed my lead, and when Mike found out, he just let us all sleep until morning.

When we did finally wake up, I was ravenously hungry. Not one to eat alone, I woke everyone else up and we went to the restaurant for breakfast, to be followed by a trip to meet Mike at the base. We all arrived at the restaurant, and the first person I saw was Jarhead! And then Bear! We all shouted each other's names at the same time, and then Bear gave me one of his Bear hugs, which came close to breaking my ribs. I introduced them all around, and everyone started swapping stories. The crash was bad, and the tally was really high. Out of twenty-nine on board, ten were dead and nineteen wounded including the crew of three. A few just slightly hurt like Bear and Jarhead, and some required evacuation to Japan. Thanks to the quick-acting ground crews at Naked Fanny and the pilot and copilot, the entire plane-load was not killed. I felt like the luckiest guy in the world having only a few scratches for all my time in country. Then the last two arrived, Mr. Russell and Mr. Harris the class trainers from my training days. We greeted them with handshakes and hugs as well. Harris filled us in the details of the crash and who had bought the farm. It was pretty bad; it decimated the entire class.

Russell said, "So, Red, on the first day, I didn't think you would make it through the training, but you sure are full of surprises. It looks like you turned out pretty good from what I hear. I am eager to see your famous spinning knife technique. Did Sykes teach you that?"

"No, that was my own invention. I still can't chunk a grenade for shit though." Everyone laughed. "Would you guys like to come to Bangkok with us later today?" Russell and Harris declined, saying they had several days of planning meetings to attend, but Jarhead and Bear were ready for some R&R.

When we arrived at Nash's's office, the clerk ushered us right in. Naturally, there sat the air force captain I had un-loaded on the previous day. Nash introduced us all to Captain John Roberts, and there was an awkward moment when I was a little unsure of whether I should shake the good captain's hand or not. I felt sort of bad about my behavior…not *actually* bad, just sort of. Fortunately, Mike, Pipes, and Ace were not at all embarrassed, and I followed suit. I expected I was going to be asked to apologize, but instead, Captain Roberts apologized for his language during our encounter. That wasn't what I was expecting.

Apparently, his sergeant major, when asked, suggested that we might have taken his comments the wrong way, and that without us taking the bad guys down they certainly would have taken casualties from the machine gun and dug-in NVA. He had seen the mangled bodies of the two sentries and thought we had done it, not the fire from the Dushka. I apologized for my out-of-control mouth and explained that we had indeed placed them on the trail but the rest was collateral damage from the fifty-caliber fired by the bad guys, just as his sergeant had suggested. After all, we only had about one hundred rounds of 5.56 apiece; we weren't going to waste any of it on dead guys.

"If I hadn't seen it with my own eyes, I wouldn't believe it, and I don't really know what to think." He paused. "Yes, I do know what to think. I heard you guys were really crazy, and now I know you all are really frigging crazy. With only one hundred rounds apiece, you should all be dead!"

We had expected the odds to be three versus six or eight, not twenty-six. Taking on eight was on the edge, taking on twenty-six was way past crazy. Our plan had been to harass and cause as much damage as we could and then go doggo in the bush. But that's a much less impressive story than us just going completely berserk. The time for BS had come, as we would do almost anything to improve our reputation for being crazy motherfuckers.

Moose started. "Well, we didn't just have guns; we also had knives. Bloody Snake here gave me one of his, which I am keeping, because it's really nice and very quiet for a knife. So thank you, Snake, nobody ever gave me anything as nice before—sharp as a serpent's tooth."

Then DD chimed in. "Me too! I got the smaller one, but it is perfect for my boot. I haven't used it yet, but I can hardly wait for a good chance. I won't need to carry a scalpel any more with this thing."

"Seriously, how *did* you guys do it?" asked Nash.

"Baseball, sir," I said, "and plain, ordinary luck. It was very dark, and even small lights, like a cigarette, could be clearly seen. And we have two star pitchers here. The gooks were all huddled up together working of the weapons pit for the ZPM, and when half a dozen grenades and a Willie Pete sail out of the bush at you during a black night, you can't tell where they are coming from. It was devastating. The rest is a testament to the miniguns on the Pave Low, except the two sentries and the hail of 5.56 we put on the gooks when they charged up the trail at us. But to be honest, we were just trying to slow them down so our Marine buddies could take them on. Turns out we slowed them down permanently."

• • •

Our amazing luck had held yet again. But how many more times could you roll the dice and not come up Snake Eyes?

CHAPTER 14

Bangkok and then another Tough Assignment

• • •

That which does not kill me only serves
to make me stronger. "Really?"

—FRIEDRICH NIETZSCHE

DD CAME BACK FROM A visit to his friends at the infirmary. He was carrying a box that contained vials of bicillin and syringes. We were about to get the obligatory prophylactic injections of antibiotic before our launch to Bangkok. Jar Head and Bear were surprised a bit, but everyone got their shot and off we went.

The C-130 made a quick trip from NKP to Bangkok. We landed at the airport in Bangkok took what little luggage we had and piled into four taxis and headed into the city. We asked the drivers to drop us at that Patpong Road which was at the time a center for bars, restaurants, and was becoming a center for nightlife as well.

We decided to start at Lucy's Tigers Den (and the Hobo's Roost on the second floor). This was a nice watering hole to get our feet on the ground before we descended into the dens of iniquity that lined the street. The bartender let us leave our stuff in an upstairs room and we were off. We considered going over to Petchburi Road where a lot of R&R guys from Vietnam congregated but Patpong had a certain "New" look. The Air America office was first located on Patpong along with a number of other airlines, it had not gotten the full reputation it developed in a few years later, when the offices were relocated. It was becoming a major Red Light area but it was not the only thing there. There were a number of great bars, restaurants and plain old watering holes. The Mississippi Queen had a definite Soul Music feel but they had a singer who did as good a version of The House of the Rising Sun as I have ever heard. Lots of black GIs sought out the Mississippi Queen just for the music. I can believe it. There were crazy places like Safari where the dancers used Pythons as props and The Red Door Restaurant and The Super Star were all running at full tilt. Go-Go dancing was the rage and some of these places were really rocking with large numbers of beautiful young ladies.

In general, the "Upstairs Bars" were more "raw" than the "Downstairs Bars" and some charged covers to see the shows which were pretty wild at times.

Before we got too drunk on Singha beer to navigate, we flagged down some of the taxis that cruised the streets, mostly Datsun Blue Birds, the ubiquitous taxis in Bangkok at the time. I never saw one of these in U.S. but they were very common as

Taxis in Bangkok. We negotiated the price for the ride Lucy's and on to Mamasan's down to 10 Baht each and then gave the drivers a red 100 Baht note as a tip. We had Mamasan's entire place booked, so it was nice not having a lot of strangers wandering around and like the last time, your clothes got laundered and pressed and delivered to the bath but this time there were robes hanging on the door. The ritual of morning coffee was great and we were ready for the trip back to NKP by way of Udorn. We went to the airport and we were booked on another Air America flight set up for us. Who do you think our pilot was? Yes, luck of the draw, we got Johnnie from the "Den's of Iniquity Tour". He looked a lot better than the last time I saw him. I think he must have had quite a hangover. This time he was very chipper and looked very professional in a starched and press shirt and grey AA uniform. We made the hop to Udorn and Johnnie arranged for a couple of company cars. We left through the Air America gate and stopped at O.K. Taylor's shop to pick up some new Tigers and fatigues as we were pretty hard on them and I had become very particular as to how the pockets were placed and having a couple of "Non-Standard" pockets made a difference. In particular, a compass pocket high on the shoulder, slashed pockets with drain holes covered with the same little screens as the ones in the boonie hats. DD, Moose, and I also stopped by Tony Tik's Jewelry, where Nash had arranged for us to pick up something. He would not tell us what it was but it turned out to be a silver Japanese 50 Sen Coin mounted in gold with a silver chain. Was this a play on 50 sin, I guess. This is likely as close to a medal as we ever came. Tony also gave us the eight silver cap badges he had had made up. They were "Cap Badges", circlets of silver with "*Per Caelum Per Terras*" (From the Sky and From the Ground) and Anything, Anywhere, Anytime, Professionally around the circle with lightning bolts and a hand holding a dagger in the center. This was one for everyone on Nash's "A" team including Buzz and Fuzz. Well, at least we thought we were Nash's "A" team but then you never really know with Nash. Since we were getting ready for the trip to Taiwan for the singing contest, we all had a set of Greys made up which was really good for me. Tight fitting clothes were "In" at the time, but mine were really tight across the chest to the point the jacket did not close and the trousers were tight too, because they were made up on measurements taken before training and I continued to add weight while in country which was unheard of. I did have a reputation for constantly eating noodles and fried rice. Everyone got measured and they would be done in a few days so we could pick them up on the way to Kaohsiung.

We left the shop and are headed down the street when Tony comes running after us. We had a phone call. Now this was pretty amazing since this was not the "everyone has a cell phone" era, cell phones did not exist yet. Tony and the Tailor "shared" a business phone. This was really up scale for the area. Nance gets the phone and we hear "yes sir, yes sir, on our way sir. He then looks at us and said we have been "called out" we need to get back to NKP ASAP. We had been looking forward to finding out what was in Johnnie's Real Den of Iniquity that charged for admission but not this time. I asked what "called out" meant, and Nance said they had a problem on the ground and we were part of the solution. We headed directly for operations and we go into the communications room where Nance gives everyone a sheet of paper and a pencil. This is a two-day mission. Write down your name and everything you want in your ruck and hurry, we launch out of here as soon as you are done. He takes a sheet of paper and starts writing. I go through the ruck from the bottom to the top, and ask heavy on ammo? Nance says yes, extra heavy. We hand the sheets to a clerk who begins to type at blinding speed into a Telex machine. I always worried that the slow Teletype on the other end would not be able to keep up. The telex or TWX machine transmitted typed messages over the phone lines, thinking of it now, it was the original text message. These lists were all magically appearing in NKP where someone was apparently running around packing our rucks for us. Just as we finished, the typist handed our sheets back to us since he typed so fast it only took a minute or so per page for him to enter the lists. Nance says take these with you and you can think about it more on the trip.

Moose and Jarhead did not know what to do so they just took what I had and added a bunch more grenades to the list along with another M-79 and a PRC-77 just in case they would launch with us. I did not know what the mission was but I guessed they might be involved.

Unproven people on a sensitive mission was a big problem. I now understood the concern on my first mission that was supposed to have been a walk in the Park. Now more than six guys was a really big issue in that the more people you had the noisier you would be and we generally relied on being very quiet. Since we normally kept at 10 meters between people, the length of the strung out team went from 50 yards to be close over 100 yards with 12 people in a team. This was just not workable. We would have to close up, the distance from point to drag was so long you could not hope see from the head to the tail. Actually, in thick bush you could not even see the guy in front of you sometimes. A person in camo a hundred meters away was like looking to try to see a person on a different continent. Worse still was trying camouflage the trail with so many people walking on it would be a bitch, six was bad enough but more would be close to impossible.

Johnnie was at the plane, his beloved DC-3. This particular plane had had the original Wright engines replaced with two Rolls Royce "Dart" engines, which had considerable more horses than the originals, and the props had been changed as well. The top speed of the old DC-3 was around 200 knots but the "new" bird was much better than that, it cruised at over 200. As we load up into the plane, a jeep appears and a box of hamburgers appears, with Thermos bottles of coffee, cokes, fries, and several pies in a separate box. I realize I really, really need to pee, and tell Nance man, I've got to piss. He says no problem, signals circle up, so on the runway we stand eight guys in a circle providing "cover" for each other getting ready to take a leak. As fast as I can I unbutton my fatigues and as I start to pee, I feel instant relief and then almost immediately on a signal from Nance the rest of the team just turn around and laughing walk up the stairs to the bird leaving me, dick in hand taking a piss on the runway. Naturally, Moose not to be outdone circles behind me and pulls my fatigues to the ground. Typical, I knew these guys, Whore

Mongering, Raised by Wolves, Sons of Bitches, my buddies. If I had any modesty left after being with this crew, it was by now, too little to measure, I just don't care at this point and take my time pissing standing on the runway in front of the ground crew and God Almighty, trousers around my ankles, no underwear, and then run up the stairs and we are on our way into harm's way again. But I owe Moose another one. Anything, Anytime, Anywhere, Professionally. Professionally? Really? OK, so it was pretty funny I guess. This is another time I had to question my sanity. Gee, I could be in a nice rice patty getting shot at for $300 a month with people who were not nearly as much fun.

Well, the distance from Udorn to NKP is about 150 miles (250 klicks). So with Johnnie putting the throttle at full bore open it takes us about 40 minutes for the trip. We eat the hamburgers and the fries on the way so we are all ready to go as soon as we touch down. This was not my normal pre-launch meal but it would have to do. Buzz's Pave Low was sitting on the flight line and a "Black" Huey with the usual M-60 door gun replaced with a modified Mini-Gun. A jeep arrives carrying Russell, Harris, and two guys I have not met. The first guy is a rather short fellow, but muscular and the second one is a tall, dark skinned, Tarzan type dude, both have "the look" of the jungle warrior. We quickly do the meet and greet thing. I find out Russell's bush name is Viper and Harris is Monkey. The short stout guy whose real name is Mike is called Leaky, and other guy is Custer. I later find out Leaky is a "re-purposed" Navy Seal, so the name is really Leaky Seal. Call signs are just stupid. Custer turns out to be a Sioux – Irish mix. They have a door gunner who is a really old guy called Gunny and the pilot is called Wings. His co-pilot is called Right-Side for obvious reasons. A second jeep packed with our rucks arrives and I grab mine and put it on and shake to test rattles. It is good to go. On the left strap is a new to me, but old to the world, Japanese tanto. It looks to be a fine old blade and clay tempered. This was the real deal. Where the hell did Nash get this? The canteens seem to all be full, as do the repurposed canteen covers full of magazines with rubber bands to silence them. But it was really pretty heavy pack.

We sanitize ourselves by the ritual removal of dog tags, wallets, and any id, and we give these to Nash. He already has our,"if I am dead letters". Then we strip and put on our Tigers right on the flight line standing by the birds while the ground crew are working quickly to arm the miniguns and 50 cal. Naked on the flight line seems to be becoming a habit for me. Not really keeping a low profile as the local ground crews stare at us like they have never seen a bunch of naked men blousing their fatigues on the flight line before. I put on my brand new Tigers. We pile the cast off clothes in the back of the jeep then Nash's clerk comes driving over to the birds at high speed in a pickup truck. There sitting in the passenger seat is Nance's favorite Montagnard Priest. In the bed was an 81 mm mortar and several boxes of rounds. This shit is really heavy stuff. What the hell would we be using a mortar for? I had never used one I had just seen them used in old movies. While they load the mortar and ammunition into Russell's bird we get our blessing and then the Priest blesses

Russell's team and birds. Superstition dies hard. Nance gives him a 100 Baht red note, asks the question, Everyone Happy? We all rumble out an affirmative answer and immediately crank up and lift off. Russell hands me two M-72 LAW tubes (Light Antitank Weapon, the new at the time "bazooka") from a box in the back and hands another one to DD, and asks can you guys carry these? Sure, but just what are we going to use a LAW for I wonder? I have never fired one of these either, I assume I am just humping it in for someone else to use. I am beginning to think this is really not at all the regular mission I have trained for. I have visions of rooting out NVA from bunkers and spider holes. The guys in Nam who walked up the hill and did that kind of mission really had courage. I was scared shitless.

We had traded Russell for Pipes since he will brief us on this mission en-route. This must be a really hot item to move so fast with so many people and so much equipment. I am not certain I am very well trained for a large unit operation and for us anything over 6 was "large". As we are loading up and lifting off, four B-26s (or A-26s) painted dark green one the tops and sky blue on the underbelly come roaring in and land. They have no markings; this means they must be ours. These are beasts as ground support they have eight, yes eight, 50 caliber machine guns in the nose and shit load of bombs and napalm hanging on the hard points. We never had real air support before but this is not our typical mission, it is during the day and damned overt. I noticed on the flight in that one of the Mini-guns had been replaced with a 20 mm Vulcan. Going from 7.62 mm to 20 mm (0.300 in. to 0.787 in.) gave the bird the ability to stay out of range of the NVA 50 caliber guns and but really put it on them, 20 mm x 102 mm Vulcan is small caliber artillery with a rate of fire of 6,000 rounds per minute and it is just hellacious. Probably it was good enough to go against the NVA 23 mm AAA as well, after all they were shooting up and we would be shooting down at them. The problem is how much ammo can you carry and the rate of fire means you burn 600 rounds of ammo in 6 seconds and that was all you carried. So adjusting the thing from 6 to 3 barrels was required so now you had 12 seconds of ammo.

We had launched as quickly as possible and we still had some things to take care of before we exited the bird. We immediately begin to paint up in the bird while Russell starts to explain the situation. It seems that we have a team down and surrounded. The bad guys are putting it all in on in an attempt to find and eliminate them. Their bird went down in a valley. They exited it as it lurched its way across and then off a karst and fell hitting the base of the karst in a burning heap. The pilot was KIA for sure but the six-man team and co-pilot are still alive. They have three seriously wounded but they are on top of the karst with enemy all around looking for them and it is only a question of time before they are found or just plain die. They are using the radio they have very little to transmit since they are worried about Radio Direction Finders could pinpoint their position and that they are alive. The only good thing is the NVA think the bird hit the Karst and went down, not crossed the Karst and went down. The NVA have put in several batteries of antiaircraft artillery including their old standby the 14.5 mm (0.586) ZPU around the crash site waiting for the rescue forces using the crash site as bait. Just flying any kind bird through the area drew very intense and sustained AAA. A direct helicopter rescue would be impossible until the AAA is dealt with. Russell says the downed team is afraid to use the radio because of radio direction finding. We are to land and act as a spotting and assault team and to draw them off the area. Bait, hey they want to us to as bait? Fucking Great. We normally go through a lot of planning and map study before we do anything; I see where they want us to go and where we are going to be inserted in. We were being inserted near a "high-speed" trail. The term "high-speed" trail refers to trails that have been hard packed by years of use or in some cases hundreds of years of use. They are rather like concrete at least in the dry season. We always avoid these trails for our normal mission movements since they are used so frequently by the NVA both day and night they were dangerous. We set up sensors on these and it is not easy to camouflage if you dig across the actual trail surface since you disturb the hard packed surface. It looks like we're going to move up toward the valley on one and then take a highpoint where we could see what is happening in the valley below. I don't think humping the mortar up the hill with an 80 pound ruck on your back is going to be very easy, in fact just getting to the top of the hill may be a major problem. The mortar weighs about 100 pounds with no ammo. Each round weighs about 15 pounds. 6 rounds would be 90 pounds another heavy load, so even with it disassembled into pieces and the ammo distributed it would not be simple or easy to carry and what exactly is the target? That was one advantage a 200 plus pound Moose,

Bear, or Jarhead had is they could pack a lot more than the average 170 pound American or 110 pound Montgnard. Still 60 to 65 pounds not including your weapon is a pretty good load in the hot humid jungle and this was a "normal "heavy" load. The two limiting items were usually ammo and water. You can reduce the water if it available from a stream or river but no one really wanted to be drinking Klong water even if it was treated with twice the iodine pills it needed to sterilize it. The ammo was an essential item and you really could not have too much, but, with a 12 man team maybe one PRC-77 radio was enough that saves 14 pounds and the spare battery another 2 pounds so here is a 16 pound offset or one mortar round. I just have to assume Russell and company know what they are doing and I will just do my best to hump whatever I am asked to hump. But the mortar is good to 3000 meters and I assume the LAW was a line of sight weapon, a hundred yards or so. The question in my mind was what we're planning to do with these? I guess I would find out soon enough and I was correct.

The helicopters flew nape of the earth just skimming over the treetops. Below, you could see an expanse of green spread out across the world. It was beautiful and strange, almost alien looking landscape. In the distance, as we wound our way through the valleys you could see the occasional karst pillars and cliffs jutting out of the green jungle and the small rivers, all tributaries of the great Mekong winding through them. It had all had a surreal look, almost a fairy tale like landscape you just cannot capture in a photograph. Soon, we would be in the reality of it, a hot, humid, backbreaking hike through "Indian

Country" I wished Koob was with us, his scouting abilities and ability to see into any snipers hides would be missed but we had Mike and Russell and Sykes the best we had to make up for it.

The birds descended into a small river valley with steep sides and at a place where the water course widened across a large flat stone floor they went into a hover just off the water and as quickly as we could we exited the birds, into a few inches of running water and they left the area as quickly as possible. Russell's team had broken the mortar into three sections and Jar Head, Bear, and Moose each had a piece to carry. I had the two LAWs so I did not get a mortar shell but everyone else got at least one. Everyone had a really heavy load this time as moved into the jungle along a "High Speed" trail that crossed the little stream where we had been inserted. As I said before we would normally never use trails like this there was just too much enemy activity but today we really needed speed. We moved as quickly as possible and Russell kept the ear-plug of a PRC-90 in his ear listening for reports from aerial surveillance. In "orbit" at 25,000 feet, we had the Banshee scanning with sensors to see what it could using FLIR (Forward Looking Infrared) and optical sensors as well as the Black Crow. They saw no movement on the trail but us. We moved onto the trail and one thing became apparent a tracked vehicle, maybe a tank had been there before us, or more likely one of Russian quad mounted radar controlled anti-aircraft vehicles a ZSU-23-4, the tracks made marks penetrated into the hard packed surface. If it was tracks from a ZSU-23-4 this was really bad news as four 0.9 inch guns could really make your day really bad. We avoided these tracks to avoid leaving any of our own. We really began covered some distance quickly on the hard packed trail. In training, with a 65 pound pack, we were expected to hump about twenty five klicks (fifteen miles) in four hours, but making about ten klicks, with these heavy packs, on this uphill, was exceedingly tough and it took two hours. We then turned off the trail and into the heavy bush where the speed fell to a crawl as the Nash working as the drag man and had to really work hard to cover the trail since there were twelve of us and we all had very heavy packs. Once we broke through the thick vegetation at the edge of the high-speed trail, the triple canopy jungle seemed to have less understory and we made better time until we hit a thicket of bamboo. This shit was the thin kind and was wind blown into a tangle. There was just no way through, we had to go around it even if it made the track a lot longer. We stopped for water and a short rest break; everyone was really beat. It was hot and we had been sweating like crazy and the heavy pack cut into your hips and shoulders. I drank a liter of water and ate my fruitcake. These little fruitcakes were full of sugar and fat, they came in a small "C" ration can and I removed one from the can and shoved it into one of the heavy zip lock bags I got from supply so I did not have to carry the can or use the tiny P-38 can opener well known to anyone who has ever eaten "C-rats" which I carried on a dog tag chain around my neck to open it. There was no time for that this time since someone else packed the ruck for me, so I just ripped the top off as quickly as the little P-38 could. The sugar gave me a quick surge of energy and the fat gave it a little more staying power, plus it was silent and did not rattle like M&Ms. It was time to go, we helped each other get the rucks back on our backs since they were so heavy, then it was back on the trail which was getting to be really steep, it was like walking up stairs except there were no stairs, just an increasingly rocky, rough ground. Pretty soon, we could not continue unseen since there was less and less cover as we came up toward the crest of the hill. The jungle thinned and you could see ahead. There was no thick cover like you had at the edge of the high speed trail or a stream or river, the trees just thinned and we would be very exposed in another hundred meters. Nash, Russell, and Harris huddle in to discuss the options and plan. This is a great time for a "standing break", stopped, bending over with hands on the knees. There was a karst cliff ahead somewhere and we attempting to get to the top of it along a spine that connected it to the ridgeline we were working our way toward. The cover had become sparse enough you could see small patches of sky through the canopy above us and blue sky was becoming dark. Then, the rain started, a torrential downpour even through the trees. There was no place to go doggo so we just continued forward in the rain. The tree cover thinned but never really disappeared as we made our way across the "bridge" that connected the steep spine to a karst spire which stood like a peninsula attached to the valley walls

They had the PRC-77 set up and had a KY-38 cypher unit to scramble the communications and guarantee no listening in by the bad guys. I guess they did not trust "battle talk" to be safe enough. They might be able to understand the communications but they could still use direction finders to locate you. Someone had to pack in the KY-38, which that had the same damn heavy batteries as the PRC-77. We really had some mules in the group today for certain. The darkness came quickly as it often does in the mountains and the jungle. With night falling, the temperature also dropped. Soon it was pitch black as there was no moon. Out came two pair of night vision goggles. Russell and Nash use these to scan across to the other karsts and the valleys below. We were all silent and kept as still as possible. Russell motions to Nash to move over and they both scan the karst across from us carefully. They see movement and in the dark we see a bright light as someone lights a cigarette. The match is like a beacon in the dark night. Russell carefully places an infrared beacon to Mark our position on this karst. The light is invisible except for the FLIR camera on the Gunships. Nash cranks up the PRC-77 and sends a quick message. We hear the low rumble of the C-130 in the distance. It echoes in the Valley. And then the karst across from us explodes in a flash of light. Explosions strike the top of the karst. This is the Banshee standing off out of range of any AAA and using the 105 mm gun to put it on the bad guys. The last shell was white phosphorus and the burning phosphorus lit up the entire top of the karst. Whoever was there was probably pretty unhappy right now.

The center of our particular Karst had a cluster of trees and some large boulders that provided us cover. We circled up in the trees and a few of us had thin green ponchos, which we clustered under, three or four men to each one. Here I was again, tired, wet, cold, hungry, and thirsty but glad not be humping that pack. I was between Moose and Larry the Bear who were literally radiators actually "steaming" as they stood there. The temperature had dropped a lot with the thunderstorm, not like the monsoon rains that hardly seemed to change the temperature. Moose had taken the tube and the base plate of the mortar and was assembling it with me acted as the tent pole for the poncho. The sighting mechanism arrived with Russell and soon the mortar was completely assembled. Now to fire this thing you needed an unobstructed view of the sky. In the center of the trees, the rocky outcrop provided this since there were no trees on the rocks, just some low bushes. Sighting it on a target was more difficult since you could not directly see where to aim but with the direction and a topographic map and an idea of the distance the round would travel you could get close with the first round and then adjust from there.

The mortar rounds came out of the packs and there were fourteen in total. Not a lot in reality. In addition, we had three LAW rockets, two M-79 grenade launchers and about 25 rounds for each of these. Everyone had either a Car-15, M-16, except Leaky and Nash who were armed with the Stoner 63s and we had all humped in a lot of 5.56, at least 500 or 600 rounds per person and a lot of grenades and several claymore mines. We were, as they say, armed to the teeth. Because of the rain everyone had filled back up the water supplies to 100% and hydrated to 100%. Food was going to be sparse but no one was too hungry yet and we had dehydrated LURP rations, but we were all pretty much soaked to the skin and as usual, I was cold until the temperature came back up after the storm passed, then I was just wet.

Several more explosions came across the valley close to the ridgeline. Flames and secondary explosions now lit up the sky from the ridgeline and outlined the shape of what looked like a small tank. From the sky, 40 mm shells streamed onto ridgeline and the little tank exploded. Nance continues to occasionally give a short message to the planes.

A finger of light arches down from heaven and scours across the ridgeline with a great howl. Next, the finger of light moves and comes up to our little karst. Well, it was close to our little pinnacle but not actually on the top of it. The fire from the sky scoured the "bridge" from the ridgeline and the approach and along into the jungle's edge. There were a lot of tight sphincters in our little hideout, but if you were headed our way I bet you had a very bad day indeed. At this point the question of what the hell am I doing here, crossed my mind again. I am still sure a line unit taking on the NVA to kick them off a particular hill was much worse than anything we did but this was still pretty intense and not really what I was trained for.

There was return fire from what had been camouflaged anti-aircraft artillery (AAA) clearly seen because of their tracers, and as fast as a C-130 can, which by the way is not so very fast, Banshee gained both distance and altitude away from us but as she turned into a new orbit, one last 105 round of WP marked the position of the AAA just as the sun began to rise.

As soon as the light came, so did the air support. Skimming across the treetops, three black A-26s came in so low the radar from the AAA could not get a lock on them, the first two strafed the AAA position with their eight 50 caliber machine guns and the last one hit the site with Napalm. The fire from the napalm burned brightly for over five minutes and ammunition cooking off added to the noise.

Our site was high and we could see parts of the trail in the distance where the jungle canopy was thin because of the size of the trail or the places where it crossed rocky outcrops. Banshee was still in orbit as evidenced by the occasional 105 rounds impacted the jungle in the area of the trail. Several WP rounds marked the spots for attention from the A-26s, and they came in like avenging angels really putting it on whatever was there. Nash and one of the guys from the second team made something moving in the jungle below us and they fired a mortar round in the general direction to get the range and then fired six in quick succession. One of the A-26s dropped a cluster of fragmentation bombs in the area and anything in the general area was toast.

The A-26 had the ability to fly "Low and Slow" and they were very accurate for ground support and had the ability "Loiter" for a long time over a particular area. The problem with them, helicopters, and the AC-130s was they were easy for radar controlled anti-aircraft artillery (AAA) to target and destroy. Until the NVA brought up Russian ZSU 23-4 quad mounted 23 mm (0.9) radar targeted AAA, we owned the night with the AC-130 and the A-26. Even so, by flying at treetop levels the A-26 could generally prevent radar lock because of the ground clutter but this kind of flying was damn risky at anytime, but at in the dark it was just crazy, maybe some distance beyond crazy and to be honest I don't know how they did it.

Yes, things got constantly more difficult and dangerous and maybe the truck kills and planes downed are not exactly comparable but A-26 was number one. Southern put at least six on their books, maybe some were flown as Royal Lao planes, but three with black paint and three with two-color camouflage had no markings. In any event, it was clear even to a no nothing like me that and they were just exceptional ground support aircraft.

From our vantage point we could see a lot of activity now along the high-speed trail. This was just what the A-26s wanted and they strafed then they bombed the convoy on the trail. There were numerous secondary explosions and as soon the blacks had expended their bombs, the two-tone planes came in and finished the job. With Nance acting as a forward observer, a lot of ordinance was put on the target with great accuracy by the A-26s. The weather was deteriorating and soon the rain came on with a vengeance. Real Monsoon rain poured from the sky and we were all soaked completely. Not that it made any real difference, as I never really dried out from the previous thunderstorm. The air support had to be called back and we all just went doggo as best as we could. I pulled out a can of commercial corned beef and ate the entire can in just a few minutes. The protein and fat was tasted really good. I was still hungry and opened a LURP ration of Pork and Scalloped Potatoes and added rainwater to reconstitute it. I carefully put it inside my jacket next to my belly to allow it to warm up to body temperature and hydrate. This was as good as I could do during a rainstorm. In about 45 minutes, I judged it "done" and I consumed it completely. It looked like hell but I really needed the carbs. This particular pack had a bar of the infamous "tropical" chocolate. I decided to save it for later. Well, now I was done with lunch and dinner. Time had come for the worst part of being in the jungle, I needed to take a shit. It was raining but just lightly; the ground was about 2 inches of dirt on top of rock, not ideal conditions to say the least. Well, at least I had toilet paper from the LURP package. I found the "Latrine" area behind one of the boulders and scrapped a trench about three inches wide and about foot long, straddled it and took care of business. While my trousers were around my ankles the rain suddenly came down in buckets. The direction of the rain also changed now it was hitting me directly in the face and pouring into my trousers which acted to funnel more water into my boots, no fucking problem, were already pretty much full already. The TP was soaked completely and was mushy. I didn't care. I then covered the hole as best as I could and put a flat stone on top. Not that it really made any difference, if the NVA found this we would all be dead already. It just kept others from stepping in it.

It was my turn at watch. I took off my boots and dumped the water out and took off my thin wool socks and squeezed them dry. I got into the hide and got as comfortable as possible but I was wet and cold. I used the binoculars to scan the area of the trail leading up to our hide as well as what I could see of the trail. Most of the trail here was really very improved to be used by trucks and most of it even had a "camouflaged roof" of trees and leaves to keep the trucks out of the sight of aircraft. There was nothing much to see, just green trees and bush. Then, I saw what looked like movement at the same time that Leaky the other lookout saw it. Leaky and I peered through our binoculars intently. We knew something was moving out there on the trail we but we could not identify it through the heavy rain and we were beginning to lose the light. I went to Nance and he had the entire team watching for any more signs of movement. Then we saw it, a tank like tracked vehicle slowly moving up the main high-speed trail. Leaky says he thinks it is a Russian ZSU- 57, an anti-aircraft weapon consisting of two 57 mm cannons in a twin mount. It lumbered slowly off the trail and up toward the ridge which would eventually lead to our hide. There are a good number of troops with it, probably around thirty. We count at least 20 and this was not all of them. This was really bad news. The karst pillar we were on did not really provide us a "backdoor" and if we stayed and were detected, we could be murdered by this thing and by mortars as well. As soon as the darkness came we needed to get the hell off this place and into the jungle where we stood a chance of evasion and escape or at least setting a trap for these guys.

Darkness came and so did the plan. Harris, DD, Ace and Monkey would man the mortar and provide additional support. Custer, Pipes, Lyndell, and Nance with LAWs, an M-79 and claymore mines would set up an ambush along the track, and four more, would act as a flanking force above the track close to the top of the ridge. Moose, Pipes, Leaky, and I drew this last flanking force job; we had a couple of LAWs and an M-79 as well.

To fire the LAW was really pretty simple. The design is a tube in a tube. You open the out to its full length by simply pulling out a safety lever and then the tubes are pulled out as far as possible. This allows the front and rear sights, which are spring loaded, to pop up. There are two switches both in black rubber waterproof sheaths, the one forward is the trigger and the second one back on the tube from the trigger is a catch to allow the tubes to be collapsed back together. I really had no intention of using this thing, this was Leakey's job; I had never used one before and now would be a really bad time to practice. Moose carried Leakey's Stoner 63, everyone else had a CAR-15 or M-16. Each assault team had a pair of night vision goggles each to help keep us on the path. Leaky was to lead us up to a position above the flat "lip" which then fell down a steep cliff to the valley floor below. From this position we would provide flanking fire down onto anything that moved after they ran into the blocking force of Custer, Pipes, Bloop, and Nance. Getting the forces into position at night through the often very thick understory was going to be very difficult task and not silent by our standards, but we had little choice in the matter.

We left before the thin crescent moon rose. Moving like a centipede, the man with the Night Vision (NV) goggles leading and the three "followers" holding onto the pack of the man in front of them. We did not have the beta lights (Tritium lights) we had the last we used the night vision goggles so we had to make do. It worked but it was so dark you could not see the man in front of you. If you let go it was all over, you would have to call an audible halt to get to "reconnect". No one let go. We made the most difficult and dangerous part of the hike, crossing over from the karst pillar to the area between the cliff and the ridgeline. Once over the cover provided by the thick understory along the edges of our track acted to camouflage us and at the same time make movement very difficult. Finding the track and keeping on it was not easy. At this point the two teams broke up and we began the climb up the hillside toward the ridgeline. It was very difficult made much worse by the darkness. I remember thinking how much noise we made compared to our normal "silent" routine. It did not matter, it had to be done, and quickly, we had to be in place by dawn. The jungle was thick in places but a lot of the area was just rock and we chose a position sheltered by large boulders and karst outcroppings. The boulders and the outcrops were a godsend and overlooked an almost clear 100 meter hillside down to the cliff and the small 15 meter lip of flat ground just before the almost vertical drop to the valley floor 75 meters below. This was a perfect ambush site, the blocking force had good cover while the enemy force would be without cover and without anywhere to go except up a very steep hill. Except if an armored vehicle with two 57 mm guns was able to kill you. It is important to remember 57 mm is 2.6 inches a very big bullet indeed with high explosive (HE) rounds this could be very unpleasant indeed. The ZSU-57 had to go and pretty much first thing, especially if we wanted air support.

We sat down in our positions and did what we could to improve them but digging was out of the question, the ground was only a few inches of soil on top of rock. We did stack up some stones into low walls. Now, we finally had a few minutes to eat and get ready. I took my boots off for the first time in two days. My feet had been wet and were in pretty bad shape. I dried the boots out with the small towel I carried around my neck and I had some Columbia Medicated Powder that I applied pretty thickly to the swollen and split feet and passed it around to everyone else. It really made my feet feel better. I managed to get them back into the boots this time with socks and got ready for the coming dawn and the battle we knew was on the way.

Dawn came and the NVA were up early moving the ZSU-57 and the towed ZSU-23-4 a 23 mm (0.90 inch guns in a quad mount). Now we just had to wait. Waiting is always difficult, you cannot help but let the adrenalin begin to build in spite of trying to calm it down with breathing and clearing the mind as much as possible. I just wanted this mission to be over.

About 25 NVA soldiers in a large group walked along beside and behind the tank like ZSU-57. As they approached the ambush, Custer fires a LAW from about 100 meters directly into the side of the ZSU-57 and it amazingly penetrated whatever armor there was and damn thing just exploded in a large gout of black smoke, while at the same time Lyndell dropped several 40 mm grenades into the ZSU-23. The three claymores triggered and they scythed through the troops. At this time, another contingent of NVA exited the woods and moved forward at a run to help their comrades. They likely could not really see any of us as they charged across the relatively open area. In what seemed to be seconds, seven mortar rounds were on the way and landed right on target on top of the ZSU-57 and ZSU-23 and while seven more landed on the troops rushing to help their comrades. It was a devastating strike.

Four A-26s arrived and began to bomb and strafe first the area where the NVA were and then the trail just below our position. Eight 50 Cal guns are really death dealing bastards. When they figured that they had taken care of our bad boys they moved on to other targets. They used bombs, Napalm and the 8 x 50 caliber machine guns each plane carried in the nose to really put it on the trail only a few miles from where we were.

Suddenly, an enormous explosion rocked the earth and a massive blast wave ripped through the jungle below flattening it for over 100 meters around the center of the explosion that was down on the jungle floor and miles from where we were. They must have hit a very large ammo dump. Flying debris from the explosion damaged one of the planes. The plane arced around and a single person managed to "punch out" and the parachute carrying them down drifted in the wind landing them on the Karst pillar we had been on while the plane impacted the jungle below us in a massive ball of fire after the fuel, Napalm, and remaining bombs it still carried exploded. DD from the mortar team went back and helped the pilot out of the chute and across to meet up with the rest of the team.

I had half expected to have to go charging down the hill killing commies like John Wayne. This just did not happen. They were taken care of by the mortars, claymores, and especially the A-26s and the hail of 5.56 we provided. All I had to do was move down the hill and wait for extraction. This was a very good thing.

The first extraction helicopters came in at tree top level and flared over the karst pillar with the crashed people on it. The second set, the PAVE Low and a Huey came in for us while the remaining A-26s worked over the trail. As soon as they touched down we were clamoring aboard and we made our exit as quickly as possible, skimming the tree-tops. We were it seems remarkably unscathed. The pilot we rescued turned out to be the old Norwegian guy in his fifties who flew our DC-3 a few weeks before. He a tough old bird for sure, flew a Spitfire in the Battle of Britain, fought in Korea, and now got shot down over Laos! Well he had another story to tell of being blown out of the yet sky again. The other team we came to help were less lucky, they lost a pilot and three members of the team and after a few days on top the karst pillar wet and hungry were all in pretty bad shape, but they would all recover in a few days. I was especially glad that this one was over and we had sustained no casualties in our group, another miracle. I just wanted my R&R!

We landed at NKP and the first thing we did was get to a shower. I sat on the floor with the water spraying on my face and took my boots off. My feet were a mess after being in water for several days. The Columbia Powder had helped some and mine were far from the worst but still were cracked open in places. I realized I had missed seeing Nash. I had finally broken my streak. We showered, changed into greens and "shower shoes" and were escorted to the officers club for something to eat, since we were all starving. We trooped into the club in greens without any insignia and shower shoes. No one said anything to us about it. Having Nash and the Air Force colonel who was Nashes liason in Bangkok probably did not hurt any either.

None of the Air Commandos (the Air Force guys operating the base at NKP) to their credit, really never asked us for or about anything, and from the top on down they went out of the way to help us if they could including arming the planes and birds. They were always on board with anything we did that hit the NVA since they saw it for what it was a way to save American lives. Every bomb or bullet that did not get down the trail was one that would not be used against us.

We missed our singing competition, so we decided on a drinking completion to replace it. I lost. Puked my guts out way before anyone else.

I really had not been feeling well for over a day now. I just chalked it up to the stress and strain of the mission, too much Jack Daniels and bad food but in the evening I began to have a fever that neither aspirin nor Motrin didn't really touch. I had aches and pains and really bad chills and fever. I thought oh fuck! Dengue again but it was not like Dengue. The next morning I went back to the base and the doctor took one look at me and said probably malaria. A blood sample was quickly taken and a microscopic examination of the blood smear showed the little buggers were in my blood. Since it takes weeks for symptom to develop I had run the mission with malaria!

But doctor, I said, I am taking my chloroquine and had the depo shot of CI 501. "Son, it would seem that you have a chloroquine resistant malaria". So it was decided to go with the tried and true remedy of quinine and doxycycline. The doctor, a grizzled old flight surgeon with a long background in treating malaria, said that I should take the dose he prescribed but if it did not cause ringing of the ears I could increase the dose. I replied but doctor, my ears are already ringing! I was miserable for several days the fever broke but I had to continue the medication for another two weeks just to be sure we got it all. No nice nurse this time, but in two days the Moose joined me in my little quinine fest! Misery loves company they say. Must have been quite a mosquito; in any event in a week I was back among the living, we had caught it early. Not to mention the fact I was full of at least four anti-malaria drugs, and did a "Cathartic Purge" with chloroquin for a week as well. I was really tired of tropical diseases but I was alive again, not in good shape but alive.

Moose and I was scheduled for a trip back to the world to discuss the issues on the ground with the design team. I think I had a lot to say to them. This trip would provide a little extra recovery time before any more missions. The rest of the team was also off on R&R as well. So Moose and I gathered up some gear and took a local transport from Bangkok to Saigon. We then took a Pan American 747, the very top of the line jet aircraft at the time (so much better than the way I had come) from Saigon to Manila, Manila to Guam, Guam to Honolulu, Honolulu to L.A. and a Braniff 727 from LA to Dallas. This was First Class Travel, food served on china and free drinks.

I was glad to be back to the "Land of the Round Door Knob". We crashed in a hotel in Dallas and I slept almost 12 hours. Both Moose and I were pretty drained from the last mission followed by a round of malaria, and the anti-malarial drugs probably make you feel like shit as well as giving you some amazing Technicolor dreams. When I finally returned to the living after the flight, I realized Moose and I had a Friday, Saturday and Sunday to have some fun before we needed to get to work. I decided to take him to visit NTSU and see what was going on at the old college. Our hair had grown out for several weeks now so we had longish "crew cut" hair at best so I guess we looked like ROTC guys. It did not matter we just went anyway. I parked close to the campus at about 7:00 pm and it was just getting dark. As we walked into the campus I saw at lot of students gathered in the center of the Mall area, oh shit, an anti-war rally I thought. I was wrong. Three guys and one girl came running up the street toward us, completely naked. We had it seems discovered a "Streaking fest". Moose says if this is college now I really like it! Quite a number of people were running around naked including a number of girls. Pretty amazing.

We went to one of the old hangouts and had pizza and beer. We both still had very little stamina, and got really tired early and I drove back to Dallas and we both crashed again before midnight. The next morning after breakfast, we sat in the sauna of the hotel and sweated out the toxins from the last few weeks. We were done with the medications and I think this helped and we both felt better, but while we wanted to have some fun it was clear we needed to get ready for the meeting on Monday at TI. We really had nothing written down on paper and we would have to type the report ourselves. We were able to get most of it in a rough draft by Saturday afternoon and we went out and ate a large steak and came back and completed the task. Neither of us was very astute at report writing and even less so at typing the damn thing up. Still, we managed to have ten pages of clearly delineated field observations and a few suggestions. These we typed up and this took less time than I thought it would since Moose was a pretty good typist.

That night we went out to a little "alternative" progressive country music / blues at a small club called the Rubayiat on

McKinney Avenue. This was not really a very good place to meet girls, it was great place to listen to music but still that SOB Moose worked his magic and connected with a pair of girls and the rest is history, naturally we were late for our meeting at TI, on Monday morning. We just blamed the traffic, no one seemed to mind.

The failure of the modifications to significantly improve the range of the transmitter under actual conditions was a disappointment to the team but I wanted to see how it was tested. Sure enough, the testing was just through the "air" without thick foliage in the test. My suggestion was to test it in an alfalfa field and they agreed to try this, as well as reducing the size of the wire used as the antenna.

We had good discussions and explanation about the environment that included the Karst areas we were operating in. This was an additional issue of complication, as if triple canopy jungle wasn't enough. The fact that the NVA had people using metal detectors and dogs to look for mines and transmitters surprisingly was news to the reseach team, but it was not possible to make a transmitter without some metal in it. Removing the metal cases and using a good engineering plastic like nylon or delrin could help. When we "salted" an area with metal fragments or the area had been heavily bombed, the metal fragments disguised everything small anyway.

Making them into anti-personnel mines was also discussed and this idea might shorten their useful lives, but activating them only when the batteries went dead seemed to be a good idea.

Having just come back from Asia, they naturally took us to eat lunch at a local Chinese lunch counter just across from TI. I would have liked a hamburger but hey it was okay. The place had three cooks with woks over Chinese stoves, a menu on the wall, and their English speaking kids taking orders. Well, the food was really good and we finished discussing what changes were planned. We were done with the paperwork and free.

Watching TV and reading the papers, it was becoming pretty clear now that the war was in a downward spiral and was ending. The negotiators were giving away all our advantages and the communists were violating all their agreements. We had been pulling troops out and in 1972 the troop levels were officially reduced to 24,500 from a maximum of over 580,000 in 1968. In 1973, the official number would be reduced to a total of 50. Bombing the trails with B-52 strikes had been stopped officially and then congressional action forced all covert bombing by American military forces to stop. So the military had been pulled out leaving the mercenary corps to soldier on without them. Fucking great, but why monitor traffic on the trail if you stopped the bombing and interdiction? The answer was yes there is traffic on the trail by both day and night now, lots of traffic.

I really wanted to understand what the mission was and how much longer we planned to continue. The electronic firms had not made any plans for slowing down at all what they were producing, spend it while you can I guess

The training program in Austin had been closed, so I was pretty much in the first and last class. The war just cost too much and took too long and the political will to continue the American involvement in the war was gone, and now there were lots of under-employed Special Forces guys on the market as the military shed troop strength. These were dark days for the America's men in uniform. The returning soldiers faced people yelling things like "baby killers" and worse.

I remained unsure as to what we were going to do and what we would not do. We were "Vietnamizing" the war and were losing ground everywhere. The enemy continued to become stronger.

We had completed our meetings and now we were headed back to the nest but by way of the UK where we would meet up with the rest of the team. Pipes wanted to show us around a bit and we needed some R&R. We dropped the rental car off and the girls parked at the Braniff remote parking so we could ride the Jet Rail, a new monorail system that takes you from a remote parking lot to the terminal. Well, this was all pretty damn futuristic, a monorail and then a jet. Remember at this time flying was still a pretty special thing even enjoyable, not at all like the cattle transport we have today.

Strangely, I felt happy to be back with the team returning to Asia. This was difficult for me to understand or to explain. Why would a rational person want to go back to a war zone and potentially get their ass shot off? I certainly did not understand these feelings at the time and maybe a little better now, but I really felt it. I remembered Nietzsche's warning: "Whoever fights monsters should see to it that in the process he does not become a monster", but I am not worried. We are not monsters but bad ass motherfuckers to be sure.

I know I wanted the excitement and the feeling you get from being in a close team in the bush and the camaraderie and brotherhood. I don't know how to explain it but there is a certain crystalline clarity in the bush and in a firefight not found in "real life". In the bush it is all business, everyone knows their job and without question, everyone is always there for each other.

I knew on some level this war was not really a good thing and I knew this could not last, but while it did I was ready to run with it. I had contracted for two years and that period would be over in a few months. When the time came I would decide what came next for me. This had certainly been an interesting year for me full of first time events.

CHAPTER 15

The End

• • •

If you do not change direction, you may end up where you are heading.

— LAO TZU

THE SITUATION ON THE GROUND just continued to deteriorate. Everywhere became a hot zone. As American troops were withdrawn and American air power stopped flying sorties, the Communists became bolder and more aggressive. They shifted antiaircraft artillery (AAA) and surface-to-air missiles from defense of North Vietnamese sites to the defense of the Ho Chi Minh Trail. It became dangerous to fly anywhere near the trail in any aircraft, but in a helicopter it just became suicide. We were lucky; someone, probably Mr Nash, had some sense, and we just stopped running missions well before the bitter end. But our morale was really low as we sat around doing nothing, and boredom can be the genesis of problems, as we have seen in the past.

High altitude aerial surveillance showed that the traffic on the trail increased from some trucks traveling by night and hiding during the day to convoys both day and night, and the trail was no longer just a network of paths but was becoming a paved highway. We allowed it to occur by stopping the bombing and truck killing campaign. No reason to count the traffic really, is it was high both night and day as I said previously. This was the final buildup before the invasion and overrunning of South Vietnam by the Communists, and we were aware of it and allowed it to happen. Nixon was pulling us out of the war and ending the draft. Then in August, Congress passed the Case-Church Amendment which shut down any US military activity in Vietnam, Laos, and Cambodia. This left us really hanging out with no support at all. The war was over, and we all knew we had lost.

Finally, Nash arrived and called us all together. "Gentlemen, your group has just been demobilized. You will be officially disbanded at the end of the month. Until then, you can get your equipment packed for shipment back home to the United States and make a trip to Bangkok if you want. There will be another assignment for you, if you choose to take it, but probably not in Asia, so think about what you want to do and where you want to go. I'll let you know as soon as possible what options are available."

So just like that, we were done. I had known it was coming, but I was not really ready for it. Now the question became would the Brotherhood of the Tigers be broken up or just relocated to a different place? Where else could we go? I still had several months left on the ironclad contract I had signed, so I didn't have a lot of options, even with Nixon ending the draft. I decided to talk to Mr. Nash and Mike and get their advice.

Mike had paid the right people and got Koobs and his family relocated over the border into Thailand where they continued to help the Thais by looking for Khmer Rouge, the Thai Communists, who were infiltrating across the border into Thailand. At the same time, he was able to help some of his villagers relocate. Mike understood the Communists taking over Laos and Cambodia would be a bloodbath for the local Montagnards who had helped us and couldn't leave. We tried to take care of our comrades as best we could. Years later, Koops died and his son took over the role of shaman. We heard he had a very fine funeral, which is an important thing for a shaman.

Unfortunately, America did not take care of her friends; we left them behind to suffer and die. Graham Martin, the new ambassador to Vietnam, was in denial and perhaps just plain stupid. He refused to allow documents to be shredded until the last moment, and as a result many fell into the hands of the Vietnamese, which caused many agents to lose their lives. Worse still, he refused to allow the extraction of the Lao leader Vang Pao's men until the last minute, meaning many had to be left behind. Some refused to surrender and fought on as guerrillas against the Communists for many years.

We did not know what to do so, we decided to spend a week in Bangkok, a final fling with the team. Off we went in Buzz's bird, but my heart and head weren't really in it; there were too many things up in the air. Well, at least until the first few drinks landed in my belly. Then I loosened up and focused on having a good time.

Thailand was changing: demonstrations by students were starting, and the old guard was beginning a McCarthy-like hunt for Communists. The government was headed for a crisis. The red light businesses didn't seem to care, however, and the clubs and bars were not crowded but were still running at full tilt, even though much of the clientele had returned home to the U.S. of A. The handwriting was on the wall; the boom times were over.

We did a reprise of my first trip to Bangkok, complete with the trip to Mama-san's. The next morning, after coffee and croissants, we sat around the breakfast table with Nash talking about what we would do in the future. I asked Nash, "Where do you think they would want us to go?"

"Well, I hear things are really heating up in South America, but you would not be part of a military augmentation. We would be CIA mercenaries, and I, for one, am not going to go in that direction. If you want my opinion, here it is. But I warn you, it is a pretty low opinion. The government has changed. We have political leaders who are only interested in staying elected and in power. We have second-string incompetent people like Martin making decisions now, and I don't think it will get better in the short term. I am done now, this will be my last hurrah. I will probably just retire; I belong to the last generation, not this new one. I can't work with these guys; they don't give a shit about the law or American values—just keeping power and getting rich."

"So what are you boys thinking? I'd like to spend some time in Korea studying martial arts," said Mike. "I have plenty of money saved and could live for ten or fifteen years over here if I wanted. Maybe I will open a Karate studio later."

Lyndell said, "I know what I am going to do. I'm going to dental school."

DD chimed in, "Well, it's medical school for me if I can get in." Buzz and Fuzz were planning to run a helicopter charter service in Hawaii they had talked about for years.

Moose said, "Well they offered me a job in Dallas, and I might try that for a while. Good-looking women in Texas, you know," he said. "What about you, Red?"

"Well, I guess I'll go back to school since they can't draft me anymore. I still owe them two months on my contract, but I don't plan on becoming a mercenary and killing our South American brothers. So I don't know what I'll do."

"You will have to buy the rest of your contract back, Red Dog," said Nash. "And it won't be cheap. Double what they pay you. Do you have the money? I'll help you if you need it."

"Well, yes, I think I have the money. It will take a lot of what I've saved if it's double the pay, but it's a bargain at any price versus getting killed in fucking South America."

I thought to myself, *none of these jobs back in the world have any real excitement in them. How will we all adapt to moving back into the real world? We can't even talk to people about what we were doing here. I know I am not the same kid who started this adventure and then came to Thailand a year ago. I don't know how I will fit back into the academic world…or just the plain old world, for that matter. I'm worried I won't fit in at all, but then I'm not really a mercenary either.*

We went back to our little base and started packing everything up in the camp and then a team "bean counters" from the US of A descend on us. They packed up suppy and without ceremony gave Fredrick Barbosa, our supply clerk, his pink slip. We took him for a night on the town and gave him a "bonus" of five hundred dollars, a small fortune in Thailand at the time, I suppose. He could retire on this bonus and his savings.

Then it was finished and done. The Bean counters supervised loading everything for us. As I recall, they were particularly amazed and rather grumpy about all the extra weapons and stuff we had acquired and refused to allow any personal weapons to be transported except in wooden crates which would be inspected upon arrival. If you are not in the military there are no "war trophies", so according to them we did not officially "own" all our "excess weaponry acquitisitions". Fortunately, SAT pilots were not so "by the book".

I realized my adventures in Asia will have to become a closed chapter of my life. You could not talk about it with anyone except the team of course, so when it was done, it was done and it really remained.

We were scheduled to fly commercial from Bangkok to San Francisco where we met for drinks and dinner with Nash at "Henri's Room at the Top", the restaurant at the top of our hotel, with a great jazz club. Nash was always a first class guy and this evening did not disappoint in any way at all.

I don't recall what I ate but I do recall the waitresses all wore hot pants and as expected with Nash, everything, even the jazz, was first class top shelf great. As the meal came to an end Nash says: "Well I have to tell you this to get the meal and your rooms on my expense account, I may have some jobs for you all and not the ones in South America either".

Oh my, Mr. Nash, Jesus what great guy you are I thought.

The End

Epilogue

• • •

Happiness in intelligent people is the rarest thing I know.

—— Ernest Hemingway, *The Garden of Eden*

By the way, all the Tigers became successful in their own way. My old boss had offered me a job at the university. I would be working and taking graduate courses as well, at least that was the plan. Moose would be working in North Dallas and I would be in Denton, so we would only be an hour from each other but Moose was always on the road all over the place, so we did not see each other that much, but we always had a great time together whenever we did.

It seemed a lot of the guys ended up in Texas. Lyndell went back to South Dallas but got admitted Baylor, finished his degree, and got into the Baylor dentistry program and became a dentist.

Buzz and Fuzz actually went to Hawaii to work on their helicopter tour idea. DD went back to California to get a degree and then get into medical school, and became an ER Physician. Mike made it to Korea to train in the martial arts and got the crap beaten out of himself on a daily basis by some old Korean man.

That left Mr. Nash. He took his own advice and retired to San Antonio, where he and his wife lived happily ever after. So we all finally made it back to the world and the team's amazing luck held out to the end or maybe is was the Montgnard Shaman's magic.

I worked ten-hour days and self-medicated by drinking a lot and smoking dope with a friend every weekend for over a year before I finally settled down, sobered up, went back to school full time, and finished my doctorate.

For many years, we all got together once a year and spent a few days doing something crazy. The reunions were always like stepping back in time. We never forgot Thailand and our adventures there. Eventually, we all got old, and then people started dying off. Mr. Nash had a stroke. DD skied into a tree in Colorado, probably while looking for an adrenaline rush. Lyndell had a massive heart attack and died in his dental office. Fuzz died of AIDS, and Buzz died in a plane crash in Alaska while on a back country hunting and fishing trip. Mike was killed somewhere in Burma, where he was working as a freelance war photographer, and my best friend Moose died from complications of diabetes. I trusted Moose like no other friend I have ever had, but then we had a lot of history. I still miss just talking to him on the phone, and it is hard to accept he and the rest of the team are gone, it is an empty hole in my life.

I'm still here and kicking, not high some days, but still kicking and still working. I finally got rid of a nasty low-grade infection that kept me constantly sick for about five years after they took out a lymph node and finally got a correct diagnosis. Several months of antibiotics managed to cure it but I got down to 145 lbs first. Then there are the heart problems. I've kept my Cardiologist Dr. Nemeth and my electrophysiologist Dr. Razavi in business for a decade or more now, not to mention my primary care doctor Dr. Kershenbaum who can't retire until I do. Getting old sucks.

At three o'clock some mornings, the "Hour of the Tiger" in the oriental philosophy, I dream that the Tigers are all still together, fighting in the jungles of Southeast Asia. Don't think these dreams are nightmares, they are not. I really loved my time with the team and wouldn't change it for anything. This is my happy place, where everything is simple and clear, black and white because when we Tigers are together, we are happy and safe from any harm.

Happiness is when what you think, what you
say, and what you do are in harmony.

— MAHATMA GANDHI

Appendices

• • •

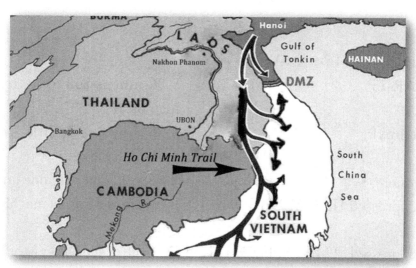

Map of Thailand, Laos, Cambodia Showing the Ho Chi Minh Trail

Organizational Chart

APPENDIX 2: TYPICAL WEAPONS

CAR-15 — 5.56 mm assault rifle, ten-inch barrel.

M-16A1 — 5.56 mm assault rifle, sixteen-inch barrel.

Stoner 63 — 5.56 mm light machine gun.

Suppressed H&K MP-5 — 9.0 mm subsonic machine gun.

Suppressed .22 (Hush Puppy) pistol — .22 caliber silenced pistol.

M18 A1 — Claymore antipersonnel mine; fires seven hundred one-eighth-inch steel balls with a killing range of fifty to one hundred meters.

M-25 AP Mine	Disk-shaped AP mine (toe popper).
M-14 AP Mine	Carrot-shaped AP mine (shaped charge).
M 79	Grenade launcher and 40 mm grenades, including high explosive, flechette, buck shot, fragmentation (mostly frag).
M-67 Fragmentation grenade	The M-67 as the extra safety wire, and is spherically shaped like a baseball.
M-26 Fragmentation grenade	Not a sphere; called a lemon due to its shape.
M-34 WP grenade	White phosphorous; shaped like a cylinder with a cone-shaped end.
V-40 Fragmentation grenade	Small, golf ball–sized fragmentation grenade; the small size made them easier to throw and allowed a soldier to carry more of them.
M 72 LAW (Light Antitank Weapon)	A small, shoulder-fired rocket with a shape charge warhead for attacking vehicles or bunkers.

APPENDIX 3: COMMUNICATIONS EQUIPMENT

A/N PRC-25

A twenty-three-pound portable radio with a range of two to three miles in the bush and a much larger range with good line of sight, not obscured by jungle: closer to ten to fifteen miles. It had an actual power tube, not a transistor device, which really increased the weight. We never used this model, it was just too heavy.

A/N PRC-77

All solid-state radio; like the PRC-25 but without any tubes. It weighed only fourteen pounds.

A/N PRC-90

Survival radio (backup for the PRC-77); small, packable radio.

KY-38

Scrambler for PRC-77 radio to allow secure communications.

AN/PPN-19

Miniature multiband beacon to allow friendly forces to find you.

APPENDIX 4: AIRCRAFT

FIXED-WING PLANES

DC-3 — A propeller-powered transport plane that could carry twenty-one people. Developed in the 1930s, it is still flying today. Also used as a gunship to attack ground targets with side-firing machine guns.

C-130 — A large turboprop transport plane capable of lifting seventy to ninety troops, depending on their pack weights. Sometimes converted to a gunship with large side-firing armament for ground attack, including a 105 mm cannon, the largest weapon on any aircraft.

C-7 — A short takeoff and landing (STOL) plane capable of lifting about six thousand pounds.

A-26

Ground attack plane; a WWII B-26.

The air force had replaced the A-26 with the F-104, mostly because of the politics. Jets were always better than propeller planes to air force jet jockeys. The idea was that high and fast was better than low and slow, and they also wanted to get rid of the self-styled Air Commandos, the *get it done* boys out of NKP just caused them too much indigestion. The agency kept several A-26 planes, often as Royal Lao Air Force—marked planes.

The same thought patterns nearly got rid of the A-10 before the Iraq war, where it proved to be exceedingly valuable. Low and slow is deadly accurate for ground support, and an A-26 can just hang around for a long time and carry a lot of bombs, not to mention having eight fifty-caliber machine guns in the nose, which are just devastating to anything they hit. They could also land on pretty rough landing fields, unlike a jet. They had the highest rate of truck kills and lowest rate of being shot down, but then they were taken out of service anyway. It is true the airframes had had a lot of service, but they were still sound, just like the DC-3, unpressurized meant little reason for stress cracking.

PC 6

A Pilatus Porter was a short takeoff and landing (STOL) transport plane. Seats for nine passengers and capable of landing on rough fields and extremely short runways.

HELICOPTERS

Pave Low Sikorski

A large and very powerful helicopter capable of carrying twenty-five to thirty men and often armed with two or three miniguns.

Huey Bell UH-1   The standard helicopter used in Southeast Asia. Unarmed (except for a door gunner), the Huey could carry up to two six-man teams.

Appendix 1: Sensors

SO WHAT EXACTLY WERE THE sensors for? They were devices to detect and target traffic on the trail. There were a number of different types. Probably the most common were seismic sensors, which could listen to footsteps or to trucks as they moved along the trail. These would go active when they "heard" something and send out a radio signal or a hard wired signal to another unit, which sent the data up to circling planes that rebroadcast it to NKP or perhaps even the huge, electronically steerable antenna array called a Wullenwebber at Camp Ramasun, which was a listening post for communications across the entire area (named for the demon of thunder, Ramasura), The data was decoded and intelligence regarding the noise was created from the information collected. This could then be used to target the convoy or troops.

A major problem with this setup was that the distance a radio signal from a sensor could travel in the bush is only about one-half mile, at least using the most common bands of 129.0, 134.5 or 148.02 MHz. Wired sensors were more prone to detection, and if the base box was found, all the sensors would go dead. Another major issue was battery life, which was generally only a few weeks at most. Air dropping of sensors was another method of implanting the devices, but this still left out the antenna wires at best and more of the relatively large device at worst. Some actually attempted to camouflage the antenna as a plastic plant, dog shit, or wood. Well, dog shit might be common on a lawn in Virginia, but it did not exist on the Ho Chi Minh Trail. Likewise, plastic plants stood out in the jungle to anyone who has "jungle eyes," or even plain eyes for that matter.

Other sensors could detect radio frequency engine noise (Black Crow) and even magnetic anomaly detectors (MADs) to detect metal like trucks and bikes. It was possible to detonate mines with such devices as well.

Another kind of sensors were People Sniffers, which could detect chemicals like ammonia and gunsmoke. These were either man-packed or, more often, flown in helicopters.

These were less useful in the jungle, since the Viet Cong and NVA hung buckets of urine in the jungle to confuse the devices. Millions spent and they failed because of a low-tech counter measure—a bucket of piss.

GLOSSARY

AN/PPN-19	A radio beacon to allow friendly forces to find you.
A/N PRC 25	A man-packable tube type radio.
A/N PRC-77	A man-packable solid-state radio.
A/N PRC-90	Small packable survival radio (backup for PRC-77).
A-26	Ground attack plane from WWII.
AAA	Antiaircraft artillery large-caliber (greater than fifty caliber), designed to be used against aircraft
ALICE Pack	Army pack and other load-carrying equipment that allows you to clip things like canteens and ammunition pouches etc. onto the outside of the pack. Pouches to the outside of the pack or onto a belt.
AN/PPN-19	Miniature multiband beacon to allow friendly forces to locate you.
Bird	A helicopter or plane.
Bird (2)	Aussie speak for girl.
C-130	A large turboprop transport plane capable of lifting seventy to ninety troops depending on their pack weights. Sometimes converted to a gunship, with large-side firing armament for ground attack.

C-7	A short takeoff and landing (STOL) plane capable of lifting about six thousand pounds.
CAR-15	5.56 mm assault rifle usually with a short ten-inch barrel.
DC-3	A propeller-powered transport plane that could carry twenty-one troops. Developed in the 1930s and 1940s.
Drag	The last person in a line of soldiers moving in the jungle.
Exfil	Get the hell out of Dodge and go home.
Frag	Fragmentation grenade or bomb.
FNG	Fucking New Guy a derogatory term applied to a new team member who has not seen combat.
Ghillie suit	A mesh covering which you can attach plants like grass or leaves or strips of cloth to to act as camoflage.
Hotel Alpha	HA—short for haul ass
Huey Bell UH-1	The standard helicopter used in Southeast Asia. Unarmed (except for a door gunner), the Huey could carry up to two six-person teams.
Hush Puppy	Silenced handgun, usually a small .22 caliber pistol.

Insert	Get put onto the ground at the start of a mission.
Karst	A limestone formation with steep sides and a relatively flat top.
KIA	Killed in Action
KY-38	Scrambler for PRC-77.
Laager up	Find a defensible position.
Lie doggo	Be still and quiet. Probably British or Australian usage.
M 72 LAW (light anti-tank rocket)	A small, shoulder-fired rocket with a shape charge warhead for attacking vehicles or bunkers.
M 79 grenade launcher	Fires 40 mm grenades, including high explosive.
M-14 AP Mine	Carrot-shaped AP mine (shaped charge); similar to the M-14 but with a penetrating explosive jet.
M-16A1	5.56 mm assault rifle with a sixteen-inch barrel.
M18 A1 Claymore anti-personnel mine	Antipersonnel mine that fires seven hundred one-eighth-inch steel balls. Lethal from fifty to one hundred meters.
M-25 AP mine	Disk-shaped AP mine called a toe popper, since it would not kill but would only blow your foot off.
M-26 Frag grenade	Called a lemon but not really lemon-shaped.

M-34 WP (White Phosphorous) grenade	Shaped like a cylinder with a pointed end.
M-67 Frag grenade	Has the extra safety wire.
Napalm	An incendiary bomb (fire bomb) containing thickened gasoline.
Nape of the Earth	Flying in a helicopter at high speed at extremely low level (https://www.youtube.com/watch?v=y-ZOCQh36ic).
NVA	North Vietnamese Army
Offset bombing	Using a fixed signal and a second offset signal to determine the target.
Ordinance	Artillery shells, bombs, etc.
OSS	Office of Strategic Services (WWII version of the CIA).
Pave Low Sikorski	A large and powerful helicopter capable of carrying thirty men and often armed with two or three miniguns.
PC 6	A Pilatus Porter was a short takeoff and landing (STOL) transport plane with seats for nine passengers.
Point man	The first person in a line of men.
PRICK-25	PRC-25 radio.
PRICK-77	PRC-77 radio; basically a solid-state PRC-25 radio
Purple smoke	Usually the final mark for a PZ (pickup zone).

PZ	Pickup zone—the location to be extracted from.
Rotor-head	Helicopter pilot.
R&R	Rest and Recuperation
Ruck	Short for rucksack. Backpack.
Spook	Clandestine operator.
Spoon (1)	The firing handle of a grenade.
Spoon (2)	A metal "track" that fits onto an M-16 magazine and allows you to load ten rounds of ammunition from a stripper clip in a single push.
Stoner 63	5.56 mm light machine gun.
Stripper clip	A strip of metal that held ten rounds of 5.56 mm ammunition for both M-16 and CAR 15 magazines. which allows you to push ten rounds at a time into the magazine.
Suppressed Browning Challenger 22 (Hush Puppy) pistol	A silenced twenty-two-caliber pistol.
Suppressed H&K MP-5	9.0 mm subsonic machine gun.

THERMITE	An incendiary grenade that produces molten iron through the reaction of iron oxide and aluminum.
Tigers or Tiger Stripe Camo	A campflage pattern which consists of black stripes and lighter green, light green and brown stripes somewhat like the pattern seen on tigers.
V-40 Fragmentation grenade	Small fragmentation grenade.
VC	Viet Cong Communist Guerrillas
Whisky Delta	WD; weak dick (a pussy).
White Smoke	Often marks where to put ordnance for air attacks.
Willie Pete	WP; white phosphorous grenades.
Wire (1)	Razor wire and barbed wire used for perimeter defense.
Wire (2)	A garrote.